SPELLS & WISHES & GUN

SPELLS & WISHES & GUN

SPELLS AND WISHES™ BOOK 1

MARTHA CARR

MICHAEL ANDERLE

DISRUPTIVE IMAGINATION

This book is a work of fiction. All of the characters, organizations, and events portrayed in this novel are either products of the author's imagination or are used fictitiously. Sometimes both.

Copyright © 2023 LMBPN Publishing
Cover by Fantasy Book Design
Cover copyright © LMBPN Publishing
A Michael Anderle Production

LMBPN Publishing supports the right to free expression and the value of copyright. The purpose of copyright is to encourage writers and artists to produce the creative works that enrich our culture.

The distribution of this book without permission is a theft of the author's intellectual property. If you would like permission to use material from the book (other than for review purposes), please contact support@lmbpn.com. Thank you for your support of the author's rights.

LMBPN Publishing
2375 E. Tropicana Avenue, Suite 8-305
Las Vegas, Nevada 89119 USA

Version 1.00, October 2023
ebook ISBN: 979-8-88878-231-6
Print ISBN: 979-8-88878-692-5

THE SPELLS & WISHES & GUN TEAM

Thanks to our Beta Readers
Mary Morris, Rachel Beckford, Malyssa Brannon, John Ashmore

Thanks to our JIT Readers
Christopher Gillard
Dave Hicks
Diane L. Smith
Dorothy Lloyd
Jeff Goode
Jackey Hankard-Brodie
Jan Hunnicutt

Editor

SkyFyre Editing Team

PROLOGUE

The festivities at the EverAfter Fair were in full swing. Gleeful laughter and merry songs filled the air. Colorful stalls lined the edges of the fairground, offering enchanted trinkets, potions, and magical baubles. Townsfolk and magical beings alike wandered around, enjoying the pleasant evening.

A tumultuous roar disrupted the merriment. At the edge of the fair, near the entrance to a stone bridge, stood a hulking troll. He loomed over a terrified vendor as he shook him down for coins.

"You want to cross my bridge? You have to pay a toll!" the troll bellowed.

"But this bridge wasn't yours an hour ago!" the vendor exclaimed, clutching his collection of enchanted wares. The troll smirked, showing off his jagged, yellow teeth. "It's mine now."

Charlotte Weaver approached the two, her figure tall and commanding. "This bridge is free for all, and you have no right to demand a toll," she told the troll, her voice full of authority.

The troll turned and tried to stare her down, then sneered at her. "Who are you to challenge me?"

"I'm Charlotte Weaver, a fairy godmother," she replied, pointing in the direction of the forest. "Now, leave before you regret it."

A palpable silence clung to the air, suffocating the once-joyous atmosphere. Charlotte and the troll locked eyes, their fierce gazes stirring up an electrifying tension. Their bodies were poised for battle, and the world around them seemed to fade to an insignificant murmur.

Without the slightest hint of warning, the troll catapulted toward Charlotte. The terrifying mass of muscles and raw power hurtled across the ground like a boulder in a landslide.

With the grace of a swan, Charlotte evaded his assault. She moved like a leaf dancing in the wind, smoothly sidestepping the troll's thunderous charge. Her wand came alive, crackling with energy as it released a torrent of magic.

A wave of brilliant light filled with oscillating colors lit up the night sky. With the grace of an acrobat, he contorted his body in mid-air, evading the rain of luminescent spells descending toward him. The magical onslaught just missed, the spells shimmering as they swept past his spinning form. His pockmarked skin, a testament to battles fought and won, reflected the neon hues.

This was going to be more of a problem than Charlotte had imagined. Usually, trolls weren't this intelligent or dangerous.

He landed on all fours, his gnarled hands sinking into the soft earth and his clawed feet kicking up clods of dirt. He went back on the offensive, his dark eyes glinting with delight. "You'll need to exert more effort, puny fairy," he jeered, his voice a malevolent growl that rumbled from the depths of his chest.

"Noted," she retorted sharply, her dark eyes steely and a flicker of defiance igniting her features. In the background, the fairgoers screamed and scattered in all directions. Stalls toppled, and magical goods scattered across the ground. The clash between the fairy godmother and the troll was a spectacle of flying spells, flashing lights, and the raw power of brute strength.

With an explosive final swing of his arm, comparable to the destructive power of a battering ram, the troll assaulted Charlotte. The punch sent seismic waves rippling through the ground.

She wavered precariously, but with a flicker of her wand and a strain in her voice, a shield flashed into existence seconds before the full brunt of the troll's attack collided with her.

However, her usually impeccable spell cracked under the troll's unexpected might. The shield fragmented, its protective aura barely managing to cushion the blow, and even with the shield absorbing most of the impact, the residual force knocked Charlotte off balance. She swayed, teetering on the brink of falling as she wrestled with the aftershock of the troll's brutal attack.

The troll's face contorted into a gruesome smile, his eyes glistening with sadistic joy. His chest heaved as a triumphant roar tore through his throat, a guttural bellow that reverberated through the fairgrounds and sent shivers down the spines of the onlookers. He then turned tail and fled.

The underbrush in the forest willingly enveloped him in its shadowy embrace.

"Get back here, you coward!" Charlotte called, fire blazing in her voice. She wiped the dirt off her face with a swift swipe of her hand, determination etching lines on her brow. After she regathered her poise, her feet carried her in swift pursuit.

"This isn't over," she promised.

CHAPTER ONE

Charlotte Weaver dashed through the twisted, gnarled forest. The trees extended skeletal arms from the enveloping shadows, and the mist slithered between the trunks like a spectral serpent. Her wand pulsed with warm amber light, cutting through the gloom as she cast spells to slow the rampaging troll.

With zero results to show for her trouble.

The troll, a hulking mass of fur and muscle, lumbered ahead, leaving a path of destruction in his wake. His beady eyes, almost obscured by matted gray hair, glinted with menace as he snarled, his gaping mouth filled with jagged teeth.

"Geez, you need to brush!" Her nose scrunched as she lifted an arm.

Heart pounding like a drum, Charlotte ran faster. Her dress swished around her ankles as she deftly dodged a fallen tree in her path, her eyes not leaving the troll.

She extended her wand as she muttered a quick incantation under her breath. A bolt of arcane energy streaked toward the troll.

With a snarl, he swerved, and the bolt crashed into a tree behind him, splintering the ancient bark. The troll roared, his voice shaking the trees. A flock of birds rose and flew away.

A shiver of fear ran down her spine. Her wand glowed brighter and hotter, and she aimed for her quarry's feet this time, hoping to slow him down.

The spell shot out in a brilliant flare of light. Anticipating her move, the troll leaped to the side. The magical attack hit the ground, leaving a patch of scorched earth and a cloud of dust in its wake.

"Damn it!" Charlotte's frustration simmered. She wiped the sweat from her brow with the back of her hand as she surveyed the beast.

Did he just smirk at her?

The troll hurled a boulder at her. It was an unrefined attack, but its raw power was unmistakable. Charlotte dove, narrowly avoiding the projectile. The earth shook when the colossal rock landed, and it created a small crater.

Her wand wavered. The troll was not tiring, and his eyes gleamed with predatory satisfaction. Charlotte rose, dusted herself off, and tightened her grip on her wand.

The moonlit forest was a silent witness to their duel. There was no clear victor yet. The troll snarled, ready for another round, and Charlotte prepared to retaliate.

The creature led Charlotte deeper into the forest. The trees were taller, their branches were more twisted, and the shadows were denser. Charlotte was uneasy, but she gritted her teeth. The amber light from her wand danced over unfamiliar terrain.

He is large, not stupid, she reminded herself.

The troll stopped in front of an enormous intricate web, its silken threads glistening in the moonlight. It was home to a group of magical spiders, their bodies iridescent in the glow from her wand. Usually, they were asleep at this hour.

With a malicious grin, the troll let out a deafening roar. The vibrations shook the web and roused the spiders, and their eerie green eyes blinked open.

"Damn you!" Charlotte spat, glaring at the troll. She was caught off-guard but was far from helpless.

As the spiders scuttled toward her, Charlotte took a deep breath. Her wand blurred as she cast a series of spells, her voice steady despite her pounding heart. A shield of light formed around her and harmlessly deflected the spiders' fangs.

"Tolem Arachne!" She conjured a bright light that temporarily blinded the arachnids and darted to her left, slipping past the disoriented spiders and out of their webbed trap.

She emerged on the other side, panting heavily but safe.

Looking around, she saw the troll staring at her from forty paces away, his beady eyes wide in disbelief. His plan had backfired.

Charlotte smirked. She lifted her hand, perhaps with a little less strength in her voice than she would have liked. "Is that all you got?" she taunted, pointing her still-glowing wand at the troll.

The troll let out a frustrated roar and darted off.

She sighed. "At least I can't smell his breath from this distance." She ran after him.

She shouted, "Presto!" and a burst of vibrant green and brown energy produced a tangle of thorny vines that snagged the troll's leg. He roared and thrashed, but the vines held fast, digging into his tough hide.

"Finally," she murmured with a grin. Unwilling to admit defeat, the troll looked around, casually ripped a young tree from the ground, and hurled it at Charlotte.

Her grin dropped. "Oh, crap!" She dove out of the way and landed in a pile of damp leaves. The tree hit the ground behind her and splintered into a thousand pieces, and she lost sight of the troll.

Her head rose from the forest floor, a leaf jutting out from behind her ear as she glanced around. She had to capture the troll to restore order. That was her job. She was hunting her prey, and not bringing him in was out of the question. Where had he gone?

The silence was both frustrating and mysterious. She spat out a small clod of dirt as she rose and looked to her left, frowning. Her eyes narrowed as she scanned the tree line. The fog dissipated, and the moonlight cast a silver glow through the canopy. Her wand's glow flickered again.

She finally spotted a clearing, the swaying grass whispering secrets to the night. The troll was at the edge, his fur glistening with sweat and his chest heaving.

Got him!

Charlotte tightened her grip on her wand, and its energy surged into her fingertips as warmth. This was her moment, her chance to prove that she was more than just a fairy godmother. She was a protector, a force to be reckoned with, and she would not let this troll's rampage continue.

She stepped into the moonlit clearing. The creature's gaze met hers, and they sized each other up in a sort of mental dance. The troll snarled.

Charlotte stood her ground, wand high. "Your reign of terror ends tonight," she declared. However, as she prepared to cast the capture spell, people emerged from the shadows, startling her. She took a step back. How bad could this get?

She kept her focus on the troll, but she flicked her eyes from left to right.

Clad in loose dark garments, faces obscured by cowls, the newcomers moved with fluid grace. Their demeanor was cold and calculating as they surrounded Charlotte. "Stand down, Fairy Godmother," one commanded, voice oozing disdain. "Your meddling ends here."

Charlotte glared at him. This was not her first battle. "You expect me to let the troll continue his rampage? He's a wrecking ball. His stench alone crippled the crops."

A second person stepped forward, a wicked grin peeking out from the cowl. "That's the point, dear Charlotte. The chaos is delightfully disruptive. Don't you agree?"

"Disruptive? You call *that* disruptive?" Charlotte gestured at the troll, whose heavy breathing was causing the earth to shake. "He's nearly destroyed half the Enchanted Forest! I don't know what you're playing at, but it ends tonight."

A third person chuckled, a low, menacing sound that made Charlotte's skin crawl. "We're not playing, Fairy

Godmother. We're changing rules. We're tired of living in the shadows under the rule of others. It's time for a new order."

Charlotte's eyebrows shot up. "So, you've decided to terrorize innocent creatures and destroy homes and livelihoods in your quest for power? Have you lost your damned minds?"

"Lost? No, my dear. We've just now found our way," the first man responded, his voice dripping satisfaction. His eyes, glowing in the dark recesses of his hood, met Charlotte's, and a silent challenge passed between them.

The troll, forgotten in the exchange, got restless. He shifted his weight from foot to foot, grunting irritably, then jerked up a two-foot-tall tree and used it like a toothpick. To Charlotte, his energy was like a storm threatening to break loose.

Charlotte's mind raced as she scanned the glade. She was outnumbered, but she didn't back down. She had a duty to protect the realm and its inhabitants, and she would do that.

"You're fools if you think you'll get away with this," she snapped, her gaze flicking between the newcomers and the troll. "EverAfter doesn't need a new order. It needs peace, and I'm going to ensure it gets it, regardless of whether you like that idea."

The newcomers exchanged glances and laughed cruelly. "We're *counting* on it, Fairy Godmother. We're counting on it," the third man replied.

Charlotte braced to fight them, and the troll growled, eyes darting between the cloaked figures and the defiant woman. The forest held its breath, awaiting the impending tempest.

She finally placed the last speaker's voice. "Simon! Of course. Only you could get a band of idiots to do what you say. Fuck off, you reject from a failed fairytale. This isn't going to go well. No one will ever tell your story." Her frustration peaked. "Playtime is over. I'm writing the end of this tale."

Simon chuckled, the sound echoing through the clearing like the rustling of dead leaves. "You don't have a choice, Fairy Godmother." His tone dripped derision. "You're outnumbered and outmatched."

Charlotte bit her lip. Simon was right; she *was* at a disadvantage. *I've had worse odds, though.* With a defiant tilt of her chin, she raised her wand, the swirling colors within its crystal tip dancing across the clearing. *Not that I can remember when if I'm honest.*

"All right, then." Her voice was strong. "All of you want to press your luck? Let's go."

The troll was both confused and impatient to depart.

One of Simon's minions scoffed. "You believe you can take all of us on? That's bold."

Charlotte reached for the knife strapped to her leg. "It's not a claim. It's a promise I've kept many times." The air crackled as she focused on the necessary spell. "*Vortexum Illustrium!*" she shouted.

The dark magic cult huddled together and braced for the impact of her spell.

"This is going to be a hell of a day," she muttered. "For someone."

The glow from her wand illuminated her blade as the

tendrils of her spell snaked through the air. She wouldn't go down without a fight.

The ground began to rumble, and a whirlwind of colors burst from her wand and swirled around the clearing. The newcomers stepped back, smirks faltering.

"Your parlor tricks won't save you, Charlotte," Simon spat, but his voice wavered.

Charlotte grinned. "We'll see about that."

The troll snorted uneasily and took a step back. He glanced at Charlotte and the men, then back at Charlotte. He realized he was no longer the center of attention in this drama, and he needed to leave.

The dark magicians caught his movement. "Nice of you to join us," shouted one of Simon's minions, a tall, thin man. He sneered as he pointed at the troll. "Took you long enough."

Charlotte didn't let the jab distract her. Her duty was to protect EverAfter and its inhabitants, not banter with would-be usurpers. "Last chance, Simon," she warned. "Stand down, or face the consequences."

Simon's laughter was harsh, and it made Charlotte's skin crawl. "I don't think so, Fairy Godmother. This is *our* time."

"Have it your way." Charlotte's eyes narrowed.

Sensing the escalating danger, Simon stepped back. His minions followed, their smugness replaced by caution.

Even the troll looked uneasy.

Charlotte ignored their reactions. If Simon and his cronies wanted a fight?

She'd give them one they'd never forget.

"Fulmen Venite!" The words rolled off her tongue, powerful and commanding.

The sky crackled with energy, and bright light illuminated the clearing. The figures shielded their eyes, taken aback by the display of power. The troll growled, unsure of where to look.

Crack! Charlotte's spell burst from her wand and created long trails of lightning in the open space. A tight vortex took shape in the center of the clearing, a chaotic whirl of colors and shadows pulsing to a steady beat, then became a portal.

The robed men scattered like frightened birds. Simon led the way. Their jeers turned into panicked shrieks as they darted to the edges of the clearing, desperate to evade the portal's reach. The forgotten troll bellowed and flailed his arms in a futile attempt to fend off the new enemy.

Charlotte stepped back, caught off-guard by the portal's appearance, but she was pulled toward the hole. She dug her heels into the earth, straining against the force that was dragging her to the vortex. "Fuck me." Her voice was tight with the effort of maintaining control.

Gritting her teeth, her thoughts a whirlwind of fear and determination, she murmured to herself, "Come on, Charlotte! You can't let them win. You're stronger than this." She slipped closer to the swirling mist.

The air thrummed with the portal's energy, and her long, dark hair whipped around her face. She glanced around and saw Simon gaping. *Did he do this?* No, he was not clever enough. He was only a user of others. The portal pushed her away as well as pulled her closer, and the pressure made it hard to breathe. What kind of magic was this?

"Are you trying to suck me in or kill me?" the troll asked as he grabbed a thick trunk. "Or is it both, and you do murder clean-up really well?"

No time. Charlotte's breath came in ragged gasps, and her body ached from the strain of resisting the pull. "Troll, pull me out of the energy field, and all will be forgotten. No arrest. Come on!" She stretched her hand out.

The troll hugged the tree, shaking his head and smiling.

"That is why no one likes you," Charlotte growled.

Simon lowered his hood, and his face was white with fear as Charlotte reached the portal. *He has no idea what's happening.* The realization filled her with dread and a grim satisfaction.

"EverAfter," she yelled. She had to warn her compatriots, so she shouted a simple spell, "Find my sisters!" and spread her fingers. The expected sparkle filled the air but faded. They were too far away. Charlotte cried out as the vortex yanked her into its depths. Her body was tossed and buffeted by the raging energies within, and her world was a kaleidoscope of colors and sensations.

Uncertainty drowned her thoughts and her resolve, but Charlotte pulled her knees to her chest to protect herself. She held her wand at the ready and the knife in her other hand.

Her training kicked in. "I have to be prepared for anything."

The portal's energies surged around her, bending and twisting. Charlotte marveled at the living, breathing entity. "This is more than magic," she muttered.

The swirling slowed, and Charlotte braced herself for the unknown while reaching for her fairy godmother handbook. The book contained all their secrets and spells, and it could get her through anything. Her hand grazed her pocket, and she was surprised not to feel the outline of the small, thick book.

Magic surged, knocking the wind out of her.

Then darkness overcame her.

CHAPTER TWO

Bright sunlight replaced the blackness of the portal, making Charlotte lift her arm to shade her eyes. She was kneeling on dark pavement, and her left knee was scraped and dotted with blood.

The fairy godmother had arrived in an alley behind a block of storefronts. Next to her was a row of large dark-green metal dumpsters with Property of Wonder Brothers of Cincinnati, Ohio, painted in white on the side.

"Cincinnati?" Charlotte looked around, bewildered. The name meant nothing to her, nor were the surroundings familiar. She felt lost and disconnected from her reality, with no inkling of the gravity the word carried or its implications. "I can reverse this with the—" Her heart skipped a beat. "The handbook." She rose to her feet, ignoring the ache in her knee, and probed the empty pocket.

Nothing.

The book held all the spells known to the fairy godmothers. They were told never to misplace it, much less lose it, over and over during their training. Some of the ancient spells in languages lost to everyone but the fairy godmothers were dark and dangerous and could upend EverAfter and Cincinnati.

"I promised," Charlotte whispered. "I gave my word at graduation. I got my wand because I did." A bearded man digging in a dumpster halfway down the alley looked up and gave Charlotte a salute and a toothless grin.

He probably believed her appearance was due to the bad wine he had drunk earlier that evening.

"The book would always be kept safe." She ignored him, and he went back to rifling through the trash, occasionally throwing items over the side.

Charlotte tucked the knife back into its sheath, dropped to her knees, and peered under the dumpsters. The combined stench of rotting fruit and old kitty litter and taco meat that had been warming in the sun filled her nose. She resisted the urge to gag, swallowing hard as she scanned the ground.

Still nothing.

She winced in pain when the knee twinged as she stood, but there was no time to fix it. The book was all that mattered.

"Revelo," she commanded, and her wand emitted a soft gold light. It bounced off the grimy walls and the rusty metal of the dumpsters, revealing the cobwebs, discarded wrappers, and empty soda cans but no book.

"Did it fall into the portal?" Charlotte muttered. She moved farther down the alley, scanning the ground. The shadows shrank back, revealing a stray cat huddled next to a pile of cardboard, its green eyes glinting in the glow.

"Hey, kitty," she cooed, bending down to its level. The cat hissed, and its fur stood on end. "I'm not going to hurt you. I'm just looking for a book. It's...essential."

Unimpressed, the cat hissed again, eyes narrowing. Charlotte sighed and straightened. The cats of this city weren't as talkative as the ones she was used to.

As Charlotte continued her search, she could hear her instructor's stern voice, laced with years of wisdom and impatience. "A fairy godmother is only as good as her word, Charlotte. And her handbook."

"Damn it!" She kicked a pebble, and it clattered against the nearest dumpster, the sound echoing in the otherwise silent alley. She looked at her scratched palms and then at her wand. The light it emitted flickered as if it shared her despair.

"I have to find it." She knew she was talking to herself, but the sound strengthened her resolve.

"Once more," she muttered, casting the illumination spell again. The light was brighter this time, casting away the remaining shadows. The alley was bathed in a warm gold glow.

She resisted the urge to gag, swallowing hard as she scanned the trash that had been pushed into every nook and cranny.

She inhaled, then spoke.

"Carta mystica, *guide me true,*
Lead me now to knowledge due.
By this wand and my own might,
Reveal the pages in this strange light."

A shimmering pulse of energy that tasted like adrenaline and anticipation surged through her wand and painted the air. Her brow furrowed in concentration as she put every ounce of her will into the spell. This was it; this was her chance to find the book and correct her mistake. "Home," she whispered, her voice barely audible over the hum of the magic.

The spell faded, leaving Charlotte with a sensation of vertigo that was like a sudden drop in a fast elevator. She steadied herself against the cold metal of a dumpster and exhaled, releasing a breath she hadn't realized she was holding.

"Let's try something else." She cast again, and when the spell reached its crescendo, it exploded in a dazzling display. It was as if a supernova had exploded in the dark alley, and spots danced in her vision.

A translucent magical map floated before her, a testament to her magical prowess. Each street, alley, and building was painstakingly detailed, and the magical lines glowed. It was as if a master cartographer had painted the city using starlight.

Any first-year godmother could do a GPS spell, so she tried again.

"Carta mystica, *guide me true,*
Lead me now to knowledge due.
By this wand and my own might,
Reveal the path in this strange light."

Pinponts of light blossomed, dotting the map in a hundred places. Charlotte furrowed her brow. "Come on! Work with me here."

A car horn blared, and Charlotte glanced at the street, which was visible between two buildings. People were rushing in different directions on their way to work. Cars crept down the road toward their destinations. She wanted to go take a look, but she shook her head. "The book is all that matters."

She took a moment to center herself, then concentrated on the handbook again. Each copy was numbered to keep track of it, so she pictured number three hundred twelve, which had an alabaster cover that shimmered in direct sunlight.

The twinkling lights blazed brighter but didn't move. "How is that possible?" The book was indestructible. How could it appear to be in so many places at once?

Charlotte waved her hand through the map, and the lines and lights turned to dust and rained down on the ground. She brushed the front of her dress and gave her knee a good look. "It's nothing," she told herself, straightening her back and squaring her shoulders. She went back to her training. Prioritize, assess the problem, and implement the available solutions.

She looked toward the busy road. "Cincinnati, huh? All right, let's get on with it." She moved down the alley. "Adventure awaits, and I have to find that damn book."

Charlotte turned the corner and saw her reflection in a shop window. Her pale face was framed by a cascade of dark hair with strands of purple that glowed in the sunlight. Worry wrinkled her forehead.

"I can't afford to lose myself in this place. My people need me. Who's keeping watch over my district? No one even knows I'm gone." Charlotte bit her lip and shook out her hands. "Not the way we do things. The way *I* do things. Let it all go. Look for solutions."

A group of teenagers was clustered around a bench,

their faces illuminated by their phones. No reason to ask them for help. No one in EverAfter had a phone. They weren't needed when spells were available.

She kept expecting to see banished creatures from EverAfter slinking out of a dark corner or standing in clusters, passing information for money. She shivered. Even stripped of their magic, many posed a threat, and a fairy godmother on her own was a tempting target.

Her stomach growled with hunger, and she dropped her hand to her belly. "No time." An enticing aroma wafted toward her, and her stomach gurgled. "Always hungry." The memory of her mentor on EverAfter made her chest ache. "But I have to get home."

She stopped in front of the building and looked at the sign—Skyline Chili. "However, one cannot run a mission without proper fuel. This seems as good a place as any to start." The mouthwatering smell of chili and cheese drew her in, and she went to the counter.

The restaurant was buzzing despite the early hour, but she was greeted quickly. "Can I help you?" The bored teenager looked up, and a smile grew on his face. "Love the outfit. You doing cosplay? I'm into Dragon Ball Z myself." A name tag crookedly pinned to his white shirt read Anthony.

"This was the uniform they issued me when I graduated. Would you know where I could find the nearest police station?"

Anthony froze, his mouth forming an O. He leaned closer and whispered, "You in trouble?"

Charlotte stared at him, realizing how out of place she looked, and quietly slid her wand into her pocket.

"Nothing I can't handle. Do you have an address?" She took out a small leather purse that was cinched at the top and pulled it open, then slid a silver coin across the counter. "And will this take care of a bowl of chili?"

"Ma'am, that would take care of a vat of chili. Don't leave that here, and don't show that purse to anyone in these parts. That's a good way to get mugged."

Charlotte pressed her lips together and put the coin back into her purse. She wanted to tell him she had slain a dragon crazed by a spell and banished a warlord who had defeated two great knights, but she shivered instead. She was alone in this land and had no one else to rely on.

Anthony held up a finger. "Wait right here." He came back with a bowl of chili poured over noodles and put a top on it, then slid it into a bag with a spoon and napkin. "I'll take care of it. You be careful out there. The police station is two stops away by bus, and the bus stop is right out front." He waved his hands when Charlotte protested. "Won't take no for an answer. You ever get the chance, help someone else."

Charlotte blinked in surprise. "Thank you." She took the bag. *This is Cincinnati? Seems like a nice place. Why had she never heard of it?*

She had found a quiet corner to savor the meal. The steam rising from the bowl tickled her nose. She tentatively took a bite, and the unfamiliar spices exploded in her mouth. It was a taste unlike anything she had encountered in Ever-After. In her realm, food was often enchanted, imbued with magical properties that could do anything from healing wounds to enhancing one's magic. This chili was magic of a different kind.

She closed her eyes, allowing the symphony of flavors to dance on her tongue. The tangy tomatoes, the savory meat, and the rich, creamy melted cheese created a medley of flavors. They filled her mouth and warmed her from the inside out.

It was a stark contrast to the chilly morning air.

She took her time, savoring each bite. The cheese stretched in deliciously gooey strings from the bowl to her mouth. Despite the urgency of her quest, she allowed herself this moment of peace and indulgence. It was a small comfort in a world where she was an outsider, a stranger.

After she finished the last spoonful, a sense of satisfaction filled her. The spices lingered on her tongue, a reminder of her first taste of Cincinnati. The chili had not only been a meal but also an experience, a welcome surprise in her unpredictable journey.

Wiping her mouth with the napkin, she tossed the empty bowl and spoon into a nearby bin.

Charlotte stood at the bus stop, her taste buds still tingling from the chili. The rich aroma still hung around her, the combination of spiced meat, beans, and cheese creating a comforting warmth. The smooth, velvety texture of the chili had taken her by surprise, leaving her feeling oddly content despite her current predicament.

She was so engrossed in her culinary reverie that she almost missed the arrival of the bus. The squeal of the brakes snapped her back to reality, and she gathered her belongings. Her cape billowed behind her as she rushed to board.

On board, Charlotte was confronted with the challenge of bus fare. After fumbling in her purse, she produced a handful of small, round gold coins that were intricately engraved with a regal figure on one side and an ornate crest on the other. The glint of the gold caught the eye of a fellow passenger, a middle-aged woman with frizzy red hair and a kind, if slightly disheveled, appearance.

The woman eagerly offered to exchange the gold coins for the two dollars needed for the fare. Grateful for the assistance, Charlotte accepted the offer and handed over the small fortune without a second thought.

As the bus pulled away from the curb, Charlotte's thoughts again turned to the missing handbook, which would be a vital tool on her journey. Its pages were adorned with illustrations and enchanted text that changed to suit the reader's needs. Without it, she felt lost and vulnerable in this strange new world.

Her malfunctioning GPS spell was another source of frustration. Normally, the simple incantation would conjure a holographic map that would guide her to her desired destination. However, since her arrival in Cincinnati, the spell had been on the fritz. The distorted map flickered, and the directions it offered were a garbled mess.

Determined to try again, Charlotte closed her eyes and whispered the incantation under her breath. The familiar sensation of magic coursed through her veins, but when the map materialized, she realized that something was still amiss.

The holographic images danced and twisted, and the

formerly solid lines were a storm of colors and shapes. Her heart sank when she realized the spell had failed again, leaving her no closer to finding her way back to EverAfter. Charlotte would have to rely on her wits and resourcefulness to overcome the challenges that lay ahead.

As the bus rumbled down the uneven streets, the interior lights flickered in time with the rhythm of the engine. Its dull roar filled the bus, a comforting symphony of urban life. The sound cocooned her, a stark contrast to the quiet serenity of EverAfter.

She sat quietly, her sharp eyes picking out details others might overlook. She noted the group of teenagers in the back, whose laughter echoed through the bus. She saw an elderly woman in the front row, her gnarled hands clutching a bag of groceries, and she watched as a pickpocket wove through the crowd, eyes darting around as he slyly slipped his hand into the purse of the unsuspecting woman.

When the thief withdrew his hand with the woman's wallet in his grasp, Charlotte had to intervene. She was a protector in EverAfter, and she wouldn't stand by while someone was wronged, no matter where she was. She took a deep breath and cast a spell under her breath.

Her magic was still erratic. Rather than capturing the thief in a magical net as she had intended, her spell attached itself to a stray cat lurking under the seats.

The scruffy ginger tom was enveloped in a whirlwind of magic, and it let out an astonished yowl. His body twisted and morphed, and he grew. His fur turned midnight black, and he grew to the size of a Newfoundland dog.

The transformed cat seemed to accept Charlotte as its master, and with a powerful bark uncharacteristic of a cat, it charged the thief and knocked him to the floor, then pinned him in place.

Some passengers screamed and clung to their seats, while others frantically clambered away to distance themselves from the scene. The woman whose purse had been targeted by the thief stared at the animal in gratitude and disbelief.

Surveying the pandemonium she had unintentionally unleashed, Charlotte felt a twinge of remorse. Her intention had been to apprehend the thief, but her capricious magic had other ideas.

She gazed at the magnificent dog standing victorious over the moaning thief apologetically. "I'm so sorry for the mishap, but would you mind assisting me a little more?" With an obedient nod, the creature stood guard as Charlotte bound the thief.

"Thank you. Would you like to accompany me on my journey?" The creature attempted to purr, but a pleasant growl emerged instead. Charlotte smiled and continued, "You know, I think I'll call you 'Cat.'" A lump formed in her throat. This was not how she had expected her day to go. She was supposed to be tracking down her missing handbook, not causing chaos on a city bus.

The passengers' whispers reached her ears. "Did you see that?"

"Was that magic?"

"What just happened?"

The bus driver, a burly man who had kept his eyes on the road throughout the commotion, glanced in the rearview mirror. His eyes widened when he saw Cat standing over the bound thief, and he pulled the bus over. As it came to a stop, he turned around and looked at Charlotte, and his voice was shaky when he spoke.

"Ma'am, I'm going to have to ask you to take your, uh, dog with you when you leave." He eyed Cat warily. "We can't have any more, uh, *surprises* on this bus."

Charlotte nodded, her cheeks flushing with embarrassment. "I understand," she said, struggling to maintain her dignity as she gathered her things and prepared to disembark. Maybe she should put a hold on using magic until she got her handbook back.

She guided Cat down the steps and onto the bustling street. The blaring car horns, chattering pedestrians, and sizzling food carts created a symphony of sounds and smells.

As she and Cat walked, passersby stared at the unusual duo, unable to tear their eyes away from the towering dog and the woman in the purple dress and cape. Some pulled out their phones to snap pictures, whispering and pointing.

"Is that a bear?"

"Who is she?"

Charlotte's face got hotter with each comment, but she held her head high. She glanced at the departing bus with regret, and then she and Cat continued their trek to the police station.

The police station was tall and austere, an impressive edifice of steel and glass piercing the city's skyline, a constant reminder of law and order. The building was modern, in contrast to the historical architecture that surrounded it. Its minimalistic design stood out like a beacon among the ornate carvings and intricate stonework of its neighbors.

The station basked in the soft glow of the sun, the glass reflecting the few clouds that interrupted the cerulean blue. The spectacle stole Charlotte's breath, the beauty of the scene belying the seriousness of her purpose.

As she approached, Charlotte noticed the constant flow of people entering and leaving the station. Uniformed officers strode around purposefully, their faces stern, their eyes keen and alert. Civilians were present as well. Their expressions depended on their reasons for coming to the building, she supposed.

Each had a story to tell.

Above the entrance was a gleaming emblem of the city's police department. Beneath it, the heavy double doors constantly opened and closed, swallowing and regurgitating people in an unending cycle.

She wondered what reception awaited her within its walls.

CHAPTER THREE

Charlotte and Cat strode into the station.

The noise and activity in the lobby subsided as the officers and staff and civilians took in her purple dress and cape and the enormous dog. Clutching her wand, she approached the desk sergeant, a broad-shouldered man with a bushy mustache and a bemused expression.

"Good afternoon." Her voice was steady despite the butterflies in her stomach. "My name is Charlotte Weaver, and I'm a fairy godmother from EverAfter."

The sergeant raised an eyebrow, his amusement evident. "A fairy godmother, you say?" he asked, trying to suppress a grin. "And what, um," he eyed her again, "brings you to our fair city?"

Charlotte's cheeks flushed. "The arrival part isn't pertinent at the moment. Unfortunately, I've misplaced my handbook, which is essential for me to perform my magic correctly. Without it, my spells go awry." She gestured at Cat, who sat placidly by her side, tongue lolling. "For example, Cat here was originally an orange cat, but due to a magical malfunction during an altercation on a bus, he's now a huge dog."

The sergeant's eyes widened as he noted Cat's size. "Well, that's a new one," He scratched his chin. "Let me call Detective Alex Taylor to handle your case." He picked up the phone and turned his head.

As he dialed, the station's doors violently swung open. Two police officers, both sweating and gritting their teeth, were wrestling with a large man in handcuffs. The man, face twisted with rage, was trying to break free. His hoarse yells caused everyone to turn and stare.

"Well, if it isn't Mr. Henderson," the sergeant muttered, watching with a disapproving frown. "Always causing trouble." He turned to Charlotte. "Please wait here a moment, Ms. Weaver. I don't want you," he nodded at the struggling group, "to get hurt."

Charlotte took a step back as the officers dragged the enraged man past her. Cat growled, hackles raised, and she placed a comforting hand on his head. "Easy, boy," she murmured.

The two officers, their uniforms taut, grunted as they wrestled the handcuffed man farther into the station. "You can't do this! I know my rights!" the man bellowed.

The sergeant sighed, rubbing his temples as he raised his voice. "Henderson, we've been through this! Assault is a crime. You can't go around picking fights," he chided, shaking his head.

"Those guys were asking for it!" the man spat defiantly, his face turning an alarming shade of red as the three stepped past Charlotte and the sergeant.

Charlotte watched the proceedings. She'd dealt with trolls and magical spiders, but this was a different kind of encounter. She turned to Cat. "Stay close to me," she instructed.

As the sergeant waited for Detective Taylor to answer, he glanced at Charlotte and Cat, eyebrow raised. "Your dog doesn't bite, does it?" he asked. Cat's lips peeled back from his teeth.

Charlotte forced a smile. "Only if I tell him to." Before he could respond, Detective Taylor picked up, and he returned his attention to the phone. "Alex," he began, giving Charlotte the side-eye, "I've got a case for you."

Charlotte nodded in thanks. The police station was full of ringing phones, chatting officers, and the occasional smelly person being escorted to a holding cell.

The wanted posters and public service announcements on the walls added to her unease.

As she gazed around, a tall man approached, his gaze focused on Charlotte and Cat. Charlotte was shocked by his rugged good looks.

"Detective Taylor?" she asked, voice betraying her nervousness.

"That's me," he replied, his tone guarded but not unkind. "The sergeant told me you're a fairy godmother with a missing handbook and some...magic troubles?" He eyed Cat warily, clearly trying to reconcile the massive dog with Charlotte's explanation to the desk officer.

"Exactly." Charlotte's self-assurance returned. "I need to find my handbook and figure out how to undo the effects of my malfunctioning magic."

Alex nodded, his expression thoughtful. "All right." He

extended a hand for her to shake. "I'll do my best to help you, Charlotte."

She took his hand, and the warmth of his touch sent a shiver down her spine. She took a deep breath and recounted her story to the detective. "I was chasing a troll through the Enchanted Forest in EverAfter when I was suddenly transported here to Cincinnati."

Alex's furrowed brows indicated that he was trying to comprehend the situation, but disbelief crept into his expression as she continued, "Ever since I arrived here, my magic malfunctioned. For example," she gestured at Cat, "I tried to stop a purse thief with a simple binding spell, but it turned an orange cat into this huge dog."

The staff was shamelessly eavesdropping, and their reactions ranged from confusion to disbelief. Some people smirked and whispered to each other, finding Charlotte's claims humorous, while others were clearly unsure whether to take her seriously.

She finished describing the missing handbook and the potential danger it posed, and Alex's eyebrows rose. He rubbed his chin thoughtfully and glanced at the desk sergeant, who was leaning against the wall, arms crossed and a smug grin on his face.

"I have to ask," Alex began cautiously. "Have you had anything alcoholic to drink or taken any substances that could impair your judgment?"

Charlotte bristled. "I am sober, Detective. This is not a joke or a prank."

The desk sergeant snickered. Other onlookers exchanged glances and tried to suppress their laughter. A nearby receptionist raised an eyebrow with a tight smile as she looked at Alex to gauge the detective's reaction to the bizarre tale.

"Well, this is a first," Alex admitted, scratching the stubble on his chin. Despite the bizarre circumstances, he seemed to take Charlotte seriously. "Fairy godmothers, trolls, and magical misfires. It's unorthodox, to say the least."

A commotion from the booking area drew their attention. The burly man from earlier was shouting obscenities at the officers, his face red and veins bulging in his neck. Alex looked over, his brow furrowing as he watched the scene unfold.

"I'll be back," he told Charlotte and strode off to intervene.

Charlotte watched him go, then turned her attention to Cat. The dog was still at her feet. He was unperturbed by the chaos around them, and he glanced at her before checking out the action again.

She patted his head and eyed the nearby activity. Officers moved with purpose, and the clatter of keyboards and the crackles of radios filled the air. The scent of coffee wafted from a corner, mingling with the musty aroma of old papers and the sharp tang of printer ink.

Across the room, a woman in handcuffs was arguing with a police officer, her high-pitched voice rising above the general din. Nearby, a group of officers huddled around a computer screen, their faces lit by the harsh glow.

Charlotte overheard snippets of conversations, the chatter that accompanies law enforcement. "The

Henderson case... Evidence locker... Witness statement..." The words formed a tapestry that was both foreign and fascinating.

A child's sharp footsteps pattered on the tiled floor, and Charlotte glanced around to see the source of the disturbance. A girl no older than five with a mop of curly hair and eyes glistening like morning dew approached Charlotte, her gaze fixed on Charlotte's purple dress and the wand she held in her hand.

Charlotte knelt at the girl's eye level, her cape pooling around her like a midnight sky. In the child's pudgy hand was a tiny red toy car. "Hi there," Charlotte greeted her with a soft smile. "Do you like my dress?"

The child, captivated by the sparkling wand, whispered with awe, "Are you a fairy?"

Charlotte chuckled, her eyes dancing with mischief. "Would you like to see some magic with your toy car?"

The child's face lit up, and she nodded vigorously. Charlotte took the car and set it down on the tiles, its paint gleaming in the station's bright lighting. Drawing a deep breath, Charlotte waved her wand with a flourish. She pictured the car gliding in graceful circles, but instead of taking a neat circular path, the car zigzagged chaotically across the floor. It darted here and there, making sharp, unexpected turns, and at one point, it sped up, then performed a loop-the-loop, defying gravity before landing back on its wheels.

The child erupted into giggles, her laughter pure and delightful. Clapping her hands with glee, she exclaimed, "That was funny! Again, fairy lady!"

A gentle hand settled on the child's shoulder. It was her father, who had a kind smile playing on his lips, having witnessed the playful exchange. "Thank you for that," he said, his voice appreciative. "Truly impressive. You could be on stage."

Blushing, Charlotte gave a chagrined smile. "Sometimes magic has its own ideas," she admitted, her eyes crinkling at the corners. "Even fairy godmothers don't always get it right." She rose gracefully, beaming because she had delivered a moment of enchantment to the child.

"It was my pleasure," she replied, warmth filling her voice.

Detective Taylor had calmed the unruly prisoner and was walking back toward her.

"Sorry about that." He ran a hand through curly brown hair as he gazed curiously at Charlotte. "Now, about your missing handbook and this magic problem. I suggest we start at the beginning. EverAfter, you said?" Alex asked with a patient smile on his lips. "Where is that exactly?"

Charlotte blinked, her mind momentarily blank. "EverAfter is... Well, it's here. I mean, it *should* be here." Her voice trailed off as she took in the full implications of Alex's question. "I must have... I must have ended up somewhere else," she muttered.

Alex's eyebrows rose, and he exchanged glances with another officer. "And where might that be?"

Charlotte's eyes widened in realization. "Where are we?"

"Cincinnati," Alex replied, his worry evident.

Cincinnati. The word hung between them. Charlotte shook her head, her mind whirling. "No. I mean, what world is this?"

Alex gently answered, "Earth."

Charlotte stumbled back a step. "Earth," she whispered. "I've heard of it, but...but I don't understand how..." Her voice trailed off, her mind a whirlwind of confusion.

Alex took a step forward. "Hey, are you all right?" he asked, reaching out to steady her.

Charlotte didn't respond. She was trying to reconcile her new and impossible reality. She was on Earth, but how could that be? She was supposed to be in EverAfter. What had happened? How had the portal brought her here?

She felt confusion and fear but also determination. She was far from home, on a world that seemed alien in its reliance on technology and apparent lack of magic. That explained why her magic had been so erratic and weak since she arrived. She took the ambient magical energy available on EverAfter for granted, not realizing it was critical for her powers to work.

Taking a deep breath to steady herself, Charlotte looked squarely at Alex. "I know that what I've said must be confusing, Detective."

"That's an understatement," the desk sergeant mumbled under his breath.

Ignoring him, Charlotte gathered magic from the weak currents on this world. It was like trying to catch smoke with her bare hands, but she had to show them that she was telling the truth.

"Let me show you that what I am saying is true," she offered.

The detective maintained a guarded expression, but the desk sergeant couldn't hide his grin. A young officer who was sipping coffee by the water cooler smirked, and an older woman in the corner narrowed her eyes, unimpressed.

Taking a deep breath, Charlotte aimed her wand at an empty chair and cast a spell to levitate it. However, her magic malfunctioned again. There was a loud *whomp,* and the room was showered with glitter.

The explosion caught everyone off-guard. A middle-aged woman with glasses perched on her nose gasped and shielded her eyes. Several bystanders who were waiting to file reports stared in astonishment, and many officers chuckled.

The glitter coated everything in the lobby, causing confusion and consternation. The smirking officer's eyebrows shot up, and the woman muttered "fairytales and nonsense" under her breath.

The desk sergeant's grin had been replaced by bewilderment.

Detective Taylor studied the scene in shock, amusement, and suspicion. He eyed the others around him, who were wrestling with accepting Charlotte's story.

The evidence was clear, as was the absurdity of the situation, and the atmosphere in the police station was charged with uncertainty as everyone tried to process what they had witnessed.

The awe was short-lived.

"Nice light show, Fairy Godmother." The desk sergeant

scoffed, breaking the tension and eliciting chuckles from the other officers.

"Where'd you learn that trick, Hogwarts?" another officer quipped, shaking his head in disbelief.

Charlotte's shoulders slumped when she realized they *still* didn't believe her. Then she noticed that Taylor, who had been closer to her, was looking at the spot where her magic had erupted from the wand. His skepticism was still evident, but the flicker of doubt in his eyes gave Charlotte hope.

One person might be willing to entertain the possibility that her magic was real.

Alex was at a crossroads, torn between trusting the earnest woman and dismissing her as a troubled individual.

Charlotte stood tall, her wavy dark hair framing her face. Her gown and cape fluttered around her, making her look regal and powerful. "I'm telling you, what happened here was a result of my magic." She was frustrated, so she took a deep breath. "I come from EverAfter, a magical realm where fairy godmothers like me are the guardians. I was chasing a troll when I ended up here, and my magic hasn't worked properly since."

The officers exchanged glances, their skepticism giving way to curiosity. One was intrigued and waved an arm. "So, you're saying this glitter explosion was an accident?"

Charlotte nodded, her expression pleading for understanding. "Yes." She pointed at the chair. "I was trying to levitate that. Earlier, I accidentally transformed a cat into this dog with a misfired spell." She looked down. "I named him Cat for obvious reasons." She looked at Alex. "I've tried to reverse the spell, but without my handbook, it's not going to happen."

He had to consider that this could all be an elaborate hoax—he eyed the desk sergeant suspiciously—or the delusions of a troubled individual, but Charlotte's face implored him to believe her. She looked vulnerable, with her lips pressed together in a way that made it clear she would not back down until she had proven herself to him.

The chatter in the station continued unabated. Alex grappled with a whirlwind of thoughts. He was trained to sift facts from fiction and rely on evidence and reason, but now he was faced with a situation that defied logic and challenged his understanding of reality.

He had not eaten any augmented donuts, had he? He sighed.

The desk sergeant pulled pranks, but the bewilderment and shock on the sergeant's face seemed genuine. The other officers' reactions ranged from skepticism to amusement, but none wore the smug satisfaction of a successful and elaborate prank.

Did he really think these hooligans could pull off a prank like this?

Could it be a shared hallucination brought on by a chemical leak or an experimental drug? Alex dismissed that thought as quickly as it came. He had seen the effects of such substances in his line of work, and they didn't fit what he was witnessing.

Was Charlotte a skilled illusionist or magician, using tricks and sleight of hand to create the appearance of magic? He considered that, but the glitter had just appeared and exploded, and the wand wasn't big enough to produce enough of the substance to cover the room. That hadn't been a simple parlor trick.

Was Charlotte suffering from a delusion or psychosis that made her believe in magical abilities? Alex looked at her earnestness, her confidence, and her lack of fear or disorientation. She didn't display any of the signs he associated with mental illness.

He glanced at the chair, still glittering from Charlotte's failed levitation spell. Her surprise and frustration hadn't been an act. It had been real, as unlikely as that was.

His gaze moved to Cat, who was still sitting calmly amid the chaos. Transformed from a cat by a misfired spell, Charlotte claimed. The dog met his gaze and gave a soft woof as if in greeting. The animal's eyes held an intelligence that unsettled Alex, forcing him to reconsider his skepticism.

Finally, he considered the most absurd possibility: that Charlotte was telling the truth. She *was* a fairy godmother from a realm called EverAfter, and she *had* lost control of her magic. It was a concept straight out of a children's fantasy tale, but the recent event had been anything but ordinary.

Alex rubbed a hand over his rough stubble. His jaw was tense. He was a man of logic and reason, yet he was wrestling with the idea of magic and fairy godmothers. It would have been laughable if the situation wasn't so serious.

Charlotte was watching him, her eyes filled with anxiety and hope. He met her gaze, his mind still churning. He had a decision to make, and it wouldn't be an easy one.

After taking one more deep breath, he addressed Charlotte. "Let's say I am willing to believe you. What do you need me to do?" His voice was professional, but beneath it was uncertainty, a silent admission that he was stepping into uncharted territory.

He was uncertain of how to proceed.

CHAPTER FOUR

"I am telling you, Detective. It is not glitter. It is fairy dust," she insisted.

Alex pursed his lips. "Fairy dust?" he repeated, then snorted in disbelief. "You really expect me to believe that?" As he stared at her, he mused that she was easy on the eyes if odd in the head.

Charlotte nodded. "Yes. As I said, I only meant to lift the chair, but I ended up with this..." she gestured, "mess."

Her hands trembled as she tried to cast a spell again. The air around her fingers shimmered, and for a moment, it seemed as though she might be able to demonstrate her magical abilities to the skeptical detective. As quickly as it had appeared, the glimmer vanished, leaving the frustrated woman sighing in disappointment.

Alex's expression remained guarded, and his mind raced as he tried to make sense of the situation. If she was telling the truth, what did that mean for the world as he knew it?

As Charlotte continued to struggle with her powers, the

dog trotted over to a corner that Alex knew to have mice behind the walls before returning to her side, wagging his tail happily. Despite his canine appearance, the dog's eyes held a feline intelligence, and it was clear that he was loyal to Charlotte. She was innocent enough for animals to trust her.

Charlotte tilted her head to the side. "What if I showed you something else, Detective Taylor?" she asked, raising her wand. "Something more fiery?"

Alex scoffed and crossed his arms. "Fine. Let me see it."

She focused on the tip of her wand. A flicker of doubt crossed her mind, but she pushed it away. A small ball of flame sprang to life in her other palm, and the warm glow illuminated her face.

Alex's jaw dropped.

A triumphant smile spread across Charlotte's face as relief flooded through her. "You see, Detective? I *am* telling the truth."

Cat looked at her and gave a happy bark. His shaggy fur brushed her legs as he wagged his tail, brown eyes gleaming. The flame went out when she reached down to pet him, and her triumph vanished as quickly as it had soared.

Alex was trying to process the last few minutes. His eyes darted from the tip of the wand to the dog, and he was forced to reconsider his earlier dismissal of Charlotte's claims. "What the hell just happened?" he muttered.

Cat let out a sad whimper, and Charlotte smiled at him reassuringly. She stroked his soft fur and whispered soothing words to calm him.

The gruff desk sergeant interrupted his musings. "Detective Taylor, there has been a bank robbery.

Witnesses reported that the robber was playing a 'magical flute' and somehow controlling rats to help him. You need to get down there pronto."

Alex wondered why he was always assigned the peculiar cases. He sighed as he went to his office to retrieve his pack, still unable to process the magical display he had just witnessed.

Charlotte's eyes widened at the mention of someone acting like the Pied Piper. She knew that name well, and if that was true, her appearance in Cincinnati was far from a coincidence.

Charlotte strode after him, trying to keep up. She hardly noticed the din of ringing phones and urgent conversations. "Detective Taylor, listen to me!" Her voice was barely audible above the clamor. "You really need to hear this!"

Alex didn't break stride or acknowledge her. His mind was obviously elsewhere. He probably thought she was delusional, but she needed him to understand.

Cat nudged her ankles, his solid presence a comforting reminder that she wasn't alone in this new world.

"The fairy dust, the wand, the flame—they're all real," she told him, trying to catch her breath as she dodged a trash can that was rolling through her path for some inexplicable reason. She then had to duck a paper airplane. "I'm not crazy or making things up. It's not an elaborate hoax."

Alex stiffened at her words, but he didn't stop or turn around. She pressed on, her desperation mounting. "There's a whole other world out there, Detective. A realm filled with magic and wonder and danger."

Alex slowed down as if her words were starting to sink in.

"EverAfter isn't a fairytale," she continued, her voice gaining strength. "It's as real as this world, and if the man you are about to confront is from my world, I do not think you are prepared."

Alex halted, causing Charlotte to stumble. He turned around, his face a mask of guarded curiosity.

It was a start.

"What is it, Ms. Weaver? I cannot deal with any more strange happenings right now."

"The sergeant mentioned the Pied Piper and rats," she pressed. "Have there been other odd occurrences, like troll sightings under bridges or the mysterious glowing lights in the parks?"

Alex hesitated, then nodded. "We've had prank reports, but how—"

"It is all connected," Charlotte interrupted. "In my realm, fairy godmothers like me are guardians, like you are in yours, and it seems like some of my people are here for some reason. What if the Pied Piper is among them? We sent him and others away for their nefarious deeds, but he should not have his magic."

Alex raised an eyebrow. "You expect me to believe that?"

Charlotte's eyes held his. "Yes, because if this *is* the Pied Piper and there are more banished individuals like him in the city with their powers, you are going to need my help, Detective."

Alex mulled over her words. It was difficult to accept, but he could not deny what he had witnessed earlier and what he was hearing.

"If one of our former citizens is causing trouble, it is my responsibility to help deal with it."

He could not dismiss the possibility that Charlotte held the key to understanding the recent odd happenings in Cincinnati, but he hesitated, unsure if involving her was wise.

Charlotte saw his indecision and straightened her shoulders. "I need to help you, Alex. To protect both our worlds."

The detective's eyes locked with hers, searching for deception, and, finding none, he sighed. His reluctance gave way to resolve, and he started walking again.

He called over his shoulder, "All right, Charlotte. Come on."

CHAPTER FIVE

Alex's strong, tanned hands gripped the wheel of his black 1968 Chevy Camaro. The vintage muscle car rumbling around him was a product of his meticulous care over the years. The powerful engine purred as he expertly wove through the rush-hour traffic. The sleek vehicle was a force to be reckoned with on the bustling Cincinnati streets.

The cityscape was a blur of towering glass and concrete structures, a stark testament to human ingenuity. It was a different world from the ethereal realm Charlotte called home, which teemed with enchanted forests, sparkling rivers, and mythical creatures that danced under the twinkling stars.

Charlotte occupied the backseat with Cat. The canine's large form sprawled across the leather upholstery, leaving little room for her.

The car's cramped interior amplified the tension between the fairy godmother and the detective. The silence was a tangible entity that filled the small space, creating an almost unbearable atmosphere.

"Detective," Charlotte began, her soft but insistent voice cutting through the growing tension. "We must determine if those banished from EverAfter still have their powers. If they do, it is my responsibility to stop them before they cause chaos in your world."

Alex's eyes met hers in the rearview mirror, reflecting skepticism and trepidation. "This is still unbelievable."

She held his gaze. "I know it is a lot to take in, but I can guide you through the magical aspects of this case so we can protect both our worlds."

Alex finally nodded, and the tension in his shoulders eased. "All right. We will work together on this, but you have to understand that I am still trying to wrap my head around...*magic*."

Charlotte smiled. "I know, and I will help you."

They passed Fountain Square, its iconic Tyler Davidson Fountain proudly on display. The setting sun cast a warm glow over the city.

"I never imagined I would be in a place like this," Charlotte mused. "In EverAfter, everything is very different, and I can reach my magic, yet here I am, without fully functioning powers, surrounded by the unfamiliar."

Alex glanced at her, and his eyes softened. "It must be difficult for you, being so far from home and facing a whole new set of challenges."

Charlotte sighed, and her eyes drifted to her wand. "It is. I used to be able to protect my people with a flick of the wrist. Now I am struggling to keep myself afloat." She hesitated, then continued, "I told you. When I first arrived, I tried to use my magic to stop a purse thief and ended up turning a house cat into this big lump."

Alex stifled a chuckle when Cat raised his head as if he understood the conversation. "He seems to be handling it well. You are not alone anymore, Charlotte. We will figure this out together."

She allowed herself a small smile. "Thank you, Alex. That means more to me than you can know."

They exchanged stories from their respective worlds, finding common ground in their shared desire to protect those around them. In a moment of vulnerability, Charlotte gave Alex a demonstration of her limited magical abilities. She held out her wand, and a myriad of tiny lights streamed through the interior of the car. They illuminated their faces, creating an ethereal tableau. A couple strolling down the sidewalk paused and pointed at the car in awe, their faces reflecting the beautiful spectacle.

"It is not much," she admitted, embarrassed, "but it is something."

Alex looked at the fading lights, and his remaining skepticism vanished. "It is more than I could do," he admitted. "And it is additional proof that your story is true."

They shared a laugh, and he started pointing out the landmarks. The sun dipped below the horizon, leaving the sky filled with vibrant colors. The street lights came on, further illuminating the buildings and the occasional pedestrian who paused to let the car pass.

As they drove, Charlotte and Alex prepared to confront the bank robbery and unravel the connection to EverAfter. "So, what is your plan?" he asked, his voice uncertain. "Do we just waltz in there and demand to see the Pied Piper?"

Charlotte pursed her lips. "Potentially. However, we do not know if it is just a crazy person in a costume. We need to assess the situation and gather intel. If it is him, and he *has* regained his power, we need to neutralize him without harming innocent people."

"Easier said than done," Alex muttered, gripping the steering wheel tightly. "How do we even begin to fight him? I mean, assuming he is not just a lunatic." Alex's voice was steady despite his changing worldview. He kept his thoughts on the crime scene, working to piece the puzzle together.

"In EverAfter," Charlotte explained, "the Pied Piper is a figure of legend who has the power to manipulate others with his music. He can control them and lure them toward him or send them away."

Alex nodded. "And he used this power to..."

"To steal, kidnap, and create chaos," Charlotte replied. "His flute is his weapon, and his music is his magic. If he has power here, he could control people."

Alex's jaw tightened. "That's terrifying."

"It is, which is why we have to stop him."

Alex turned to look at her. "We will."

"Perhaps something in this world can counteract his magic," Charlotte suggested. "But first, I need to learn more about the rules of magic here."

"All right." His voice was calm. "We'll do that together."

"Together," she repeated. As they got closer to the bank, Charlotte considered their task. They had to find the Pied Piper and stop him.

The crime scene was a sea of flashing lights, uniformed officers, and onlookers behind the yellow tape. The crowd clogged the sidewalks, some trying to get a better view, others scrambling out of the way as the Camaro approached.

Alex hit his siren to get the onlookers to move out of his way.

Teenagers had their smartphones out, hoping to capture footage for social media, adding to the chaos. Charlotte had a moment of sensory overload, the blaring sirens, flashing lights, and murmuring crowd making her head spin.

Alex expertly navigated through the chaos, his years of experience as a detective coming into play. His focus was unwavering as he scanned the scene.

The gravity of the situation sank in as they approached. The scene was a stark reminder of what was at stake. As Alex parked the car and they prepared to step into the madness, Charlotte and Alex shared a glance, then got out.

CHAPTER SIX

Alex placed a firm hand on Charlotte's shoulder. "Stay behind. You don't have a reliable weapon, and we have no idea what we're walking into."

Charlotte bristled at the suggestion, her pride stung. She wanted to argue, but she couldn't deny that her magic was still unpredictable and unreliable. As she scanned the bustling scene, her eyes locked on an officer loitering near the yellow tape. After a discreet flick of her wand, the officer's gun disappeared from his holster and materialized in her hand. The officer's eyes widened as he patted his empty holster.

Alex, who had witnessed the exchange, stared at Charlotte in disbelief. "Wait in the car," he ordered, his tone strained. She would probably not obey the order, although she did get back in the car.

As soon as Alex walked away, Charlotte got out again. Her curiosity and eagerness to prove her worth as a fairy godmother in this unfamiliar world propelled her to do so.

Alex did not look back. Charlotte wanted to help, and she wouldn't let her unpredictable magic stop her.

Glancing around to make sure no one was watching, she took a deep breath, her fingers dancing in a practiced rhythm on her wand. A sparkle of magic flickered at the wand's tip before shooting into the sky and exploding into a dazzling array of lights that left the onlookers gasping in awe. They murmured in excitement as they tried to locate the source of the unexpected show.

Using the distraction, Charlotte slipped past the yellow tape. She was in, so now she could take a closer look at the crime scene. She scanned the area for magical activity or clues that could help them solve the case, oblivious to the concern for her safety that had prompted Alex to demand that she stay in the vehicle. She couldn't shake the sense that there was more to this crime scene than met the eye. She took in the shattered glass at the bank's entrance, the huddled whispering police officers, and the banknotes that danced in the wind.

She knelt by the broken glass and examined the shards, then poked them with her wand. Her magic mingled with another's. The residue was barely perceptible and shimmered like oil on water, a subtle rainbow sheen that would be invisible to the untrained eye. It carried a memory that hovered just out of reach.

Realization dawned. The banished Pied Piper *had* been here, so the city was in danger. That fueled her resolve to find more traces of magic, and she called upon her fairy godmother skills to aid her in the search. As she moved through the wreckage, she extended her senses. Her nostrils flared when she picked up a faint otherworldly scent that reminded her of the enchanted forests of EverAfter, a tantalizing mix of ancient wood, fresh earth, and something darker and more sinister. That told her she was on the right track.

The Pied Piper had not only found a way to restore his magic, but he was also intent on causing chaos and destruction. This had been no mere bank robbery.

Alex, who had rushed in to calm the crowd when the fireworks went off, came back and realized that Charlotte was not in the car. He was forced to try to find his possibly deranged companion and did so in the alley. He watched Charlotte as she investigated the crime scene. Her confidence and determination were both impressive and unnerving, and he couldn't help but be drawn to her.

The thought that Cincinnati could be a sanctuary for exiled fairytale characters twisted Alex's understanding of reality. It was a considerable leap from the structured, logical world of crime and punishment he inhabited. That the city was in peril was evident, but the source of that danger made his head spin. His instincts told him to rely on facts and evidence, but Charlotte's tale demanded that he suspend disbelief and step into a world where the rules of magic superseded those made by men.

He wondered how to adapt his detective skills to work with magic and fairytale characters. His pride in solving cases and delivering justice seemed insignificant in the face of these new challenges. Learning to navigate this new realm was imperative, and Charlotte appeared to be the compass that would guide him.

Charlotte had apparently stepped out of a storybook and into his reality. Was the Pied Piper truly responsible for the bank robbery? If so, what other mythical dangers lurked in the shadows? The detective's rational mind grappled with the thought of solving crimes committed by beings with powers beyond his comprehension. That prospect would make the most seasoned detective question his sanity.

Yet, if what Charlotte said was true, then perhaps together, they could stop the Pied Piper and save Cincinnati. He could no longer deny the existence of magic, not when it was being used before his eyes.

Or he could simply be going mad. Occam's razor was a sharp bitch at times.

"Charlotte," he called, his voice more forceful than he intended. She turned, surprised by the stern tone in his voice, and he strode toward her. "You can't just do whatever you want." He kept his voice low to avoid attracting attention from the officers near the alley. "This is a crime scene. There are procedures and rules."

She gazed at him defiantly. "I can't sit idly by, Alex. Not when I can help. Not when *he's* here," she spat. "You don't understand what we're up against."

Their argument was cut short by a sudden commotion among the officers, drawing their attention back to the task at hand. The tension remained, given their differing perspectives on the situation.

"Look." Charlotte exhaled, her eyes softening. "I understand your concern. But this? This is not your average crime scene. We're dealing with something unnatural here."

Alex ran his hand through his hair, frustrated. "I get that, Charlotte. I do. But you can't just go around doing… whatever this is without understanding the consequences."

"And you can't just ignore magic," she retorted, her hands on her hips. "This is not a normal case, Alex. We need to adapt."

When Alex opened his mouth to argue further, Charlotte held up her hand. "Look." She pointed at a faint trail of shimmering dust leading away from the crime scene.

"What is that?" Alex asked, squinting at it.

"That," Charlotte responded, "is a magical trail. It might —could, should, I-hope-to-hell it does—lead us to the Piper."

Alex pointed at the path. "You're saying we can follow this...this magic dust to the criminal?"

Charlotte nodded. "That's *exactly* what I'm saying."

Alex looked at the trail again. They were stepping into unknown territory, but he had a job to do, no matter how unusual the circumstances.

"All right. Let's follow the trail. But Charlotte," he added, "we do this side by side. And you have to promise me to be careful with your," he made circular motions with his finger that she assumed mimicked waving a wand, "magic. Okay?"

She nodded, although she was surprised by his acquiescence. "Okay, Alex. Side by side."

CHAPTER SEVEN

The narrow alley had tall brick walls on either side, their surfaces pitted and scarred by the passage of time. A single streetlight stood at the end, its flickering yellow bulb casting eerie shadows on the ground. The metal pole supporting the housing was bent and rusted, a testament to neglect.

The alley appeared to be mundane at first glance, but the rubbish bins scattered throughout the space told a different story. The Pied Piper's magical rats scurried among them, their beady eyes glowing with an unnatural light. Their matted fur was a sickly green, and their long tails were covered in scabs. The rats were larger than normal rodents, and their sharp fangs gleamed from the shadows.

Charlotte could feel magical energy in the air. It buzzed against her skin like a swarm of angry bees, setting her nerves on edge and making her stomach churn. It seeped into every crevice and wrapped around her in a suffocating embrace.

As they moved deeper into the alley, the magical energy got stronger and the rats got bolder, creeping closer. Their eyes seemed to bore into her soul. Charlotte squared her shoulders and steeled herself, fingers tightening on the hilt of the knife strapped to her leg. Its sleek silver blade was sharp enough to slice through the thickest of hides.

Several rats darted toward them. Charlotte immediately drew her knife, her grip tightening around the hilt. Alex, though taken aback, followed her lead. The first rat bared its teeth, and Charlotte sidestepped and slashed at it with her knife. The rat screeched as it leaped back into the rubbish. Alex kicked another rat away as it lunged toward his leg. He wasn't as graceful as Charlotte, but it was effective.

The other rats scattered.

She and Alex saw a tall young officer frozen halfway down the alley, and they hurried toward him, with her in the lead. She waved her blade, and the rats hissed and chittered, their beady eyes narrowing as they watched the newcomers. The blade was a comforting presence, a solid reminder of her strength and skill.

Charlotte was ready for whatever would come next, so she glanced over her shoulder at Alex, whose expression reflected determination as well as concern. She gave him a reassuring nod and gestured for him to stay put.

The rats moved toward the police officer, their mottled fur crackling with static electricity. Cat heard them from the car, and his ears perked up as his hackles rose.

The large canine bolted through the open window toward the fray, his massive paws pounding the pavement. His size and musculature made him a formidable foe. As he neared Charlotte and Alex and the officer, his lips curled in a snarl, revealing his sharp teeth. He would defend Charlotte and her new human friend with every ounce of his being, whatever form that took.

The police officer yelped in terror. "What the hell are those things?"

Charlotte's lips pressed together as she focused on the swarm. With her knife at the ready and Cat at her side, she saw a particularly large rat break away from the swarm and charge Cat. In response, Cat crouched, claws digging into the pavement, waiting to pounce.

With a snarl, the rat leaped at his throat. Simultaneously, Cat lunged forward, his massive jaws wide. The two collided in mid-air in a flurry of fur and fangs. Cat's powerful jaws clamped down on the rat's body, but the rat twisted and sunk its teeth into Cat's shoulder. Cat let out a pained yelp but didn't release his grip. He shook his head violently, flinging the rat into the brick wall. The rat squeaked, dazed, and Cat pounced on the stunned rat. With a swift bite, he ended the rat's struggles.

The other rats peered at them but did not advance. Panting, Cat looked at Charlotte, amenable to continuing the fight.

Rather than observe from behind, Alex joined the battle. He reached for his gun but realized that if his bullets missed or ricocheted in the tight confines of the alley, he could hurt Charlotte or the officer. He scanned the debris for an alternate weapon, and his gaze landed on a discarded metal rod.

He snatched it up as the rats attacked again. *Rude*, he thought.

The adrenaline coursing through his veins propelled him forward.

Charlotte was a deadly-precise whirlwind. Her silver blade reflected the dim, flickering light as she sliced through the monstrous rats. This situation was like something conjured from the most horrific nightmare, yet it was unfolding before his eyes.

She spotted a rat that moved with an unnatural speed, its movements unpredictable. It circled her, looking for an opening, then lunged at her ankle, its nasty teeth bared. Charlotte dodged at the last moment and pivoted on her heel, knife slicing the air where the rat had been a second ago.

"Dammit!" she hissed.

The rat had been too quick. Its movements were so fast that it was almost a blur. Charlotte focused her senses on the creature and waited, still gripping her knife.

A slower rat snuck up behind her, and Alex's rod arced down, swatting it away like he had just hit a par five from the blacks on Hole 7.

Then Charlotte struck her foe. Her blade met resistance as it impaled the rat. The creature squealed, and its body went limp as she pulled the blade out. The beast lay motionless on the ground, glowing eyes dark.

Charlotte took a deep breath and looked around. The police officer was face to face with an ugly rat. It was covered in sores, and its fangs were grotesquely long.

The officer swung his baton at the rat, but it darted out of the way with surprising speed. The rat lunged, sinking its fangs into the officer's leg, and he let out a loud cry of pain as he stumbled back, clutching his bleeding leg.

The rat lunged at the injured officer again, but just before it struck him, a large blur intercepted it in mid-air. Cat's powerful jaws clamped down on the rat, and with a swift shake of his head, Cat ended the rat's life.

The officer collapsed, his face pale from pain. Cat, with the dead rat still in his jaws, glanced at Charlotte and Alex, then confirmed that no other rats were coming at the police officer.

Glimpsing Charlotte's fight as he stayed busy, Alex felt awe and respect. He was coming around to the idea that she wasn't crazy, and he was now sure of one thing now: she was a damn good fighter.

Swinging the metal rod with all the ferocity and skill he could muster—*thank God for tennis lessons in high school*—Alex knocked away a group of rats that were attempting to outflank Charlotte as she fought two others that had taken up the challenge.

This wasn't what he had expected to deal with this evening. He grunted as his makeshift weapon connected with another rat, sending it flying into the brick wall. Panting, he turned to Charlotte and shouted over the rodents' chittering, "I never thought I'd say this, but I'm glad you're here, Charlotte!" He realized his world had irrevocably changed.

She flashed him a grim smile as her knife continued its deadly dance. "Likewise, Detective!" Her voice was clear and steady amid the chaos.

Cat dispatched the last rat.

Charlotte's heart hammered like a war drum, and her breaths were short and shallow as she sucked in the cold, fetid air in the alley.

The battle had transformed the mundane alley into a battlefield strewn with the lifeless bodies of the Pied Piper's magical rats. Their green glow was gradually fading, leaving ordinary rodents with severed tails behind.

Despite the odds against her and the limitations imposed by her missing powers, Charlotte had protected the group. Her eyes darted around the alley, her brow furrowing as she bit her lip in contemplation. There was a sinister undercurrent to the magic she had encountered here, a darkness that transcended anything she had encountered before.

Cat stood by her side, his presence a soothing balm amid the chaos, as Charlotte knelt and used her knife to turn two of the deceased rodents over. Her fingers tingled from the residual adrenaline coursing through her system. Her gaze hardened as she scrutinized the rats for traces of the magical energy that could lead her to the perpetrator of this vile attack.

She picked the faintest of glimmers and found an almost invisible thread of magical energy woven into the fabric of the rats' existence.

It pulsed with the Pied Piper's dark signature.

A dry chuckle escaped Alex at the thought of trying to explain the magical rats to the arriving EMTs. The rodents had attacked with a ferocity and coordination that defied explanation and overwhelmed the officer who had stumbled into their path and needed medical attention. The EMTs would have a hard time believing that magic had played a part in the attack, let alone that a fairy godmother and a transformed cat had saved the day.

Alex flagged down the incoming EMTs. "Over here!"

As they approached, their expressions became concerned. "What on earth?" the first muttered, surveying the alley.

"The rats. They attacked us," Alex explained. "Monstrous things. One of them bit the officer."

The EMTs exchanged glances, their eyebrows arching simultaneously. "Monster rats?" the second asked skeptically.

Alex nodded solemnly. "Yes, and it wasn't a normal bite. It's bad."

The EMTs immediately shifted into professional mode. "We'll need to treat him for possible rabies as well as infection," the first said, moving toward the officer.

"We'll get him to the hospital," the second added, pulling out his medical kit.

Alex sighed in relief as the EMTs took over and approached Charlotte with a wry smile. "You handled those rats like a pro. I think it's time we sat down and talked about what's going on here and what we need to do next."

Charlotte glanced at her dog and managed a tired smile. "I did what I could. I couldn't have done it without Cat."

"After this shit show, I need to ask questions with an open mind." She raised an eyebrow, and he shrugged to indicate that he had been wrong. "There's a diner not far from here called The Echo." Alex gestured at the street beyond the alley. "We can grab a bite and discuss things further."

Charlotte agreed and headed to her left. Alex gave a soft whistle and pointed the other way, and she turned back and headed toward him.

He chuckled as he looked around. How could he even begin to describe their new reality to his fellow officers, and he now wondered if he should. If he chose to, how would they react to the news that a fairy godmother would now be involved in their investigations?

His future was going to be very different.

CHAPTER EIGHT

Charlotte and Alex sat in a cozy corner booth at The Echo, a retro-style diner that seemed to have been plucked out of a simpler time. The checkered floor, vintage posters, and lively atmosphere were comforting, and the aromas of coffee and fried food filled the air as they sipped from their steaming mugs and discussed recent events. The other patrons sat in red vinyl booths, chatting or reading the paper or something on their phones.

"I still can't believe what we saw at the bank." Charlotte shook her head. "Those rats and the magic controlling them were unlike anything I've ever faced."

Alex nodded, his green eyes intense as he contemplated the implications. "I've never seen anything like that. At least we're both confused."

Charlotte picked up a fork and hesitantly poked the plate of hotcakes the waitress had brought her. It was her first time trying the dish, and she was curious to see how it compared to the Cincinnati-style chili she'd eaten earlier.

Cutting off a small piece, she brought the bite to her lips and tasted it.

Her eyes widened in surprise. "This is so different from the chili," she said, savoring the sweet, fluffy bite. "In EverAfter, we have something similar called fairy cakes, but they're not nearly as sweet."

Alex chuckled, his eyes crinkling at the corners. "Chili and hotcakes are about as different as it gets. I've got a sweet tooth, so I prefer this kind of breakfast."

He paused for a moment, swirling the last of the coffee in his mug. "Speaking of chili, I've always been partial to the kind without beans. It's a controversial opinion around here, but I think it lets the spices shine through better."

Charlotte raised an eyebrow, intrigued. "Interesting," she mused, then took another bite of her hotcakes. "Everyone has their own tastes. In EverAfter, we have many magical creatures with different dietary needs. It's impossible to please everyone."

As they discussed their respective worlds and the bizarre occurrences that had brought them together, it became clear that their alliance was not only one of necessity. They were both strong individuals who thrived in the face of adversity and together, they would be a force to be reckoned with.

As they sat talking, Alex couldn't deny his curiosity.

Charlotte leaned back in her seat as she mulled the rat attack. "They appeared out of nowhere, swarming like a dark, furry wave." She shuddered at the memory. "At first, I thought it was just a coincidence, but when they attacked, I knew it had to be magical."

Alex nodded. "I've seen my share of strange things in my line of work, but that was something else. I'm starting to believe everything you've told me about magic and EverAfter."

Charlotte's eyes sparkled at the mention of her home. "In EverAfter, anything is possible. Magic is an essential part of our everyday lives."

Alex was both fascinated and skeptical. She had told him that before, but now he believed her. "It's a lot to take in. I need more information before I can fully commit to the idea."

Charlotte nodded. "I know it's a lot to ask, and I will do everything I can to help you understand my world better, but right now, we need to focus on the immediate threat."

The more he learned about Charlotte and her world, the more he found himself drawn to the mystery and the potential for adventure. He took a deep breath and looked into Charlotte's eyes. "All right." He smiled. "Let's figure this out together. Tell me about your home, Charlotte."

Charlotte leaned forward, her dark eyes glowing as she described EverAfter. "It's a place of breathtaking beauty, with lush forests, crystal-clear lakes, and majestic mountains that touch the sky. The air is always filled with the sweet scents of flowers and birdsong."

Her voice was animated as she continued. "EverAfter teems with life, from the tiniest pixie to the mightiest dragon. Unicorns roam the meadows, and mermaids frolic in the seas. The members of the fairy council live in a grand palace in the center of the realm, and the fairy godmothers maintain balance and order."

Alex listened intently. He was captivated by the idea of a world where the impossible was not only possible but commonplace.

"But EverAfter faces a grave threat." Charlotte's voice was somber. "My handbook is missing, and it contains powerful spells and secrets that could wreak havoc in the wrong hands. There are enchantments for controlling the elements, potions for invisibility, and a spell that can transform a person into a fearsome beast."

Alex could see the worry in her eyes.

She ended with, "We *must* find the handbook. I can use the spells in it to understand the full scope of the situation so we can create a strategy to fix the issues that plague your city and figure out why I came here. Time is of the essence, Alex. Every moment we delay, our enemies grow stronger, and the chance of disaster increases."

"We'll find your handbook and stop whoever is behind this. I might not understand your world, but I can't ignore the danger you've described. Let's figure this out and protect both our homes."

Charlotte nodded, her eyes brimming with gratitude and relief. "We make a good team. I need someone who knows this city like the back of their hand, and you could use someone who understands magic."

Alex took a moment to consider her proposal. "You're right," he finally conceded. "I don't know the first thing about magic, so having you around could be useful. Plus, it seems like we're both in over our heads with the missing handbook situation."

She extended her hand toward him. "I'm glad you see the value in our partnership."

Alex hesitated before taking it, then shook it. "Agreed. We'll do whatever it takes to find your missing book, fix all these weird problems, and hopefully get you home."

CHAPTER NINE

As they finished their meals, the clatter of cutlery and the murmur of conversations filled the air. A burst of laughter from a nearby booth caught their attention. An elegantly dressed lady with bobbed hair was sharing a story with her friend.

"You won't believe what Mark told me last night," the lady began, her eyes sparkling with mirth.

Charlotte and Alex exchanged glances, their curiosity piqued. They leaned in to eavesdrop on the conversation.

"He claimed he saw a floating teapot at work yesterday!" the woman continued, chuckling. "Said it was pouring tea into cups and everything!"

The friend gasped, then laughed. "Oh, dear! I think Mark might have had one too many during his lunch break."

Charlotte glanced at Alex, eyebrows raised. She had seen floating teapots in EverAfter. It was a common enchantment used by fairy godmothers for convenience. But here on Earth?

Alex shrugged, his eyes twinkling. "Well, that's a first. I've heard of a lot of things, but a self-serving teapot? I'd probably find that useful if I wasn't shitting bricks."

Charlotte wasn't so sure. Could there be a trickster on Earth causing mischief, or could a pixie or two be screwing around?

Before she could voice her suspicion, the woman continued her story. "Even stranger, Mark said the teapot was singing a melody while it floated. Can you imagine? A singing teapot! I told him he'd better not be drinking on the job again."

The two women erupted into laughter. Alex's and Charlotte's expressions reflected their amusement as well. A *singing* floating teapot? That was out of the ordinary, even by EverAfter standards.

Charlotte eagerly finished the last bite of her hotcakes. Across the table, Alex took a slow sip of his coffee. As he swallowed, a loud, unfamiliar sound echoed through the diner. Charlotte jumped, knocking over her mug of coffee. The hot liquid spilled across the table, causing Alex to leap up and grab a handful of napkins to clean the mess.

"What was that?" Charlotte asked, her eyes wide with alarm.

Alex glanced out the window and started laughing as he finished wiping up the spilled coffee. "That, Charlotte, was a car honking its horn." He eyed her as he moved the wet napkins to his empty plate. "You really aren't used to Earth, are you?"

Charlotte blushed, realizing her mistake. She had heard the sound before, but in her panic, she'd thought it was some sort of alarm.

"I'm sorry," she muttered, embarrassed.

"No need to apologize," Alex reassured her, still chuckling. "It's not every day I get to introduce someone to the wonders of Earth. Just wait until I show you a traffic jam."

Charlotte looked horrified at the thought. "A traffic jam? Is that some sort of magical barrier?"

Alex snickered. "It's a lot of cars stuck in one place, but it might as well be a magical barrier, given how it stops people in their tracks."

Seeing that Charlotte's curiosity was piqued, Alex elaborated. "I can see why you might associate it with magic. A traffic jam does have some peculiar effects. For instance, it can distort time. A journey that should take minutes can extend to hours. It's as if a time-altering spell has been cast, making a short duration seem like an eternity."

"Really?" Charlotte asked, fascinated.

"Absolutely," Alex continued, warming to his subject. "And that's not all. A traffic jam can also cause a vanishing act. Patience, something which most drivers have in spades in normal circumstances, disappears as if a charm has whisked it away."

Charlotte looked surprised. "That sounds awful."

Alex chuckled. "Oh, it gets worse. With magic, teleportation is a thing, right?" He eyed her, but she just stared at him, so he continued, "Well, in traffic jams, it's as if your sanity gets teleported away. The longer you're stuck, the further away your mental peace gets."

Charlotte's eyes narrowed as she considered if he was making fun of her. "No way!"

"The most *extraordinary* phenomenon," Alex added with a grin, "is the unexpected transformation. In the magical world, someone or something can morph into a completely different entity. A traffic jam can do that to the most mild-mannered person. They turn into horn-honking, expletive-throwing creatures. It's as if a traffic jam is a dark spell."

"And I thought EverAfter had strange enchantments." She smirked, and Alex nodded, accepting that she was on to him.

He finally grinned, enjoying the moment of levity. For all the trouble they were facing, Charlotte's unfamiliarity with Earth added humor to the situation.

Alex took another sip, then set his cup down. "Do you have any accommodations lined up?" He paused. "If you need a place to crash, I've got a spare room."

Charlotte's cheeks flushed a delicate pink. "I appreciate the offer," she replied, her voice soft, "but I'm sure I can find something suitable."

Before they could delve deeper into the subject, a scream filled with desperation and fear pierced the air. The patrons of the diner fell silent as all eyes turned toward the source of the disturbance.

Cat barked frantically.

The partners exchanged knowing glances, their discussion temporarily forgotten. They rose, and Alex tossed a few bills on the table to cover their meal. The amount included a generous tip for the server who stood nearby, her eyes wide with concern.

"I can pay for myself, Alex. I have money."

"We can discuss it later, Charlotte." The duo wove through the startled patrons toward the chaos outside.

On the busy sidewalk was a bizarre sight.

An orange cat wearing boots and a feathered hat brandished a gleaming sword as he attempted to help a woman in distress. The woman, whose mascara was running down her cheeks, was dressed in a chic blouse and a pencil skirt, clearly having fled an office break-up scene. She was still crying.

She managed to choke out some words. "I just...I don't understand," she stammered, her voice echoing off the surrounding buildings. "One minute, he's asking me to grab lunch, and the next, he breaks up with me!"

She let out a wail, and the cat froze. "I thought we were solid, you know?" she continued, her voice shaky. "I thought we had something real! And to do it in the office? I had to run out in front of everyone!"

Her cries got louder as she fell to her knees. "And now I'm talking to a cat wearing boots!" She looked around the sidewalk. "What is happening? Is this a cruel joke?"

Bystanders had gathered around the pair, their eyes expressing amusement and disbelief. Some were filming the event on their smartphones while others whispered to each other, speculating that this must be a promotional stunt for an upcoming movie or perhaps a cosplayer working for tips. Many were looking for a box or hat to give him a few bucks. He was earning it.

The onlookers chuckled, but their amusement was tinged with sympathy. They were entertained by the spectacle, but they also felt for the woman. The cat sheathed his sword and approached her, boots tapping on the pavement. As he leaned in to comfort her, she looked at him, her mascara-covered face a picture of bewilderment.

"All is well, mademoiselle. Pain is fleeting, while love

lasts forever. Forget this travesty and know that on the other side of a glass of wine..." he eyed her mascara streaks, "or a bottle or two is a sunrise that will bring a smile to your face."

People shuffled closer to get a better look at the swashbuckling talking cat.

Cat eyed the feline with curiosity. His shaggy fur rippled as he wagged his tail and advanced to befriend the newcomer. Noting the dog coming toward him, the armed cat hissed and swiped his sword at the dog.

Startled, Cat sought refuge behind Charlotte's legs, then glanced cautiously at the cat.

The cat saw her and raised his eyebrows, then straightened his hat and cleared his throat. "Greetings! I am Sir Thomas," he announced with a flourish of his sword. "You are a fairy godmother, I presume? I can sense the magic within you, though it's not at its full strength."

Alex ran a hand through his curly brown hair.

"Well, shit." His world had gotten even stranger with the appearance of this suave cat, who seemed as at home with a sword as he was with wit. He mused that he now had enough evidence to believe Charlotte's otherworldly origins. Or maybe he should check into an asylum.

At least at an asylum, he would be able to sleep, and there would be no paperwork.

Clutching her wand, Charlotte asked the newcomer, "You're not a villain. How did you end up in Cincinnati?"

Sir Thomas took a few steps toward her. "I was hunting down a bounty in EverAfter, a werewolf who was tricking young girls out of their picnic baskets. I was caught up in some sort of whirlwind and found myself in this city."

He sighed, his eyes weary. "I've been here for a couple of weeks, living off the streets and doing my best to remain discreet."

Charlotte's expression softened. Alex raised an eyebrow, intrigued by the feline's tale and the circumstances that had brought him to their world.

"You've managed to avoid capture all this time?" Alex asked.

Sir Thomas smirked and flicked his tail in amusement. "The net people—I believe they call themselves 'animal rescue,' which is a rude term if you ask me—have tried to catch me a few times, but my sword has kept them at bay so far."

The mental image of Sir Thomas fending off animal control officers with his sword elicited a chuckle from Alex. He realized he hadn't heard of any strange paperwork out of that group, either.

Charlotte focused on the potential connection between her arrival in Cincinnati and the presence of another EverAfter native.

"Sir Thomas, since you're the first good person from EverAfter I've encountered since my arrival, I think it's best if we stick together. Perhaps we can figure out why we were both brought to this city."

The cat considered her proposal, clearly weighing the pros, the cons, and the dog before nodding in agreement. "Very well, milady. I shall join you and your companion in your investigation."

Alex's phone buzzed with an incoming text. He glanced at the screen, and his eyes widened.

"Speaking of the net people, someone's posted a video

of a sword-wielding cat on social media, and officers are on their way here," he warned, looking around. "We need to leave if we want to keep Sir Thomas out of jail or perhaps the pound." Alex glanced at the gleaming sword in Sir Thomas' paw and shook his head. He could only imagine the baffled expressions the animal rescue personnel must have worn as they faced him.

As they hurried away, Charlotte was hopeful.

In Sir Thomas, she had found a connection to Ever-After and a lifeline in the chaos of Cincinnati. Now, she, the talking feline, Cat, and Alex had a fighting chance to unravel the mysteries that had brought them all together.

CHAPTER TEN

Alex unlocked his car's doors and herded the ragtag group inside.

The Camaro's interior was small and uncomfortable, but there were no complaints about personal space. As Alex started the engine, he spotted a suspicious black SUV in his rearview mirror. The vehicle had followed them from the crime scene, remaining in the background.

Was the car following them, or was it a normal black SUV? "We might have company," Alex muttered, tightening his grip on the steering wheel. He swerved into a narrow alley, the sudden movement throwing his passengers off-balance.

Sir Thomas, who had been lounging on the console, was catapulted onto Charlotte's lap. His tail poofed out in surprise. "By the gods, sir!" He scrambled to return to his spot, only to be tossed to the other side as Alex took another sharp turn. "I didn't sign up for a carnival ride!"

Cat struggled to maintain his balance. His paws skidded

on the leather seats, and he ended up sprawled on top of Sir Thomas, who protested, "Get off, you oversized furball!" his voice muffled by the dog's bulk.

Charlotte clutched the door handle for dear life. She was seated next to a disgruntled cat and a flailing dog, trying to keep calm. She bit back a curse of her own.

Alex continued his high-speed evasion, taking sharp turns that threw his passengers around like rag dolls. Every swerve was met with a new curse from Sir Thomas, his colorful language getting more creative each time.

Despite the high-stress situation, the sight of the dignified cat and a graceful dog struggling sent her over the top. "You two are comedians!" She earned a grumbled "harumph" from Sir Thomas.

After a hair-raising chase, Alex turned into a deserted parking lot, and the car skidded to a halt. As a black SUV drove past, seemingly having lost their trail, Alex let out a relieved sigh. He turned to his frazzled passengers with an amused grin. "Everyone all right back there?"

In response, he got disgruntled meows, barks, and a soft chuckle from Charlotte. The crisis had passed... for now.

Alex pulled back into traffic a few minutes later. As they drove, he anxiously scanned his mirrors for signs of pursuit as the car whizzed past shops and homes.

Sir Thomas continued making sarcastic comments. "Ah, the noble steed of the modern world!" He scanned the interior. "So spacious and comfortable."

Eventually, they reached Alex's apartment, which was situated above a busy deli. He parked the sedan in a shadowy nook and ushered Charlotte, Sir Thomas, and Cat out of the car, throwing a final suspicious glance at the street.

The neighborhood was lively, with small shops lining the streets and happy voices filling the air. The aroma of fresh bread wafted from the deli, teasing their senses and making their stomachs grumble despite the adrenaline coursing through their veins.

As they entered the apartment, relief washed over them. The immediate crisis had passed, and they were in a safe haven for now. Charlotte's eyes were drawn to a painting of three dogs playing poker, its vibrant colors and vintage charm capturing the essence of the room. Sir Thomas and Cat reacted to the dog caricatures, their fur bristling in displeasure.

The living area had mismatched furniture, each piece telling a story. The wooden coffee table had peeling varnish, the faded green armchair was patched in several places, and the Persian rug was worn, but all contributed to the room's unique character.

Adjacent to the living area was a compact kitchenette. A stout refrigerator stood in one corner, humming softly. A microwave and a toaster oven sat on the countertop, their surfaces speckled with crumbs from past meals.

The chipped white paint on the cabinets, repurposed from a farmhouse, revealed the dark, grainy wood underneath. The scent of warm spices and lemon cleaning solution mingled in the air.

Charlotte found the place endearing. The warm lighting shrouded the space in a cozy ambiance. Personal touches were scattered throughout: a collection of colorful fridge magnets from various places, a small framed photo of Alex with a woman, presumably his sister, on a side table, their smiles frozen in time. The room was a tapestry woven from threads of Alex's life, so it felt like a home.

Sir Thomas, with an air of feline nonchalance, sauntered toward the couch. The worn brown corduroy seemed to beckon him, its rough texture perfect to hone his claws. As he was readying for a satisfying round of scratching, Alex scooped him up with practiced ease.

"Thomas!" he chided, but his eyes twinkled. "My couch is not a scratching post."

Sir Thomas innocently blinked at him and produced an almost inaudible purr. He extended his claws, then withdrew them as if he were testing Alex's resolve.

"I beg to differ," Sir Thomas retorted, his tone dripping feline entitlement. "It's corduroy." He waved a paw. "Irresistible. And it is 'Sir Thomas,' Detective."

Alex couldn't help but chuckle at the cat's audacity. "Well, your highness, you'll have to resist. This is not EverAfter, and that's not an enchanted tree." Despite the rebuke, a faint smile lingered on Alex's lips.

The group settled in to process their situation. Charlotte's eyes darted around the room as her mind flooded with thoughts and worries. How was she going to get back to EverAfter? What about the troll she had been pursuing when she was yanked into this world?

Sir Thomas, who was still in Alex's arms, twitched his tail as he searched for an escape route. Cat sat on the floor next to the coffee table, his new form still a source of confusion and annoyance for the once-graceful stray cat.

One thing was certain. Everyone's life had taken an unexpected turn.

Something beeped behind them, and Alex excused himself. "I need to check something in my room. Don't move," he instructed them, but his eyes were on Sir Thomas before he disappeared.

Charlotte glanced at Sir Thomas and Cat, mirroring their confusion. The silence was broken by Alex's mutters. The beep got louder and more insistent. They all felt a sense of impending trouble.

"What do you think is going on?" Sir Thomas asked.

"I'm not sure," Charlotte admitted, her eyes on the hall down which Alex had disappeared. "I don't like that Earth noise, though."

Cat whined and looked around in concern.

"We should be prepared for anything." Sir Thomas looked grim. "This world is full of surprises."

Charlotte nodded. Her hands were glowing. Then she noticed, and the glow snapped out.

They could hear Alex pacing in his room, accompanied by the occasional muffled curse. Whatever was happening, it was clear that he was worried.

"He needs help," Charlotte decided, standing up. "We shouldn't just sit here."

As they were about to head down the hall, Alex reappeared. His face was flushed, and he looked frazzled. He held a small device, apparently the source of the beeping.

"I need to handle something," he said, avoiding their eyes. "It's...complicated."

"And that is?" Charlotte asked.

Looking down, Alex scratched his chin as he read a text

to the group. "Another robbery in progress, this time at a bank on Fifth Street. Rats are involved again, and two officers are injured." His jaw tightened as he looked up. "I am going to check it out, but I want you all to stay here. It is too dangerous for you to be involved."

Sir Thomas sarcastically chimed in, waving a hand at the three of them. "Yes, because leaving a fairy godmother, a cat, and a giant dog alone in your apartment is a *brilliant* idea."

Charlotte's eyes flashed as she crossed her arms. "We are not helpless, Alex. We might not fully understand your world, but we can help."

Cat let out a low whine. He was not keen on staying behind either.

Alex sighed. He knew he was fighting a losing battle. He met his visitors' eyes and tossed a hand up. "Fine," he conceded, his voice weary. "But you have to stay out of harm's way."

Charlotte nodded. "We'll do our best, but we *will* help, Alex. This is our fight, too."

Sir Thomas smirked. "I've always been partial to danger."

They all trooped back outside. As Alex was locking the door, Sir Thomas looked at the sports car with a skeptical tilt of his head. "Are you sure we'll all fit back in?"

Alex chuckled. "We managed to squeeze in before, didn't we?" he replied, not bothered by the challenge.

Charlotte sat in the passenger seat to make room for the others. Cat curled up in the backseat, his eyes excited. Sir Thomas resignedly leaped onto the console.

"Try not to put the drive into 'crush the kitty,'" Sir Thomas quipped.

"No promises." That earned Alex a playful swat.

"Humans," Sir Thomas hissed, causing Charlotte to laugh.

For a few moments, they were lost in their thoughts. Charlotte was worried that her magic would fail when she needed it most. Sir Thomas pondered the dangers they might face. Alex was preoccupied with his responsibility for the group's safety, as well as his growing attraction for Charlotte.

Their collective worries hovering, there was a subtle shift in the eclectic group. Nervous eyes met in shared understanding. The corners of their mouths twitched upwards in hesitant but genuine smiles, small beacons of reassurance amid the uncertainty. An unspoken pact was forming, melding their fates. Adversity, a harsh and relentless blacksmith, hammered at the iron of their resolve, tempering it, shaping it into a bond as solid as steel. It fortified them, a wellspring of strength they could all draw from.

The car coasted to a stop at the crime scene. The bank, once a proud brick edifice, looked wounded. Its windows, shattered like a boxer's dreams, were gaping holes. Debris, like the aftermath of a storm, littered the sidewalk in a testament to the recent attack.

Blue and red lights danced over the scene, the police cars' strobes slicing through the darkness. Officers, their faces urgent, wove through the chaos. Yellow tape formed a barrier around the scene that the curious onlookers could not cross.

Alex maneuvered the vehicle into a quiet parking spot, and the car's engine stuttered to a halt, plunging its occupants into silence. The pause provided a brief respite to gather their thoughts and steel their nerves for what was to come.

They then stepped out into the cold reality of their situation.

CHAPTER ELEVEN

Alex's eyes held Charlotte, Cat, and Sir Thomas captive as they huddled in a dimly lit alley near the bank. It was a maze of discarded boxes and shadowed corners, an urban hideaway.

His gritty tone reinforced his order. "Stay in the shadows while I intercept the heist. I'll be back as soon as I can."

After Alex vanished, Charlotte's fingers tightened on her wand, and ten seconds later, she glanced at Sir Thomas. "What do you think? Should we wait here, or should we investigate?"

The feline tilted his head. "Despite his attitude, I have no reason to doubt the detective's abilities. I also know that fairy godmothers have their own way of doing things. You have a sense for these situations."

Charlotte made her decision and flicked her wand, which threw out sparks and sizzling arcs of electricity that danced in the air. The storm was contained within the alley's grungy walls.

Caught off-guard, Cat let out a startled woof. Sir Thomas recoiled, hissing.

Drawing her lips into a thin line, Charlotte muttered an apology. "I'm sorry, both of you." She winced at the remnants of her spell. "I didn't mean for it to be quite so...loud."

Then she saw a trail of magical breadcrumbs that flickered purple and blue. Cat's eyes followed the moving lights, and he sniffed the air, intrigued by the magical scent.

"Those are enchanted," Charlotte murmured, her brow furrowed in concentration. "Perhaps someone from EverAfter was responsible for this."

Sir Thomas' whiskers twitched. "We should follow this trail but tread lightly. We wouldn't want to send an alarm to whoever's conjured this magic." His tail curled around his paws as he added, "That would be a rather ironic twist, wouldn't it? Following breadcrumbs to our prey while they use them to discover us."

Charlotte nodded. Not informing Alex about their discovery was a risk. However, if this was the work of someone from EverAfter, they needed to act swiftly, and the detective was tied up with the heist.

The trio emerged from the alley onto the street, following the purple and blue line.

They scanned the crowd and the nearby buildings for danger but found nothing to alarm them. The breadcrumbs' glow brightened as they advanced. Their journey led them to the Ohio River Bridge, an architectural behemoth that spanned the broad river that separated Ohio and Kentucky. The water's surface reflected the sky, creating a mesmerizing canvas of shifting blues and grays.

Charlotte paused, captivated by the sight. Ever the energetic explorer, Cat bounded ahead, making light work of the bridge's expanse.

As they crossed, an impressive glass tower came into view. Its design was reminiscent of a cresting wave, a testament to human creativity and ambition. The building reflected light in all directions. The stunning spectacle made Charlotte catch her breath.

The breadcrumb trail led to the building. As they neared their destination, Charlotte's gaze swept over a gathering outside. A man stood out from the crowd, his silhouette oddly familiar. His nose was as cruelly hooked as a hawk's beak, and his grin was twisted and malicious. His greasy hair hung over his eyes, concealing a glint of dark mischief. Charlotte was uneasy since he resembled the sly and crafty Rumpelstiltskin from EverAfter.

A woman loomed beside him. Her sculpted chin jutted out arrogantly, and her piercing eyes had an icy edge that could freeze a person's blood. The venomous curl of her painted lips made her the image of Cinderella's wicked stepmother, and her high-pitched laugh clawed at the tranquility of the night.

The sight of the familiar figures amplified Charlotte's sense of foreboding. "Do you see them?"

Sir Thomas followed her line of sight. "It appears our EverAfter foes have found us," he murmured. "It is not chance."

Cat's tail mirrored his emotions, twitching in a blend of excitement and apprehension.

The group exchanged cautious glances as they carefully moved toward the building, which had a large, ornate sign titling it The Ascent. The breadcrumbs brightened again when the tower loomed above them, its glass façade reflecting the cityscape.

The familiar figures were gone. Pausing at the entrance, Charlotte absorbed the scale and design of the building. "We cannot let those inside go about their business without knowing what that business is. Let's go in and figure that out."

A middle-aged woman with short, curly red hair and a bemused expression stopped to stare at the unusual group. "Well, are not you all a delightful sight!" she exclaimed, laughing. "It is a bit early for Halloween, don't you think?" She eyed Sir Thomas. "How did you get your cat to do that?"

Charlotte met the woman's gaze and replied coolly. "We are not dressed for this 'Halloween.' We have important business to attend to."

"Hmmph." The lady continued down the sidewalk. "Young ones are so rude."

Charlotte redirected her focus to The Ascent, but Sir Thomas spoke up. "Charlotte, it is evident that we stick out like sore thumbs on this world." His eyes darted around. "Are you sure we should continue?"

She shrugged and tried for a reassuring smile. "Do not worry, Sir Thomas. After we are inside, I am sure we will blend in with the crowd. Besides, we need to locate the source of the enchanted breadcrumbs and determine its connection to the bank heist. There is no other way to accomplish that."

Charlotte pushed the front door open, and they stepped into a lobby filled with people of all shapes and sizes.

Though they still attracted curious glances, they made their way deeper into The Ascent, scanning for danger.

As they rounded a bend, someone caught their attention. A lanky man with a sinister grin, dressed in a tattered black cloak, was leaning against a wall, his eyes fixed on the trio. His greasy hair fell into his eyes, and his fingers ended in sharp yellowed nails. Charlotte recognized him as another minor villain from EverAfter.

"I know him, too," she whispered to her companions.

They couldn't walk by him, so Sir Thomas pointed out another option. Unfortunately, that way was blocked by a locked door.

Charlotte stepped up, brandished her wand, and whispered an incantation. The air buzzed with magic, and the tip of her wand spat tiny blue sparks that danced their way to the door, which she had blocked with her body.

The lock protested with a groan before succumbing to the spell. Then the door grudgingly opened. "After you two," she whispered. Sir Thomas went first, and she followed Cat through before shutting the door.

No one was in the hall, which led to another door at the end.

Their next challenge was the building's surveillance hub. Multiple cameras were trained on various parts of The Ascent, their electronic eyes vigilant. The room was alive with the hum of technology and flickers of lights.

Sir Thomas scanned the screens, then advanced to the console, whereon his paws swiftly navigated the buttons and switches, drawing on his knowledge of EverAfter's technical systems. His movements were assured and precise, a silent symphony of technical expertise.

The screens flickered, then, one by one, they faded to black, their watchful gazes temporarily suspended.

With the cameras neutralized, the group moved through the room and the rest of the building undetected.

Alex burst through the bank's doors, his pulse thundering in his ears. His gaze darted to the alley where he'd left his companions, but it was empty.

"Damn it, where have they gone?" His voice bounced off the uncaring walls of the alley as he paced, and the sharp clack of his boots on the concrete was a metronome marking his frustration. He ran a hand through his hair, the strands tangling in his fingers as he pulled on the roots.

A crackle snapped him out of his spiraling thoughts. His radio, forgotten in his hand, sprang to life. "There is some sort of…troll on the Ohio River Bridge. I thought it was a prank, but the caller was very distressed."

His heart sank. "Trolls now, too? What's next?" he groaned in disbelief and resignation. Then he shook his head. "Just another day in paradise," he mused with a sarcastic chuckle.

He squared his shoulders and retreated to his car. The engine roared to life, the purr of the motor a harsh contrast to the swirling chaos of his thoughts. With a final lingering glance at the abandoned alley, he sped toward the bridge, leaving the mystery of his missing companions behind to confront a troll.

Charlotte, Cat, and Sir Thomas were in a serpentine maze of corridors. The sterile smell of polished marble filled their nostrils, and the identical hallways challenged their sense of direction, making progress difficult.

Charlotte was on point, absorbing every detail of their surroundings. Her footsteps created an eerie soundtrack for their quest. Cat, his paws making no sound, sniffed the air. His flaring nostrils captured a whiff of dust and cleaning products, and he used those to guide them through the architectural enigma.

As they ventured deeper into the heart of The Ascent, the maze-like corridors seemed to close in on them. The first trap presented itself as an innocuous stretch of hallway. Then there was a sharp click, and gleaming spikes shot up through the floor.

Sir Thomas, who was now leading the group, sprang back. "Well, that was unexpected," he muttered, eyeing the deadly spikes warily. "Pretty sure those would have claimed all nine of my lives."

Charlotte stepped forward, wand high, and uttered a soft spell. The spikes retracted, leaving a clear path forward.

"No time to dawdle," she warned, scanning the hall ahead as they hurried away.

"Fairy godmothers," he whispered. "Can't find them when you want them, but you can follow them to your death, no problem."

He glanced at Charlotte, who was either not paying attention to him or didn't care.

The second trap was less obvious and more cunning. A barrier slid down behind them, cutting off their retreat.

Simultaneously, the floor tilted, threatening to send them sliding into a pit that had opened up at one end of the corridor.

Quick on his feet, Cat pressed his paws to the slanting floor, managing to stay in place. Charlotte grasped a ledge, but Sir Thomas slid toward the pit.

Cat pounced, fastened his jaws on the edge of Sir Thomas' cloak, and hauled him back.

Charlotte, face taut with concentration, flourished her wand in a complex pattern while uttering a counterspell. With a grinding noise, the floor leveled out, and the barrier slid back up.

"Two traps down," Charlotte stated. "Who knows how many to go? Let's proceed with more caution."

"You think?" Sir Thomas asked.

CHAPTER TWELVE

Alex navigated through the gridlocked traffic, mind filled with thoughts of trolls and his missing companions. When he reached the bridge, he brought the car to a screeching halt, let out a weary sigh, and slammed the car door.

As he made his way to the toll booth, he couldn't ignore the chaos. Drivers were blowing their horns, passengers were shouting, and bystanders were eagerly capturing the spectacle on their smartphones. At the epicenter of the madness stood a short, grotesque troll whose clothing was filthy and barely held together. This troll, whose beard seemed to have a life of its own, was demanding gold coins from the drivers in exchange for passage across the bridge.

"What do you mean you don't have any gold coins?!" the troll bellowed at an exasperated driver. "You can't cross, then!"

"I don't have any gold coins, man!" the driver shot back, his face turning a shade of crimson that rivaled a tomato. "Just let me through. You aren't a toll booth employee, dickhead!"

The troll peered at the driver, beard quivering with indignation. "I'll have you know that I am the official Troll Toll Collector, and I take my job very seriously, thankyouverymuch!" He gestured at his attire with mock pride. "I'm an employee of the highest caliber, even if my uniform is somewhat unique."

The driver's frustration mounted. "Look, man, I don't care if you're the damn Goblin King! I have to get across this bridge, and I don't have any gold coins!"

The troll leaned closer, his voice dripping sympathy. "Dear traveler, I understand your predicament. Truly, I do. But rules are rules, and trolls are sticklers for tradition. If you don't have gold coins, perhaps you could offer me something else of value?" He waggled his bushy eyebrows suggestively.

The driver's eyes widened. "Are you seriously asking for a bribe?"

The troll feigned innocence, clasping a hand to his heart. "Oh, no! I would never stoop so low as to accept a bribe. I am merely suggesting a friendly exchange of goods and services. A trade, if you will."

The driver threw his hands up in frustration. "This is insane! Fine. What do you want?"

The troll grinned, revealing a mouthful of mismatched yellow teeth. "Excellent! Now, what I truly desire is a lifetime supply of peanut butter and jelly sandwiches. The crusts must be removed, of course. I'll also need a steady stream of kitten videos to keep me entertained during my duties. Can you provide those, good sir?"

The driver blinked. "You want sandwiches and cat videos?"

The troll nodded. "A troll has to have his creature comforts."

The driver couldn't decide whether to laugh or cry. "All right, fine. Sandwiches and cat videos it is. Just let me through."

With a triumphant cackle, the troll waved the driver through the booth. As the car passed, he added, "Make sure the sandwiches are crustless, or I may reconsider."

The man threw him the middle finger as he gunned the car.

"Not sure that negotiation is going to hold." The troll harrumphed.

As Alex approached the toll booth, he overheard a woman's frantic conversation. Her voice trembled as she spoke into her phone. "You won't believe what's happening, Jess. Some lunatic hijacked the toll booth and is demanding gold coins from everyone. I'm scared, Jessie. I don't know what to do."

The troll, oblivious to Alex's arrival, was in the middle of an animated exchange with another frustrated driver. "You expect me to believe you don't have any gold coins?" The troll leaned over to the driver, his beard touching the car's window.

The driver's face was flushed with irritation. "I don't have any gold coins, and I *don't* have time for this nonsense. Just let me through!" He punctuated his sentence with an exasperated hand gesture.

The troll grinned maliciously. "My dear friend, it's not nonsense. It's tradition! Trolls have collected tolls on bridges for centuries. We're preserving history here!" He raised an eyebrow as if to convince the driver of the importance of the situation.

The driver rolled his eyes. "Look, buddy, I don't care about your traditions. I need to get to work, or my boss is going to have my ass. For the last time, *I don't have any gold coins!*"

Alex, concerned about the escalating situation, stepped forward and addressed the troll. "Excuse me. You need to step away from the toll booth."

The troll turned to Alex, his lips curling into a contemptuous smile. His matted hair swayed as he shook his head. "You do not have any power over me, copper. I am in charge here, and if you want to cross my bridge, you have to pay the toll like everyone else."

Alex's eyes flashed. "I am here to remove you from this toll booth and secure safety and order for the people on this bridge!"

Their heated argument became a clash of wills, their words flying like artillery barrages. Features contorted with anger, the troll defended his bizarre occupation, insisting taking tolls was his rightful job. "*Tradition! Duty!* Those are the pillars upon which I stand, mortal!"

Alex met the troll's fierce defense with his own unrelenting conviction. "The pillar you are standing on holds up this bridge!" he retorted. "A bridge that ain't yours, jackass!"

The air crackled with tension. The troll's breath came out in furious gusts, and his hair danced with each utterance. Alex's brow furrowed as he locked eyes with the troll, refusing to yield.

The onlookers held their breath, caught between the fantastical and the rational.

The troll's voice was hoarse from his fervent defense, and his gnarled hands clenched and unclenched in frustration. Alex's words were sharp as a sword, slicing through the troll's arguments with precision. The battle raged on, and the bridge itself seemed to hold its breath, suspended in a surreal moment of discordant harmony.

The troll's fury erupted like a volcano. A guttural growl emerged from the depths of his chest, shaking the toll booth as his gnarled hand retrieved a concealed club and slammed it on the asphalt.

Alex's performed a tango of survival in the face of certain death. As the troll's club hurtled toward him like a battering ram forged in hell, Alex's reflexes kicked into overdrive, and he escaped the devastating strike by a whisker's breadth. The wind from the club's passing made his clothes ripple like flags of valor.

Alex had no choice. He drew his concealed weapon.

The Glock 26, chambered in 9mm Parabellum, fit snugly in Alex's hand, its ergonomic grip designed for comfort and control. Its matte-black finish exuded unassuming authority, perfectly suited for discreet carry. The pistol's low-profile sights, illuminated with faint tritium dots, allowed for quick and accurate target acquisition.

As he aimed the Glock at the troll, the metallic slide clicked back with a sharp, distinctive sound. The pistol's firepower was anything but diminutive, unlike its frame.

The pistol was renowned for its reliability, and at this moment, it was a symbol of Alex's authority and his last line of defense. His finger rested on the trigger as he faced the bizarre creature that had disrupted the bridge's tranquility. He was prepared to use the Glock to restore order and protect the people caught in the supernatural situation.

He reminded himself that the paperwork he'd have to file for firing his weapon was a bitch, and he wasn't sure the troll knew what was in his hand.

Alex quipped, "You know, buddy, I've dodged traffic jams that were scarier than you." Then he yelled, "Oh, shit!" and searched for a spot to hunker down.

Alex darted behind a nearby car, pulled out his collapsible baton, and extended it. The troll, angered by the detective's persistence, had flung debris at the detective with a wave of his hand.

Frustrated drivers honked their horns while onlookers filmed the fight, their faces expressing their shock and fear. The troll's magical gusts sent trash and debris swirling across the bridge, making it difficult for Alex to predict the creature's movements.

Despite his tactical skills and military training, Alex struggled to land a solid hit on the troll. The creature's brute strength and simple magic were more than a match for the detective's arsenal. In desperation, Alex aimed his Glock at the troll's eye and squeezed the trigger.

The shot hit its mark.

The troll howled as blood poured from his ruined eye. His furious screams filled the air, drowning out the honking horns and the gasps of the horrified onlookers. Alex's heart pounded with relief, but the battle was far from over.

The troll, driven into a frenzy by the pain in its eye,

swung his club with greater ferocity. The bridge shook beneath the mighty blows, and chunks of concrete tumbled into the river below. Steel beams groaned and twisted under the strain, and the glass in the toll booth shattered. With each strike, the structural integrity of the bridge weakened further.

Alex charged toward the troll, taser in hand, aiming for a patch of exposed flesh on the creature's leg. The taser's prongs struck their target, and electricity surged through the wires. To Alex's shock, the troll did not flinch, just glanced at the taser with disdain and swatted it away with a meaty hand.

A young woman with a baby clutched to her chest sobbed into her phone. A group of teenagers huddled together, recording the chaos on their smartphones. An elderly couple clung to each other, the woman whispering prayers for their safety. Amid the panic, a man in a business suit attempted to flag down a car, desperate to distance himself from the supernatural creature.

The troll, sensing its advantage, unleashed a powerful gust that sent several vehicles skidding across the asphalt. With a guttural roar, it leaped onto the railing, teetering above the churning waters. It looked over its shoulder at Alex and, with a snarl of defiance, launched itself from the bridge and disappeared beneath the water, leaving a whirlpool behind.

Frustration surged through Alex as he scanned the bridge. The toll booth resembled a toy flung away by a petulant child. Its twisted metal frame, bent and contorted, bore the scars of the troll's strikes, and glass no longer graced its windows.

The bridge, once a sturdy passage for commuters, was in dire disrepair. Its steel beams groaned, their integrity decreasing with each passing second. Chunks of concrete dangled perilously over the churning river, a portent of the amount of reinforcement that would have to take place if this bridge was going to stand.

The acrid scents of gasoline and smoke filled the air, a reminder of the violent clash that had just taken place. A pungent cocktail of burned rubber and charred debris added to the sensory assault.

Car alarms wailed, and sirens in the distance added to the cacophony. Alex's jaw clenched. In the midst of this surreal nightmare, his duty was unchanged. It was his job to restore order, unravel the mystery of the troll's rampage, and protect the innocent who had unwittingly become witnesses to the extraordinary.

To do that, he needed to find his companions. Was it only earlier today that he had wondered if Charlotte was pulling his leg about magic? He shook his head as he eyed a man whose head was bleeding.

"I will find you," Alex vowed, his voice barely audible above the chaos. "And when I do, you will pay for what you did here today—assuming something else doesn't get in the way, which, if this continues, is likely."

"Detective!" He turned his head when someone called for him.

Alex sighed. No rest for this weary detective. He wasn't supposed to have taken the call, but everyone else had been busy. He holstered his weapon.

His captain walked up, his tall frame topped by a neat crop of salt-and-pepper hair. His piercing blue eyes surveyed the wreckage with disbelief and anger. The glitter on his shoulder seemed out of place. "Report."

Alex braced himself as he explained the bizarre battle that had just taken place. "Captain, I know this sounds crazy, but I was attacked by a troll. Not an internet troll, but a real, honest-to-God troll." He waved at the bridge. "It nearly destroyed the entire structure."

The captain stared at him and shook his head. "A troll, Detective? You expect me to accept that a mythical creature was responsible for this mess?" The disbelief in his voice wounded Alex.

"We have it on video, Captain." Alex pointed at people with their phones out.

The captain walked away, muttering, "Fairytales." Alex took a moment to survey the damage the troll had caused. Cars had been overturned and crushed, their shattered glass glistening in the moonlight. The people who had witnessed the battle huddled together. Some whispered among themselves, their voices low and filled with wonder, while others stared at the carnage, unable to comprehend what they had just seen.

"I saw it with my own eyes," one woman insisted, her voice trembling. "It was like something out of a nightmare."

A man, his hands shaking, recounted the troll's relentless assault. "It just kept coming, no matter what he did. It was unstoppable."

More officers appeared and calmed the crowd. Alex sighed as he put away his weapon. He was sure that in a few days, some story would come out that would chalk this up to a mundane criminal. Perhaps that was for the best.

He looked across the bridge as his radio crackled to life. "We have a major disturbance at…"

It had been a hell of a day.

CHAPTER THIRTEEN

When the trio stepped into the grand ballroom, they saw magical creatures of all shapes and sizes mingling and conversing. Goblins chatted with fairies, and a group of elves laughed at a towering troll's joke.

Charlotte took it all in. "Is this a celebration?"

"I have an inkling." Sir Thomas gestured at banners hanging from the banisters, bearing the words REPEL FOR MAYOR OF CINCINNATI! in bold letters. Below the text was a familiar face that made Charlotte's jaw drop.

"No! It can't be," she whispered, staring at Prince Repel, a despised figure from her homeland. Her mind flashed back to the day he was banished. He had walked through the portal that led to the human world, but here he was, seemingly thriving in his new environment.

Charlotte turned to Sir Thomas and Cat. "I was there when he was banished. I saw him step through the portal. How did he end up here, running for mayor?"

"You might wish to keep your voice down, milady," Sir

Thomas warned, glancing around. "Remember where we are."

Charlotte took another look at the partygoers. Their attire fused elegance and grotesque extravagance, a visual representation of their twisted characters. Silken gowns shimmered under the grand chandeliers, their fine embroidery reproducing monstrous features. Luxuriously tailored coats adorned scaly, inhuman skin.

The room buzzed with anticipation and shared malevolence that clung to the air, making it heavy and difficult to breathe.

"I have never seen so many poisoned apples in one place," a witch cackled, gesturing at a table laden with cursed fruit.

"At last, an opportunity to show these pathetic mortals who is in charge," the Big Bad Wolf barked, his sharp teeth glinting as he spoke.

An evil queen, her dark beauty enhanced by her form-fitting black gown and ornate ruby necklace, surveyed the room with an air of superiority. A woman with spider legs strutted by in a gown made of shimmering webs, and a man with a vulture's head pecked an hors d'oeuvre with his sharp beak. The conversations that floated past Charlotte's ears made her skin crawl.

As the trio observed the gathering, it became evident this was more than just a party. It was the start of a sinister alliance. The villains in the room had a common goal. They all wanted power and control, and Prince Repel was offering them the opportunity to seize it.

"Is not this just our luck? We stumble upon the villainous gathering of the century, and all we brought were a wand with dubious magic, a cat who is now a dog, and another cat with an attitude problem," Sir Thomas opined dryly.

Charlotte glanced at her companions.

Sir Thomas was watching the crowd. "I knew these villains were up to no good, but I did not anticipate that they were so organized."

"Not a fan of the other team being smart," Charlotte agreed. "I prefer them stupid and dumb."

Cat growled at the Big Bad Wolf, who shot him a scornful look.

At the center of the room was a twisted tree trunk that served as a podium, adorned with banners proclaiming Prince Repel's mayoral candidacy. In stark contrast to his noble brother Prince Charming, Repel was the black sheep of the royal family in EverAfter. He stood proudly before the crowd, his dark hair falling over eyes that gleamed with triumph and malice. A wicked grin spread across his face as he addressed the villainous assembly.

"Welcome, my esteemed confederates of cunning and malevolence!" Prince Repel began, his voice rebounding off the grand ballroom's walls. His charisma was evident, commanding the attention of everyone in the room. "As we gather in my new lovely building in this fetid new realm, let us mark this occasion as the dawn of a new era—an era where we, the true forces of power and cunning, will rise to reign supreme!"

A wicked grin spread across his face as he continued, "In a matter of weeks, the title 'Mayor of Cincinnati' will be mine. Not one I longed for in my previous life, but it shall serve our purpose in this world. Once I am in that position of power, we shall initiate our grand plan to take control and let those mundane mortals know they are no longer the ones holding the reins."

The crowd erupted into cheers and applause. The Big Bad Wolf howled in approval, the evil queen laughed wickedly, and Captain Hook raised his artificial hand in salute.

"I extend my deepest gratitude to each and every one of you who stands before me today. Whether you pledged your allegiance willingly or I had to pull you from the comfortable confines of our homeland of EverAfter, know that your move has not been in vain. In time, you will see the wisdom of my actions, for in this new world, we will rewrite the stories in which we were the defeated. Here, we will be the victors!"

Repel's words resonated with power and promise, leaving the room charged with an electric energy of anticipation and malevolence. As he stepped down from the twisted podium, he was swarmed by his villainous supporters, each vying for a moment in the presence of their charismatic leader.

Charlotte processed Repel's words. Had he forcibly brought people to this world? How was that even possible? Anger and shock washed over her.

Sir Thomas was deep in thought. "Why is Cincinnati the epicenter of all this magical activity? What attracts those beings to this city?"

Charlotte barely heard him. She was searching for an exit. "We need to get out of here," she whispered tensely.

Beside her, Cat's fur stood on end, and he growled as he eyed the crowd. The trio was vastly outnumbered; their anonymity was their only shield. They had to act quickly and cautiously to avoid facing the wrath of the most malevolent forces EverAfter had to offer.

Sir Thomas murmured, "Perhaps we can slip through the crowd unnoticed and make our way to that side entrance by the ice sculpture." He calculated their course through the sea of villains.

Before they could put their plan into action, the ballroom doors flew open and hit the wall with a bang, drawing the attention of everyone present. A squirrel, its fur electric blue, burst in, its tiny face determined. As it surveyed the room, its beady eyes sparkled with a defiant mischief that challenged the opulence and arrogance of the crowd.

After an acrobatic leap, it landed on a lavishly set table. Crystal goblets tumbled, causing expensive wine to flood the tablecloth.

"Asshole! That was three-hundred-year-old goblin wine!" cried an ogre in a tuxedo, his face turning a deeper shade of green.

"What in the name of Fat Jack Merlin's beard is going on?" wailed a witch who had probably dressed in a gas station bathroom. She retrieved a spellbook drenched in mimosa.

The blue squirrel bounded from table to table, scattering hors d'oeuvres and toppling crystal decanters. The once-elegant ballroom was now a scene of bedlam, with the clatter of shattered crystal and the outraged cries of the villains as a soundtrack.

"What the devil!" a short gnome cried sharply. A wheel

of some pungent cheese had rolled off a nearby platter onto its head.

"I'll turn that blasted rodent into a brooch!" threatened a witch, aiming her wand at the squirrel. After she loosed a bolt of lightning, a pissed-off wizard whose conical head decoration had caught fire glared at her. She muttered, "Oh, dear," as she disappeared.

In the eye of the storm, Charlotte, Cat, and Sir Thomas exchanged glances. They now had an opening, so, like specters dancing in a moon-drenched landscape, Sir Thomas led them through the throng.

The side entrance got tantalizingly closer as they wove through the crowd, the gigantic ice sculpture a marker shimmering under the chandeliers' glow. The disgruntled murmurs and clattering faded, replaced by thoughts of reaching the exit.

As they neared the door, their hopes were dashed. A loud shout pierced the din, followed by a booming, "*Stop! There they are!*"

CHAPTER FOURTEEN

The squirrel leaped at a large orc with a scar crossing his face who was dressed in a dark, finely tailored suit that strained against his massive frame. The rodent landed on his shoulder with the agility of a gymnast, causing the orc to emit a bellow of surprise and anger that echoed off the high gilded ceiling.

"What the—" the orc sputtered, reaching with a meaty hand to try to swat the squirrel away.

The squirrel was too quick. He darted around the orc's neck and leaped off, then bounded toward Charlotte.

Sir Thomas was ready. With his sword drawn and gleaming in the light, he was prepared to strike down any threat to Charlotte. The squirrel proved to be no threat, only ran between Charlotte's legs, its tiny claws brushing against her ankle. Charlotte yelped in surprise, her dark eyes wide.

To her astonishment, the squirrel looked up at her, its bright eyes filled with regret. "My bad, lady! Had to be done. Did not mean to spook you," it said in a high-pitched voice that was incongruously deep for its size.

Charlotte stared, mouth agape, and Sir Thomas raised a quizzical eyebrow. "Was that who I think it was?" he asked.

The lull in the chaos came to an abrupt end when the scarred orc locked eyes with Charlotte and snarled, "That's the bitch who ruined me in EverAfter! Get her!"

The ballroom erupted into a melee as villains of all shapes and sizes converged on Charlotte and her companions. Sir Thomas moved like a whirlwind, his sword flashing as he parried and struck, sending villains flying with every expertly placed blow.

Cat, the duo's fearsome canine companion, leaped into the fray, his powerful jaws clamping onto the arms of villains, sending weapons clattering to the floor.

Charlotte focused on disabling the attackers' guns. She muttered a spell, her wand weaving intricate patterns in the air, but something went wrong. Instead of disarming the villains, the guns transformed into a bouquet of flowers, a rubber chicken, and a turtle. The villains stared at their former weapons, nonplussed.

"What the hell?" one exclaimed, holding the bouquet as if it were a bomb.

Before the situation could devolve further, the doors to the ballroom burst open, and the Three Billy Goats Gruff trotted in. Their fur was matted and dirty, and they wore ammo vests. They looked like they had just stepped out of a war zone. The largest of the three snorted aggressively, pawing the ground before charging into the fray.

"By the twinkling stars in my tiara!" Charlotte exclaimed. "Those guys, too?"

Sir Thomas glanced at the rampaging goats and rolled his eyes. "Really? Ammo vests? None of you has any fashion sense." Despite his sarcastic comment, his eyes showed fear as the largest goat barreled toward them, his horns lowered menacingly.

Cat stood his ground, growling at the new entrants with his fur standing on end.

Charlotte willed her magic to cooperate, but when she waved her wand, only sparks appeared. She needed to regain control of her magic and fast. The ballroom had turned into a battleground, and she had to take charge before the situation spiraled even further out of hand. She longed for a little control and more results at this moment.

From the corner, the squirrel watched the chaos unfold, munching on a nut it had found. It made a comment about the scarred orc's appearance. "Wow, did you get dressed in the dark, or is that just your face?" it quipped, causing a few of the nearby villains to snicker before they were silenced by the orc's glare.

Sir Thomas was engaged in a fierce battle with the Three Billy Goats Gruff, his sword meeting the horns of the largest goat in a shower of sparks.

Cat was battling the orc's henchmen and failed to notice one of the goats sneaking up behind him. The goat lowered its head and butted Cat into the crowd.

"*CAT!*" Charlotte screamed, her heart in her throat. Then she heard a woof and blew out a breath of relief as Cat ran past her, having recovered from the blow.

A group of talking mice appeared from somewhere and was creeping toward Charlotte, their beady eyes gleaming with malevolence. When they saw Cat, they stopped in their tracks. He sprang at them, and the mice scattered, squeaking in terror.

"Charlotte, we need your magic!" Sir Thomas called over the din, his sword clashing with the horns of the largest goat.

Charlotte raised her wand, muttering a spell, but only sparks appeared. She cursed under her breath, her frustration mounting.

An imp, its scales bloody and clutching a knife, locked eyes with Charlotte, snarling in rage. Before it could make a move, a large foot kicked its ass, sending it flying into the crowd. One moment, it was there, and the next, it was gone.

Charlotte looked around for her next challenge. Whatever had happened to the little bastard, it was not her problem. She had bigger fish to fry.

The ballroom had transformed into a pandemonium of clashing swords, flying spells, and outraged cries from the villains. In the midst of the chaos, the blue squirrel continued its reign of mischief, leaping from one table to another, knocking over glasses, spilling drinks, and sending plates of food flying into the air.

"Damn that rodent!" a witch in a tattered robe cursed as a piece of cake splattered on her pointed hat. She sent a bolt of purple lightning toward the squirrel, but it nimbly dodged the attack, its tiny body moving with an agility that was almost supernatural.

Sir Thomas, Charlotte, and Cat were locked in a fierce battle with the villains. They parried and struck in a dance of death, using every ounce of their skill and strength to fend off the attackers. The ballroom floor was littered with the bodies of fallen foes, their crumpled forms a testament to the trio's prowess.

"Over there! The exit!" Charlotte shouted, pointing at a set of double doors that seemed tantalizingly close yet impossibly far away. They fought their way toward the doors, their progress slow but steady as they cut through a sea of villains that seemed endless.

The squirrel, having completed its mission of sowing discord among the villains, made a beeline for a window. With an acrobatic leap, it reached the sill and turned to look back at the chaos it had created. Its bright eyes gleamed with satisfaction, and with a cheeky wink, it leaped out the window, disappearing into the night.

Charlotte, Sir Thomas, and Cat finally reached the doors, but as they were about to make their escape, a massive troll blocked their way, club high and ready to strike. As a last-ditch effort, Sir Thomas raised his sword and brought it down on the troll's leg.

It screamed in agony and fell to the side, creating a path to the doors. Then another figure stepped into their way—a tall man wearing a black cloak, his face hidden in the shadows of the hood. The room seemed to darken as he approached.

Charlotte felt a chill run down her spine as the man lifted his hand. He had a ball of fire dancing on his palm. She raised her wand to cast a spell, but the fireball exploded. When she could see again, the man was gone.

Panic clenched Charlotte's chest as she looked around the ballroom. The villains were fighting among themselves as much as against the trio's spells and blows. Reinforcements poured in from every door and window, their faces twisted in rage and their weapons glinting in the light from the chandeliers.

The squirrel had disappeared, its mission to create chaos complete, leaving the trio to fend for themselves. Charlotte almost despaired when she realized the enormity of the task. They were outnumbered and outmatched, and escape seemed impossible.

"Fight!" Sir Thomas yelled, his voice cutting through the din. "We must fight to the end!"

Charlotte agreed, not that there was much choice. They would fight, or they would leave themselves to whatever fate these nefarious creatures had in store for them.

Considering how many wanted her dead, she had a good idea of where that would lead.

CHAPTER FIFTEEN

Magic pulsed through the room, and raw energy surged from every corner, bathing the space in color. Enchantments were cast haphazardly, with wildly varying success.

Seemingly having a mind of its own, Charlotte's wand continued to defy her commands, channeling an unruly magic that created humor amid the chaos.

As Charlotte attempted to cast a binding spell on an enemy, her wand sputtered rebelliously and turned a nearby potted plant into a hostile vine. The new vegetation monster rose and flexed, then whipped its muscular tendrils at the villains. They recoiled, distracted from their original targets.

"On the wings of wayward pixies," Charlotte yelled, fighting to keep her magic under control. She was both frustrated and resigned.

Sir Thomas slid through a villain's legs. "We aren't winning, Charlotte."

"Tell me something I don't know." She punched a man with a glass eye. "Any suggestions?"

"Run?" Sir Thomas half-asked, half-answered.

"Where?" Charlotte asked after an explosion on their left flung two people onto a pig that was bitching from the sidelines.

Emboldened, Sir Thomas charged into the tumult anew. A sinister-looking wolf with a scar marring its muzzle was his target. The wolf bared its teeth, swinging a spiked club threateningly. Sir Thomas evaded the attack, retaliating with a slam of his paws that turned the dangerous weapon into so much firewood. The wolf snarled and retreated.

Sir Thomas then engaged in a battle with a hulking orc who wielded a hammer so massive that it seemed to defy gravity. Sir Thomas executed a well-timed leap over its head.

Problematically, the orc was trying to do the same thing.

They collided in mid-air, and both hit the floor, the orc with a thud. The hammer slipped out of its hands and slid across the marble floor.

From the corner of her eye, Charlotte saw the hammer careen toward a mouse sporting spiked hair who was watching from the sidelines.

The mouse was skittering around the edge of the room, perhaps hoping not to be noticed. Charlotte could imagine its horrifying end, and she turned away, not wishing to watch or get wounded for not paying attention.

Her magic continued to perform in odd ways, transforming an enemy's blackjack into a rubber duck, its bright yellow body incongruous amid the blood in the room.

A whirlwind spell cast by a villain wearing a purple and

yellow pantsuit went comically awry. A torrent of soap bubbles danced in the air, their iridescent surfaces providing a moment of beauty amid the turmoil.

More adversaries emerged. A wicked witch with a crooked nose and a malevolent grin cackled as she conjured a ball of fire.

Charlotte saw the witch's fireball and aimed her wand at it.

"Torrent of Tides!" she commanded. Her intent was to douse the fireball.

However, as if it had a taste for chaos, the wand resisted her command. Instead of water, it produced butterflies, each more colorful than the last.

Their delicate wings, which resembled stained glass, fluttered in a captivating dance. They caught the light from the fireball and reflected it in a myriad of dazzling colors, creating a spectacle that was as enchanting as it was surprising.

The witch, thrown by beauty, stumbled back a few steps, and her confident cackles choked off when the butterflies approached her face. Their iridescent wings picked up the fireball's glow, illuminating her surprised countenance.

"W-what in the hells?" she stammered as she tried to swat the swarm away, her fireball forgotten. "By Morgana's Scales, what sorcery is this?"

In the midst of the pandemonium, Charlotte's voice cut through like a knife. "Thomas, chandelier! Hurl yourself toward the witch!" She didn't need to say more.

Quickly, Sir Thomas deciphered Charlotte's plan. His eyes darted to the grand chandelier swaying precariously overhead. With a swift motion and determination etched onto his face, he leaped onto the ornate fixture. His paw gripped one of the delicate chains, the cold metal biting into his skin. Using the inertia, he swung forward, his body soaring through the air toward the wicked witch. As he closed in, he shouted defiantly, "Your reign of terror ends now!" His weapon was drawn, reflecting the eerie glow of the room, and he slashed at her with a fervor born of both strategy and desperation.

In another corner of the hall, Cat faced a grotesque troll clutching a massive hammer. It took all of Cat's strength and agility to dodge its blows as a low growl resonated from his throat, a subtle but clear warning to his opponent.

He sprang at it, his jaws clamping down with an iron grip onto the hilt of the troll's weapon. He held on, teeth clenched, which prevented the creature from using its weapon. His eyes flashed with an unspoken challenge, silently daring the troll to reconsider his choice of weaponry.

With a yip of surprise, the troll flung Cat off. Unfortunately, he didn't let go of the hammer, and he disappeared into the melee.

The attacks continued, each villain more menacing than the last.

Sir Thomas had a savage gash on his left shoulder. His eyes, usually filled with mirth, were clouded with pain.

Cat was also the worse for wear. His fur was disheveled and an ear was split, a painful memento of a close encounter. His face was covered with scratches that left raw maroon trails in his fur, but despite the physical toll, his eyes glowed.

"Cat." Sir Thomas' voice was brusque. "We need a way out."

Charlotte thrust her wand at a veiled woman who seemed intent on stopping them, and a dazzling shower of pink and purple sparks exploded outward like a supernova.

The burst caught their adversaries off-guard. The veiled woman staggered backward, shielding her eyes from the blinding display. Others in the crowd faltered, disoriented. The trio had finally gotten a respite.

Sir Thomas lunged at the nearest adversary, and his fist connected with the villain's jaw. The villain grunted as he staggered back, surprised by the strength of the diminutive cat's attack.

Sir Thomas darted toward the next opponent and landed a swift punch to the gut that left the enemy doubled over. A well-placed kick sent a third adversary sprawling. Each move was precise and effective, a seasoned fighter taking advantage of the confusion.

Crouching, Cat crept along the edge of the ballroom, his nose twitching as he sniffed the air and analyzed the chaos. The thrill of the chase made his fur bristle with anticipation as he tracked an anomaly amid the rich scents of perfume, wine, and villainy.

He paused by an unassuming section of the wall, nostrils flaring as he inhaled the odd scent—dust in a hidden passage. His ears pricked up, his body went rigid, and he let out a low bark. It wasn't loud, but it cut through the commotion, a signal to his friends that he'd found something.

His tail wagged. To anyone else, it would have seemed like canine joy, but for Charlotte and Sir Thomas, it was a

Morse code message promising escape. Charlotte and Sir Thomas rushed to him, casting wary glances over their shoulders. The air was thick with magic, but no one attacked them.

Charlotte had a wry smile on her lips. "It's as if the EverAfter magic is a first-time tourist, lost in translation," she remarked. "It's trying to adapt to this alien world. The slew of misinterpretations? Well, they weren't what I intended, but it got the basic idea."

No sooner had she finished speaking than the validity of her statement was hammered home. A villain who was attempting to render himself invisible ended up looking as conspicuous as a peacock in the desert. The eye-catching plaid suit would've given a tartan enthusiast a run for his money.

She pointed at the corner, where another villain was wrestling with a magical faux pas. Intended to summon a fire-breathing dragon, his ambitious spell backfired. The result was a creature that spewed glitter, not flames. The room now wore the shimmering residue of the creature's belch.

"We must remain vigilant," Sir Thomas cautioned, scanning their surroundings. "Humorous as those hiccups are, we cannot let our guard down."

He ducked a cannonball. "See?" The ball went through the wall where his head had been.

"Yes," Charlotte replied. "You almost dropped your guard."

Cat added his mite to the conversation with a growl of agreement.

"I'm thinking that's not a way out." He pointed at the

hole, and Charlotte saw a seriously large eye looking at them.

"Well, ice dragon tits." Charlotte glanced at the glittering villains, who were slowly getting their wits back. A few looked at the party crashers with malice.

Charlotte nodded, accepting the responsibility for ruining their night. "We can get out of here."

"Seriously?" Sir Thomas slashed his sword in a figure eight. "I'm not sure what they give you to drink at fairy godmother gatherings, but I'd like some."

"Deal!" Charlotte yelled, then wielded her wand like a sword, casting spell after spell at the villains coming at them. Her wand created animated flowers instead of the disarming spell she had hoped for.

They cascaded from the villain's former sword, dancing joyously in the air. Startled, the villain flung them away, muttering curses that bordered on poetic. Charlotte shot him an impressed look, surprised by his imagination.

He smirked, then went ass over appetite when an errant chair caught him upside the head.

Choosing to trust the unpredictable nature of her magic rather than abandon it, Charlotte continued casting spells. Each resulted in a different and often hilarious outcome, further confounding their foes.

Then sirens pierced the air.

"Oh, thank god! It's the police!" Sir Thomas smiled, then frowned. "We weren't supposed to leave that alley."

"How would we have known about this gathering if we hadn't?"

Alex burst through a door with a team of heavily armed police officers. Their appearance forced the villains to stop harassing the trio for a moment, but then one of the criminals sent a torrent of dark energy at Charlotte.

That grabbed everyone's attention.

Fortunately for Charlotte, the spell backfired, and the energy exploded around the criminal.

Smoke filled the room, and just like that, the fight was back on.

CHAPTER SIXTEEN

Alex took in the chaotic scene. Unpredictable magic created otherworldly tableaus, and the scents of incense, ozone, and a dozen other things stung his nostrils.

His gaze went to Charlotte, whose eyes glowed like fire opals. Their intensity was as mesmerizing as it was terrifying, and his image of a damsel in distress shattered.

It was replaced by that of a warrior who was wielding magic as lethal as any weapon.

The presence of the police team ratcheted up the stakes of the conflict. Gritting their teeth, the cops prepared for a blitz attack.

Amid the chaos, Charlotte moved with speed and precision and grace and fluidity. Her magic cast an almost holy aura around her, and her gleaming hair floated in the glow of her magic.

The battlefield was forgotten as Charlotte sprinted to meet Alex, her cloak billowing behind her. The scents of lavender and magic followed her, a heady and enchanting blend that encapsulated her essence.

Alex got caught in her gaze.

Her voice rang out, steel-wrapped silk slicing through the bedlam. "We have a serious fight ahead of us." The urgency in her tone sent prickles down Alex's spine and reminded him of the danger he and his team were in.

Charlotte's features were drawn with worry. "We're dealing with Prince Repel," she told him, her voice strained. Her words cast a dark cloud on the battlefield.

Alex's heartbeat stuttered. A prince? From the look on Charlotte's face, he was not one of the kind and virtuous figures from normal fairytales.

"Prince Repel has always desired power, unfettered by constraints." Her voice was serious and grim. "In EverAfter, we stopped him before he could pull off his plan, then banished him after a stay of execution. In exile, Repel has apparently turned his sights to this world."

She looked around to make sure no one was targeting them. The cops had gotten involved, but fortunately, no one was shooting. "A reality free of the mystical checks and balances that held him at bay."

As Alex pieced together their predicament, his frown deepened. "So, the mayor-to-be is an evil prince. That is less surprising than one would think, considering politics." The realization turned his blood to ice. Remembering the recent headlines that had sent ripples of unrest throughout the city, he added, "I don't know his goals, but I'm guessing we don't want him to succeed."

The thought of Prince Repel, a villain from a fairytale land he had recently scoffed at, holding a position of authority in his city was as ludicrous as it was concerning.

Charlotte frowned. "If he wins, he'll gain control on a level he's never had before. Tangible political power."

The sirens' blare redoubled, signaling that reinforcements had arrived.

For a brief moment, their gazes locked, and a silent vow passed between them. Then she charged into the melee. She darted through the chaos, her movements as fluid as they were swift. Her inner warrior emerged with a force that was both terrifying and awe-inspiring. Each action was a lethal dance imbued with a deadly grace.

Beside Alex, Officer Mellows, a gruff man with a stoic exterior and a heart of gold, watched the spectacle with fascination. "Never thought I'd see the day when fairytales came alive," he muttered, his eyes on Charlotte as she pirouetted around an opponent, wielding her blade.

"Welcome to the club," Alex replied. "But she's not your average fairytale character. She's more."

Her dress billowed around her, and the smells of lavender and ancient scripts wafted off her, a unique perfume that was as bewitching as the woman herself. She looked like a celestial being who had descended into the melee—a fairy turned warrior.

Charlotte dodged a bolt of dark energy, twisting in the air with a gymnast's finesse. She retaliated with a flick of her wand, her magic pulsing out in a wave of light.

Mellows grunted in agreement, his focus on the battle. "Also never thought I'd see a fairy godmother with a lethal right hook." He chuckled, but the sound was lost in the fray.

"Trust me, Mellows," said Alex, smirking despite the situation. "That's just the tip of the iceberg."

Alex was calm amid the chaos. Charlotte couldn't help but steal glances at him, her heart pounding. He was awe-inspiring, his stance as unyielding as oak and his moves as fluid as water.

His fists pummeled the gut of one unsuspecting villain. Then he roundhouse-kicked another. It was like witnessing a deadly ballet. Each punch and kick landed sent an enemy sprawling, giving the trio a fighting chance to get away. His hair, disheveled and sticking to his forehead from sweat, made him look like a warrior of old, and the scent of his exertion, a heady mix of adrenaline and determination, filled the air around him.

Her admiration grew, as unexpected as it was enthralling.

Her attention was wrenched back to the fight by Sir Thomas, whose voice carried over the din. "Charlotte, incoming on the left!"

She twirled and slashed her wand to send a magic-fueled blast at some advancing villains. There was a loud crack and they hit a wall, sending a cloud of dust and the acrid smell of burned cloth and leather into the air.

"Good catch, Sir Thomas," she said, her breath coming in gasps. She caught sight of Alex again, embroiled in a hand-to-hand fight with a villain. She watched as he ducked a swing and retaliated with another roundhouse kick in almost the same motion.

Her breath hitched when he landed a blow that sent his enemy crashing into a table laden with food, and an array of canapes and pastries flew into the air. The smell of fresh bread mingled with the smell of sweat and magic.

"Wondered who would brave the food," Sir Thomas quipped.

"Alex is holding his own," Charlotte stated with satisfaction. He rose from a crouch, his ears red with exertion but his eyes bright, and the spark within her got brighter.

Though he was a novice in inter-realm war, Alex was proving to be a valuable ally. His actions spoke louder than his disbelief, which sparked not just admiration but also hope in Charlotte.

Alex ducked a crushing blow, the gust of its passing ruffling his hair. In reply, he sent a swift fist into the gut of his opponent, his brows furrowed in concentration.

Gradually, their fights brought them closer, their movements and actions integrating into a synchronized dance of survival. Alex stole a glance at Charlotte as she cast a spell that sent an enemy sprawling. She was mesmerizing. She moved with the grace of a seasoned martial artist, and each flick of her wand was as deadly as a skilled swordsman's strike.

Charlotte and Alex fixed their gazes on Prince Repel, who was circled by a throng of dedicated followers in the farthest corner of the ballroom. There in the flesh stood the leader of these nefarious magical beings. His malevolence was as legendary as his cunning. The air around him seemed to thrum with the power of a spell, intricate and elaborate, weaving a web of magic that held those near him in thrall.

Seeing Charlotte and Alex making their way toward him, Prince Repel's lips curled into a sinister smirk, but he made no move to confront them. Instead, he dispatched a cadre of henchmen to intercept the duo. His dark eyes glinted with amusement as his minions did his bidding, the spell he was weaving seemingly unaffected by the diversion of his attention.

"Let's take the fight to him!" Alex nodded at the prince as Charlotte turned to him.

"Alex!" she shouted over the din and pointed behind him. "Giant on your six!"

Alex looked over his shoulder and saw a snarling behemoth lumbering toward him. His eyes widened at the sheer size of the creature, but he didn't run.

She liked that in a man.

"Got it!" he called, pivoting on his heel to face the oncoming threat. Alex attacked from the front to draw the beast's attention while Charlotte wove her magic around it, the spells binding and weakening the creature.

It was nice when her spells went right—or right enough —for a change.

With a roar, the giant swiped at Alex, who narrowly avoided its huge, gnarled hand. Charlotte's voice rang out crisp and clear, her final spell creating magical chains trying to bind the giant.

As the pandemonium raged, Alex grounded himself, acutely aware of his surroundings. The acidic scent of smoke, coupled with the sharp tang of fear, created an unsettling cocktail that invaded his nostrils and prickled at his senses.

He spotted a momentary lull in a thug's attack. Seeing Officer Bennett nearby, he yelled and held out a hand. "Bennett! Your taser!"

Bennett, his eyes as wide as saucers amid the chaos, heard the command. With a nod, he whipped his taser from its holster and deftly tossed it to Alex.

The detective caught the device in mid-air, its familiar weight creating a point of stability in the madness enveloping him. The buzz of electricity filled the air as he charged it, and the sparks at its tip illuminated his face with their blue-white glow.

Alex lunged and jabbed the sparking end of the taser into the giant's exposed side. The sizzle was followed by the acrid smell of burning cloth and flesh.

The brute jerked violently, and its eyes bulged. Its roar filled the room as its legs buckled, and it crumpled to the floor.

Bennett, who was busy subduing a smaller villain, looked up in time to see the giant crumble. "Damn, Detective. You took down the big guy with just a taser!" He stared at Alex in disbelief.

Charlotte saw the giant twitch and reached for a heavy, ornate candlestick on a nearby table. Then, with a battle cry that rang through the ballroom, she sprinted forward and brought the makeshift weapon down on the giant's head to ensure it wouldn't get back up.

The creature groaned, its eyes rolling back as it went out cold. Their combined efforts had succeeded in toppling the giant.

Alex smirked, his chest heaving with the effort of the takedown. "Modern technology," he managed to wheeze out. His triumphant grin was infectious as he readied himself for the next wave of attackers.

He turned to the other officer and yelled, "Reload me,

Bennett! It's time to give them a shock treatment!" The humor in his voice belied the gravity of the situation.

"Impressive teamwork," Alex noted.

Charlotte nodded. "We do make a pretty good team, don't we?"

Sir Thomas and Cat arrived, and Charlotte and Alex turned their attention to the new arrivals. "Everyone okay?" Sir Thomas asked. His eyes darted to a glass that was tossed across the room and back to the group. "Anyone need throwing stars? The guy I took them from isn't going to use them anymore."

Charlotte reached out. "I'll take some."

"You know how to use throwing stars?" Alex asked.

She nodded. "It's similar to my dagger, yet nothing like it."

Alex looked toward a noise that seemed to be coming from a wall forty feet away. "That's not very helpful."

Part of the ceiling collapsed when a massive hole was punched through it in the direction Alex was looking.

"Perhaps it's time to leave?" Sir Thomas asked. "Given the new support for Prince Repel."

Charlotte nodded, then asked, "How many legs do those things have?"

"More important," Sir Thomas replied, "why are they looking at us?"

CHAPTER SEVENTEEN

The quartet sprinted through the corridors in The Ascent, their heavy breathing reverberating off the walls.

"Hey, is it considered a retreat if you're running for your life?" Charlotte asked.

Sir Thomas looked thoughtful as he slashed at a minion who got too close. "I'd prefer to think of it as a tactical repositioning," he replied, punctuating his words with grunts of effort.

"Ah, a good rebranding. I like that, Sir Thomas! Makes it sound less like we're about to soil our britches," Alex chimed in, then looked at Cat, who had just bitten a minion.

"Guys," Charlotte interjected as she sent a bolt of energy toward a minion. The creature shrieked as it was thrown back, colliding with its comrades. "Less banter, more battling."

"Hey, your magic is working!" Sir Thomas exclaimed. After the next spell Charlotte cast, the hallway's ceiling produced rain for ten feet in either direction. "Strike that. Celebrated a bit too early."

Every step was a gamble that drew them deeper into danger, but paradoxically, those steps were their lifeline—the path that inched them closer to respite from the onslaught.

Numerous legs skittered on the stone floor behind them, and arachnid creatures emerged from the shadows, their bodies grotesque parodies of spiders of unnatural size. Deadly spikes gleamed in the corridor's overhead lights.

"Damn it," Charlotte muttered. "I thought we lost those bastards." She readied herself for the next wave of battle, her eyes meeting her team's.

Her magic was still erratic, but Charlotte cast basic spells to blast the arachnid minions back. She also drew her dagger and used it when the opportunity presented itself.

Sir Thomas darted between the legs of the spider minions, using his sharp claws to tear through their soft underbellies. Cat leaped onto the spiders' backs and crushed their exoskeletons with his powerful jaws.

Charlotte faced a particularly challenging adversary. "Well, aren't you the charming one," she quipped, narrowly dodging as it lunged at her, ripping the wall in three places with its spines. "I'd say you're compensating for something, but I'd hate to give you a complex."

The creature hissed, its blood-red eyes narrowing. Charlotte dodged the swipe of a spiked leg. "Not a fan of humor?" she gritted out, weaving her way around another aggressive lunge. She drew a throwing star from her belt. "How about sharp wit?"

She flung the star, and it lodged it in the creature's eye. It gave a horrific screech as it stumbled back, its legs buckling beneath its weight. It collapsed in a heap, twitching and writhing. Finally, it went still.

"That's for ruining my favorite boots," Charlotte said, using the short reprieve to catch her breath.

The last arachnid of the attacking group turned and fled. Charlotte noted that it went in the opposite direction from the ballroom. "Look!" She stabbed her finger at the retreating figure with a triumphant smile.

The smile had barely formed on her lips when a massive luminescent ball of ice hurtled toward them. It slammed into the ceiling and showered them with sharp shards. The shockwave rippled through the air, rattling their eardrums and their bones. It reminded them of their perilous situation.

The team whirled to face the new attacker, and their hearts sank when they recognized the person. Sir Thomas grimaced at the tall woman. "Well, I'm quite positive this is going to be unpleasant." His voice was heavy as he eyed the newcomer. "She's not known for her soft touch."

Confused, Alex turned to the others. "And who might this be?"

Charlotte and Sir Thomas chorused, "The Snow Queen."

Sir Thomas added, his voice thick with disdain, "Prince Repel's right hand. Has a penchant for torturing fairy godmothers."

The stark reality of their situation struck them like a tidal wave of frigid water, gnawing at their tenacity. The icy air crept into their pores, mirroring the cold, pitiless scrutiny of the Snow Queen, a brutal precursor to the imminent storm.

Charlotte turned to her companions, her voice barely a whisper. "Get ready. This is going to be a frosty one."

"Oh, just what I always wanted," Sir Thomas' voice dripped sarcasm. "A snowball fight to the death."

The Snow Queen advanced smoothly, her eyes shining with malicious delight. Her fingers tightened on the hilt of her ice-blue katana, which gleamed ominously in the corridor's lighting. Her lethal elegance horrified her opponents.

Still not speaking, she flung her free hand forward, sending a barrage of razor-sharp icicles spiraling toward Charlotte. They whistled toward the fairy godmother, sharp points glinting.

Charlotte sidestepped the freezing projectiles, her brow creasing in determination.

The Snow Queen laughed, the sound cold enough to freeze their blood. "Oh, how delightful! A bit of a dance now, is it?"

Her frosty breath fogged the air as she continued, "You really think you stand a chance, Fairy Godmother?" Her voice echoed, a taunt wrapped in a rumble of amusement. Charlotte steeled herself. The Snow Queen's combat skills were renowned in EverAfter, and she had to duel with the cold monarch.

As the women's katana and knife clashed in a lethal

symphony, Sir Thomas watched with a blend of worry and amusement. "Things seem to be a bit frosty over there," he remarked, his voice oozing sarcasm. "Be careful, Charlotte. You would not want to catch a cold!"

Despite the humor in his comment, Sir Thomas was uneasy as he watched the duel unfold. Charlotte was giving it her all, wand and dagger working in perfect harmony, but the Snow Queen's relentless attacks were tiring her. The woman also did not seem to have nearly the same difficulty controlling her magic that Charlotte did.

Sparks flew as Charlotte blocked another strike from the Snow Queen's katana with her dagger. The Snow Queen's lips curved into a menacing smile, and her frosty breath was visible in the air.

Charlotte's hair whipped around her face as she dodged a vicious swipe. The cold air stung her lungs as she struggled to maintain her footing on the frost-covered marble.

The shrill crackle of a police radio cut through the battle. Alex, whose radio had somehow remained intact amid the chaos, grabbed the device. His face went pale as he listened to the transmission.

"All officers vacate the building." The transmission abruptly cut off, replaced by static.

"Damn it," Alex swore, shoving the radio into his pocket. "What are they doing?! They can't retreat now!"

"It must be Repel," Charlotte warned. "He must have one of the officers under a spell. How is his magic so strong?"

The new development was a punch to the gut. If their backup in the ballroom was compromised, the tide of the battle had just turned against them.

Her shout for a tactical withdrawal was barely audible over the clashing weapons and the hum of the elemental magic. "We need to pull back!"

Sir Thomas and Cat, half-blinded by the swirling snow in the hall, scoured their surroundings in a desperate bid to find an exit.

Charlotte narrowly evaded some razor-sharp icicles while returning fire with her own spells, a delicate ballet of survival.

Alex's voice reached Charlotte. "There! Over here!" he hollered, pointing at a half-concealed door down the hallway.

Charlotte had a split second to react as the Snow Queen lunged at her. She twisted away from the gleaming katana and flung a bolt of energy at the Snow Queen. The spell collided with the magic blade, creating a bright flash that threw the queen off-balance.

Seizing the opportunity, Charlotte sprinted toward the door with her companions hot on her heels. They darted through it as the Snow Queen resumed her fighting stance and slammed the door shut behind them. The four barely had time to catch their breath, hearts thudding wildly against their ribs.

"This way!" Sir Thomas called. Everyone followed him with alacrity. Charlotte just hoped the Snow Queen didn't chase them. After the first battle, she had few reserves left to face the lady again.

They tumbled through the rear entrance of the building in a frantic rush after kicking the door open, emerging into the narrow confines of an adjacent alley. The harsh glare of city lights and the discordant symphony of car horns and distant sirens slammed into their senses.

"On your toes!" Charlotte commanded, her voice bouncing off the dank brick walls. "The Ice Queen might not be far behind!"

"Car's this way!" Alex shouted over his shoulder, motioning them toward the northern end of the alley. The ensuing sprint ended at his Camaro. Alex unlocked the doors and they all piled in, beaten and bruised heroes all.

As they buckled their seatbelts, Alex made a distress call to headquarters. "Safe for the moment," he reported, his voice steely. "Got a team of battered knights here. I'll try to get there...soon."

Now they knew he was not in the building, and he couldn't be blamed if he didn't get his paperwork done right away.

Lungs burning and bodies bruised, the quartet stumbled through the door into Alex's apartment. Their limbs were heavy with fatigue and their bodies screamed in protest as they sank onto various pieces of furniture or the floor.

"Is it just me, or does this place look better after an escape from death?" Charlotte asked, a wry smile playing on her lips.

Alex chuckled, his laugh a small spark of warmth in the cold aftermath of their fight. "You just might be onto something, Charlotte," he replied, his eyes twinkling with tired humor.

As small and homely as it was, Alex's apartment was a

sanctuary—a comforting antithesis to the chaos they had just left. Familiar scents permeated the air: old books and a faint hint of morning coffee, a soothing undertow to the adrenaline still coursing through their veins.

From a bathroom cabinet, Alex retrieved a medical kit filled with the necessary supplies and set it on the coffee table. They got to work and tended to their injuries in silence. The soft rustle of bandages being unwrapped, the faint sting of antiseptic, and the comforting murmur of reassurances filled the room. The warriors exchanged fleeting touches, a squeeze of a hand, or an encouraging nod, all signs of a bond that ran deep.

Charlotte winced as she tended a wound in her shoulder where a shard of ice had burrowed into her flesh. The skin was an angry, inflamed ring around the wound, and each beat of her heart seemed to pulse in tandem with the pain.

Cat was unnervingly silent. His fur was matted with blood from a cruel, deep gash that ran across his side.

Normally the picture of health and vitality, Sir Thomas' bright eyes were dull, their usual sparkle dimmed by fatigue and pain. He didn't even make any pithy comments.

Charlotte glanced at Alex. His usual humor was absent, replaced by a weariness that lined his face. His clothes were splattered with blood. Charlotte found her gut twisting with worry, unable to discern if the blood belonged to him or one of their fallen foes.

Each smear was a testament to the battle they had survived and a reminder of the dangers that still loomed. Exhaustion and pain filled the room, but beneath it all was a resolve to win born of necessity and shared experiences.

Charlotte broke the silence, and her voice rang through the room. "We cannot let him succeed." Her gaze swept over her friends. "He threatens everything we hold dear, everything in this world and EverAfter. Our fight is far from over."

CHAPTER EIGHTEEN

It was the day after the battle, and Alex had just come home from the station. With everything going on, Charlotte had few options about where to stay with her small team while being available to work with Alex. So, as much as she would prefer to have stayed at another place, she had to agree it was best for the three of them to stay with the detective.

Starving after waking up and realizing the pizza they had ordered from the all-night pizzeria was gone, the three searched the kitchenette and found a small selection of canned goods, instant noodles, and a few packets of stale crackers. It was clear that the detective had not planned on hosting magical beings.

Alex came in after changing, eyeing Sir Thomas, who held a can of Star-Kist out beyond Cat's maw.

Cat bumped him, and the two got into a heated argument. "I saw it first!" Sir Thomas snarled.

The fur rose on Cat's back, and he growled.

"Absolutely not!" Sir Thomas hissed. "The sardines are mine." He grabbed the bag of saltines and put them in front of Cat. "You can have the crackers."

Alex let out a weary chuckle at the absurdity of a cat and a dog who was formerly a cat arguing about canned fish.

"Don't worry, Cat. I'll get you something."

When they reassembled in Alex's living room, the tension from their recent battles faded for a moment. The group settled down to eat their makeshift meal on mismatched plates, and their conversation shifted from playful banter to the matter at hand—their next steps in the battle against Prince Repel and the Snow Queen.

"We will need to find a way to track their movements," Alex began, his voice serious as he swirled a forkful of noodles. "If we can anticipate their moves, we will have a better chance of stopping them."

Charlotte nodded in agreement as she nibbled on a cracker. "We should also try to figure out how they are pulling characters from EverAfter into this world. If we can stop the flow of reinforcements, it will weaken their army."

The group watched in amazement as Sir Thomas leaped onto the computer desk and, with surprising dexterity, typed in search terms and clicked on links on Alex's desktop computer. He went from news articles to dark corners of the web to gather information on Prince Repel and his growing army.

Alex created a timeline of events on a pad of paper. He noted the first sightings of Prince Repel in Cincinnati, the emergence of the Snow Queen, and the growing number of fairytale characters surfacing in their world, like the Big Bad Wolf and the Troll under the Bridge.

Charlotte shared her suspicions with the group, suggesting that Prince Repel had somehow managed to tap into the magic of EverAfter and was pulling characters into this world against their will. She wondered if he had found her handbook.

Charlotte stared at Alex, anger and resolve flickering in her eyes. "We need to talk about Prince Repel," she declared, her voice carrying a hard edge.

"The charming runaway prince?" Alex asked, arching his eyebrows skeptically. "What's there to talk about?"

"My suspicions," Charlotte replied brusquely. "And they aren't pleasant."

Alex folded his arms, leaning back. He raised an eyebrow in silent encouragement. "All right, shoot."

Charlotte began her tale, her words painting a vivid picture of a magical ball in EverAfter. "It was like a scene from a fairytale," she said. "The kingdom was abuzz with anticipation. The reason? I was tasked with securing a bride for Prince Repel, just like I did for his dear brother, Prince Charming."

Alex squinted at her, his forehead creasing in thought. "Let me guess. Prince Repel wasn't as charming as his brother?"

"No, he wasn't," Charlotte confirmed, her words heavily laced with bitterness. "A monster disguised in princely attire. Once I stumbled upon his true colors, the arrangement was promptly dissolved."

Sir Thomas, who had been quietly observing the exchange, interjected, "And how did our not-so-charming prince take that, Charlotte?" His tone carried a slight hint of mockery toward the absent prince.

"Just as poorly as you might imagine, Sir Thomas," she retorted, playing along with his light-hearted banter to ease the tension. "His pride was severely bruised, and as years passed, his humiliation gradually twisted into insanity."

Alex, his playful demeanor replaced with a hard seriousness, asked, "And you reckon he's out on a vengeful hunt now?"

Charlotte cast a glance at Sir Thomas, nodding gravely before turning her eyes back to Alex. "Yes, he's nursing an old wound, one that has decayed into a lethal vendetta. I fear we could be the targets," she confessed, her tone acknowledging the grim reality of their situation. Sir Thomas, silent once more, nodded in agreement, his eyes reflecting the shared apprehension.

Sir Thomas joined the group by the timeline, and they all studied it. The evidence of Prince Repel's sinister plan dared them to find a way to stop it.

"We need to be careful," Charlotte warned. "We do not want to expose EverAfter's existence to the world. We need to handle this discreetly."

As their conversation evolved into strategic planning, a silent dialogue seemed to unfold between Charlotte and Alex.

Green irises met dark ones, an invisible cord woven with shared strength and an assertive autonomy stretching between them. Their dynamic was a complex puzzle, the pieces interspersed with a sizzling undercurrent of something more than platonic.

A rush of warmth suffused Charlotte's cheeks, coral staining her fair skin as she quickly looked away.

Charlotte's gaze was drawn to the intricate masonry of the wall, her mind as busy as her fingers, which were absently fiddling with her wand. She could sense the tension in the room, a thick, palpable thing that seemed to choke the air.

Alex shifted beside her, the scrapes of his boots on the wood floor echoing in the silence. His throat-clearing was an unspoken testament to his discomfort, a familiar call to action.

"We need to stop Prince Repel and the Snow Queen," Charlotte declared, breaking the silence. Her grip tightened around her wand as she turned to face the rest of the team. "Their reign of terror continues because we haven't been able to locate my missing handbook. We need to find it and thwart their plans."

Sir Thomas, his gaze piercing, nodded in solemn agreement, the weight of their collective mission in his gaze. "Indeed," he affirmed, the words heavy with the truth of their predicament. "We shall have to draw from our combined knowledge of EverAfter and this realm to thwart their malefic intentions."

"Their what?" Alex asked.

"Malefic intentions." Sir Thomas eyed him.

"Like, Maleficent?" Alex replied.

"You are messing with me, aren't you, human?"

"Yes," Alex agreed with a smile.

The urgency of their task was as clear as the glassy surface of a still lake. They needed to uncover the depth of Prince Repel's wicked plans and his unholy alliance with the Snow Queen.

"In our quest," Sir Thomas began, his voice carrying a hint of intrigue, "perhaps we should explore the resources we have in this realm. The owner of the enchanted bookstore, for instance, might hold crucial information that could aid us."

Recognition lit up in Charlotte's eyes at the mention of the bookstore. "Yes, absolutely," she agreed, her spirit ignited. "He could indeed prove to be a useful ally. Especially so if he has been keeping tabs on EverAfter through his texts. We could also try to enlist the aid of witches. They could hold sway in their circles."

The spark of recognition in Sir Thomas' eyes flared at the mention of the witches. "Yes, those old crones could prove to be influential allies in our mission."

Charlotte continued, her gaze unyielding as she met Alex's eyes. "Not to mention the other fairytale figures in EverAfter, like Cinderella's stepsisters and Snow White's dwarves, to name just a few. If they are here, and we can convince them that we're defending not just our world but theirs too, they might come forward."

With a contemplative look in his green eyes, Alex added, "Indeed, it's as if their sole aim is to create chaos in both our worlds, dragging the mystical and human realms into the open."

"But to what end?" Charlotte wondered aloud. "Is it a

power play, revenge, or is there a deeper, darker purpose behind their actions?" She eyed the group. "We cannot let Prince Repel succeed."

Sir Thomas leaped onto a windowsill and scanned the dark streets for any sign of their enemies. "Not to mention the Snow Queen. She will not go down easily."

Charlotte gripped her wand tightly, the wood warm and comforting in her hand. "We will do whatever it takes."

"Well." Alex broke into their reverie. "Not before we get some good food into us and another couple of days of rest. Not all wounds are obvious, and we all need to be healthier."

Charlotte eyed him. "Are you trying to get out of us helping you?"

"No," he admitted. "I have paperwork. The force operates on paperwork, I believe."

"Fish," Sir Thomas turned toward them from the window. "The next pizza needs extra fish."

"Anchovies," Alex corrected.

"Whatever." Sir Thomas turned back to the window. "Make it so on the next one."

Charlotte studied the timeline. "I'll see if I can think of who else might be on this world who could help us."

Just then, Alex got a message. "Dammit." He looked up. "More paperwork. Do you need me?"

Charlotte shook her head. "It's just a different world, Alex. Talking to problem people is my normal line of work."

Alex stared at her blankly. "I have to remember that you aren't a normal citizen."

They shared a smile as the trio stepped by him on their way out of the apartment.

As the door shut, Alex heard Charlotte ask for directions and "Trust me" from Sir Thomas. He shook his head and went to grab the clothes he had changed out of when he got home.

CHAPTER NINETEEN

Prince Repel paced in his luxurious apartment at The Ascent, his irritation as clear as crystal. It had not been nearly enough time since the debacle at The Ascent to lower his blood pressure.

The Snow Queen's presence had wreaked havoc on his carefully decorated living room, an amalgamation of modern and fairytale-inspired pieces. The plush velvet sofa, which was deep royal purple, bore a pale blue stain from her frosty touch, and the ornate gold mirror that hung over the marble fireplace had a spiderweb of cracks. The palm tree in the corner drooped, its leaves brittle from the sudden chill.

It didn't take much time for her wintry presence to affect his plants.

The Snow Queen lifted her hands and conjured an extraordinary ice sculpture of a dragon in the center of the room. Its wings were outspread, poised as though it were on the brink of soaring into flight. The dragon's scales were intricately detailed, each one a testament to her chilling power. Its expression was fierce, almost lifelike, making Prince Repel halt in his tracks to admire the craftsmanship.

Yet, before his eyes could fully appreciate the icy spectacle, the Snow Queen, with a wicked glint in her eyes, flicked her wrist. In the blink of an eye, the ice dragon was no more, shattered into thousands of shards that scattered across the polished marble floor.

Caught off guard, Prince Repel jumped back with a gasp, a reflexive magic shield flickering to life around him, warding off the icy shards that ricocheted in his direction. His heart pounded in his chest, his usually calm demeanor momentarily unsettled. The remnants of the ice dragon glistened under the chandelier, a chilling spectacle that demonstrated he might not hold as much control over the situation as he had initially thought.

Arms crossed and a frown on his face, Prince Repel was a picture of exasperation. He watched as the Snow Queen continued her flurry of icy antics, his patience wearing thin. His plush royal accommodations were being turned into a winter wonderland, and the sight of it was equal parts absurd and infuriating.

He glanced at the scattered shards of her recent icy creation. It had been beautiful, but at what cost?

"Sincerely, *Your Majesty*," he began, massaging his temples as if to ward off a burgeoning headache. His words dripped sarcasm as he continued, "Your talent for turning everything into a winter spectacle is unparalleled. However," he paused, shooting her an acid glance, "it's wreaking havoc on my decor."

His gaze fell on the drooping frost-kissed palm tree in

the corner. He shook his head, letting out a resigned sigh. "I've got a splendid idea for you. You know, there's this charming little place called Antarctica," he quipped, a mocking smile on his face. "Unlimited ice, endless snow... I think you would fit right in." He paused for effect. *"Endless."*

With a dramatic roll of his eyes, Prince Repel uncurled his arms and stepped away from the Snow Queen's frosty spectacle. The elegant space that had reflected the warmth of his personality was now a shimmering ice rink. It was time to regain control of his residence.

Extending his hand, he summoned a soft, golden glow in his palm, a stark contrast to the chill and focused it on the sad palm tree.

He continued speaking to himself in a high voice. "Really, Your Highness? Antarctica? The humidity would ruin my complexion." His words were veiled in a sarcasm that was masked by the concentration his magic required. As the warm glow from his palm engulfed the frozen tree, the ice began to melt, droplets cascading onto the marble floor below.

The tree slowly but surely regained its initial vibrancy, the leaves straightening as the frosty grip on them was released. However, as he turned his magic onto the scattered ice shards, a sigh escaped his lips. "I should not be the one dealing with these ice-cleaning duties," he grumbled, the gold light flickering in annoyance.

His eyes swept the room, transforming it back into its original state one magic pulse at a time. The shards of the shattered ice sculpture melted, the frost creeping up the drapes withdrew, and warmth seeped back into the room, replacing the chilling aura. All the while, Prince Repel continued grumbling, a scowl etched on his face.

It wasn't just the cold that was getting under his skin. The Snow Queen's frosty attitude was proving to be more than a minor inconvenience.

The Snow Queen smiled, her eyes full of mischief as she toyed with her frosty powers, unaffected by his irritation.

The prince strode toward a cabinet in the corner. The dark oak, polished to a high shine and adorned with intricate silver details, occupied his attention. He ran his fingers over the surface, murmuring under his breath, and the cabinet door swung open to reveal magical artifacts and tomes. The air around the cabinet shimmered, hinting at the powerful enchantments placed upon it.

With care, Prince Repel retrieved a worn fairy godmother handbook from its resting place. The pages were frayed and the bindings were loose, evidence of years of use. He hesitated, gazing at the book with both disdain and fascination before replacing it in the cabinet. With a few more muttered words, he re-enchanted the cabinet to ensure prying eyes could not access its contents.

Returning to the room's center, Prince Repel poured himself a glass of red wine. The liquid shimmered like blood. The crystal goblet was a work of art adorned with silver vines that seemed to come to life in the candlelight. He took a slow, deliberate sip, savoring the rich taste.

The Snow Queen stood with icy elegance, her floor-length gown shimmering like fresh snow. Her long silver hair cascaded down her back, framing her cold, beautiful face, and her piercing blue eyes seemed to see through him.

As Prince Repel strode toward her, his eyes flicked

over her, taking in the way the candlelight danced over her frost-coated skin. The Snow Queen raised an eyebrow, her expression unreadable as she met his gaze. "Enjoying your drink, Repel?" she asked, her voice as cold and sharp as the ice she liked to cover her surroundings with.

He smirked, holding the glass of wine loosely in his hand. "Of course, Your Majesty," he replied, his voice heavy with sarcasm as he took in the ice that was slowly beginning to form again. "This fine vintage perfectly complements the...unique ambiance you have created."

The Snow Queen's eyes glowed with amusement, and her lips curved into a mocking smile. She clearly reveled in the chaos she had caused, delighting in the discomfort it had brought her supposed ally. As she tilted her head, her frost-covered fingers traced patterns in the air, leaving delicate etchings of ice behind.

The air crackled with energy and the promise of conflict.

"That fundraiser was crucial to my campaign," Prince Repel said, his voice smooth and self-assured. "With the right connections and enough money, I can secure my position as mayor and exert control over this city."

"What about the officers who were part of the fight?"

He waved a hand. "Issues. We can solve them with money, time, and magic." He paused. "I would prefer money. Even given our advantages, magic is more sacred and scarce."

She nodded in understanding.

He took a sip of his wine. "Plus, it seems we have included an annoyed fairy godmother in our machinations.

I've heard plenty of stories about her and that lunatic troll-fighting detective."

The Snow Queen grimaced. "Indeed, but we must not underestimate the threat posed by the detective and the freakmother and their team."

Prince Repel pulled his thoughts together. "Detective Alex Taylor," he mused, his brow furrowing. "He and his team of magical misfits have been quite the thorn in our side. Charlotte, in particular, seems to have taken a liking to him. They must be dealt with before they can disrupt our future plans."

The Snow Queen's icy gaze met his. "We cannot allow them to continue to interfere," she agreed, her voice as crisp and cold as the frost patterns she left behind. "I will do what it takes to ensure victory."

Prince Repel led her to a large screen and displayed footage of the recent brawl involving Detective Taylor and his team.

"Nice picture." The Snow Queen admired the 8k TV Screen.

"LG." Repel smiled. "Wonderful quality. Earth has excellent technology. Much better than scrying over a huge bowl of water."

"Where did you acquire the video?"

"Security," he admitted. "It's how we figured out those miscreants came into the building, bypassing our watchers. They also affected the security footage of them passing by. Our security troll was indisposed at the moment they went through."

She eyed him as he glanced at her, answering the unasked question. "I sent him to the Desert for a year."

Pursing her lips, she nodded. "Good punishment."

The Snow Queen and Prince Repel watched intently, analyzing the situation and noting the strengths and weaknesses of their opponents. Charlotte's tall, beautiful figure and dark wavy hair made her easy to distinguish, as were the other members of the team: a dog and the cat, Sir Thomas, clad in boots and a feathered hat.

"They are resourceful," the Snow Queen conceded, annoyed. "But we are more powerful. Together, we will ensure their downfall."

Prince Repel nodded, his expression darkening.

The Snow Queen extended her arm, and an ice dagger materialized in her hand. The weapon had an ethereal glow, and its razor-sharp edge gleamed with deadly intent. "Leave it to me," she said, her voice as cold as the weapon she now held. "I will ensure that Taylor and his team are dealt with."

Prince Repel watched the Snow Queen with a calculating smile, his eyes glittering with malice. "Excellent," he drawled, the corners of his lips twitching upward. "I knew you'd come through."

With her eyes closed, the Snow Queen was a living display of raw power. Snow and ice spiraled around her like a cyclone, swallowing her whole. The temperature plummeted as the icy gales screamed through the room, and then all was silent. She had disappeared, leaving behind a frosty mist like a shroud seeping into the opulent interior.

Prince Repel was ready. His fingers traced graceful patterns in the air, weaving intricate spells to counter her icy farewell. Gold streaks snapped in the air, warring against the wintry mist. Little by little, the icy haze broke apart, evaporating under the warm glow of his magic.

As he worked, the grandeur of his apartment reappeared from beneath the frost. Rich, velvet curtains, no longer touched with frost, framed the floor-to-ceiling windows once again. Gilded mirrors and elaborate chandeliers twinkled, freed from their icy prison, as they adorned the regal walls and ceiling.

Wiping the chill from his hands, Prince Repel muttered under his breath. Next time, he decided, there would be some ground rules about unsolicited weather changes indoors. The air in the room, once warm and inviting, now felt cold and oppressive, a stark reminder of the Snow Queen's power and the danger she posed to those who dared stand in her way.

He glanced at his wine, now a solid red ice cube in the bottom of the glass. He sighed, waving his hand over the top, and the wine started to defrost as he turned toward the kitchen.

He was going to need to call a crew in to refurbish his abode if this kept up for too long.

CHAPTER TWENTY

"Told you." Sir Thomas spoke to Charlotte, who was ahead of him as she opened the door, a bell tinkling above her. The smell of fish that hit them was as robust as the broad grin that took over his face. "Quite the tavern you've led us to, Charlotte."

Charlotte rolled her eyes as she entered the shop. The tight aisles were filled with barrels of ice and fish like snapper, cod, and an impressively large tuna. The shop was humble, worn, and heavy with the scent of brine. It was a far cry from the types of bars Charlotte was accustomed to, but she couldn't help but chuckle at the unexpected twist.

"Truly, a bar for connoisseurs," Sir Thomas continued with a twinkle in his eye.

"Very funny," Charlotte retorted, unable to suppress a smile. "You could at least pretend to be a bit more supportive."

Cat merely huffed, shaking pretend water droplets off his fur while he eyed the fish in the shop absently, his tail wagging in approval.

A familiar face appeared behind the counter. "Peter!" Charlotte's voice softened, taken by surprise. It was a face she had not seen since EverAfter. A peculiar mixture of warmth and nostalgia swept over her, compounded by the presence of her old friend—and at times foe—from her former world. She felt a wave of homesickness.

Despite the circumstances, seeing Peter was like finding an anchor in the storm. "We require answers," she said, her voice firm but underscored by a note of pleading.

Peter, a middle-aged man with pointed ears and a rough beard, looked up from his work. He put aside the knife he was using to clean a fish, his eyes sparkling with curiosity and mischief.

"Well, well. It isn't every day that an actual fairy godmother is seen on Earth! A fairy godmother and her…" he eyed the dog and cat, "crew?" Peter finished as a smile spread across his face. "What brings you to my modest place of business? And more importantly, how did you end up here?"

"We have no time for pleasantries," Charlotte stated, staring at her acquaintance with determination.

"Not even for pleasantries? It's been so long, and I'm mighty curious." Peter leaned against the table.

"We've picked up on something…unusual," Sir Thomas began, his voice cutting through the fishy air of the shop. His eyes were intense, the usually twinkling gold replaced with a sharp seriousness. "An influx of magical characters in Cincinnati at a rate much higher than the normal pattern of newcomers. Do you perhaps have any insights into this?"

Without a word, Peter moved from his spot by the fish

counter to lean against a worn-out wooden barrel filled to the brim with ice and fish. His posture was casual, but the lines of his face were drawn tight, a certain heaviness settling in his pointed elven features.

"I've heard the murmurings too and seen the newcomers," he admitted, his voice gruff but laced with concern. Peter's gaze drifted over the aisles of the shop, seeming to look beyond the walls and into the city. "It's not just the whispers. Every day, every single day, I see new faces from EverAfter. The trickle has turned into a stream."

He fell silent, letting the implication of his words hang in the air for a moment. His gaze then shifted to Charlotte. It was soft yet filled with a solemn understanding. "And Charlotte," he said, the name hanging in the air between them, "I don't think this is all random, a simple coincidence. There's almost a sense of urgency and dread, like something really big is happening."

As the group absorbed this information, Peter motioned for them to follow him toward the back of the shop. They navigated the aisles, passing a display of exotic seashells and a tank filled with live lobsters. Eventually, they reached a door concealed behind a curtain of fishing nets.

With a practiced ease, Peter's hands danced over the net. His fingers nimbly found and pressed a precise sequence of knots that were indistinguishable among the tangled weave. It was a cleverly disguised security measure crafted with intricacy, one that could be decoded only by those who knew the secret pattern.

As the final knot was pressed, a low hum vibrated through the room, the resonance barely audible.

The door gradually creaked open, resisting the years of dust that had accumulated in its hinges, to reveal what lay beyond. It seemed as if they were standing on the threshold of a different world, a bit of magic involved, a sanctuary tucked away in the heart of the mundane.

It was a dim room, the scarcity of light enhancing its charm. Shadows played on the walls, whispering secrets about magical sojourns and safe havens. Comfortable, well-worn seating was arranged haphazardly, each piece holding stories of magical beings seeking solace, seeking companionship, seeking refuge.

A myriad of colors danced from the few stained glass lanterns hanging from the ceiling, casting a warm glow over the room. The atmosphere was heavy with warmth and promise, an unspoken oath of refuge and rest for those treading the path between two worlds.

Flickering candles cast moving shadows on walls lined with shelves filled with magical artifacts and trinkets. The secret lives of its inhabitants were hinted at by the items they had collected.

Peter leaned against a bookcase and stroked his scruffy beard, his pointed ears twitching.

"I do not understand," Charlotte blurted. "How can Prince Repel still have his magic? And why would he bring these other creatures with him? There must be a larger scheme at work."

Sir Thomas chimed in. "It seems that way. This is no mere coincidence."

Peter nodded, his mischievous demeanor gone. "I have seen them before, Charlotte. They have been planning something for a long time, waiting in the shadows for the right moment to strike."

A heavy silence settled over the room.

A sigh escaped Peter's lips. "You see," he began, his gaze distant, "EverAfter was once my home, as much as it was yours. But I was banished..." His voice trailed off for a moment before he forced a smile and continued, "But that's an old tale now. I've since found solace in aiding newcomers from EverAfter, giving them a helping hand in navigating this unfamiliar world."

His gaze hardened. "It's not the same as home, but it's something. Though," he added with a hint of bitterness, "I've heard stories of a beastly character who doesn't exactly make the transition easy for those he finds." Peter waved the comment away, his smile returning. "But that is a legend, even among our kind."

The room fell quiet at Peter's tale, each person lost in their own thoughts, grappling with varying degrees of fear, disbelief, and skepticism. Charlotte furrowed her brows, a shadow of worry crossing her face. Sir Thomas remained silent, his gaze fixed on the floor as he processed the news. Cat's ears perked up, a low growl rumbling in his throat at the mention of the "beastly character." The levity of their earlier banter was lost, replaced by the gravity of their thoughts.

Charlotte finally spoke, her voice barely audible. "I never thought I would find myself in the center of something like this."

"Agreed." Sir Thomas flicked his ears. "And we cannot afford to fritter away time. Both Cincinnati and EverAfter hang in the balance."

Cat woofed in agreement.

Peter straightened, his eyes serious and determined. "Then let us get to work."

Sir Thomas nodded. "There must be someone out there who knows more about what is going on."

Peter paused, then offered, "I could reach out to my contacts in Cincinnati and EverAfter. There's a chance that someone may have heard something about Prince Repel's plans."

Their voices swirled together, throwing around options like tossing a salad. Different ideas and possible paths, yet nothing was set in stone. The room, filled with the scent of aged paper and time-worn trinkets, felt tighter, the atmosphere heavier. The ancient books and artifacts lining the shelves, silent sentinels, seemed to listen to their tentative plans and unsaid fears.

With the echo of their discussions fading, they finally decided to call it a night, the plan of action still a work in progress. A shared nod passed between them as they left the room, Peter telling them that if they happen to run into any of their kind who need a place to get their footing, to send them his way. Charlotte stated she would do just that, and they made their way back out of the shop.

They were unaware of a solitary figure quietly observing them from the shadows.

A silhouette cloaked in mystery stood enshrouded in the swirling mists, moving with the grace and agility of a cat. A pair of keen eyes, shimmering with curiosity, tracked the group's every move. Once their comforting chatter and the soft echo of their footsteps on the stone floor had receded into the distance, the figure slipped out of a hidden door, light as a feather on the wind. In an instant, it merged with the bustling crowd of the shop, disappearing as if it had never been there at all.

This silent observer drifted away, carrying with it the echoes of the group's quiet conversations. It disappeared into the anonymous throng, ready to reemerge when the time was right.

Sir Thomas cast a watchful glance around, his gold eyes seeming to search for something just out of sight. Cat held his head high, and his ears twitched as if he sensed the presence of the unseen observer.

Charlotte felt the gaze too, but she seemed unbothered. If this was an assassin, it wasn't a particularly good one. Like Peter had said, they don't get many fairy godmothers around here. Probably just a curious observer if it was another one of the banished. They would be out of the shop in a moment, and they would see how far their curiosity went.

CHAPTER TWENTY-ONE

As the sun set, Charlotte, Cat, and Sir Thomas left the busy fish market.

The air was sharp with the scents of fresh catch and sea salt, while the clatter of crates and the animated haggling of vendors created a symphony of everyday life. Gulls circled overhead, their cries blending with the market's uproar.

The cobblestone beneath their feet was slick from the vendors' attempts to clean the areas around their stalls and stubborn fish scales.

The trio's attention was drawn toward one man who stood in stark contrast to the bustling market scene. He was garbed in a cowboy outfit, with a wide-brimmed hat atop his head adorned with a feather so vibrant it could have been plucked from a tropical bird's tail.

His duster, a shade of brown that hinted at many years of hard use, cascaded down to his worn leather boots, which had the look of countless miles walked and stories untold. A scruffy beard, sun-bleached and wind-torn, framed his face, hiding the lines of age and experience.

Despite his rugged exterior, his eyes held an unquenchable fire that flickered with knowledge and wisdom.

Intrigued, Charlotte moved closer, her curiosity piqued by the man's unconventional attire.

He tipped his hat in a gentlemanly fashion, unveiling a crown of matted hair. "Howdy, ma'am. The name's Benny," he announced. "Not often one notices a fairy godmother while strolling around."

His voice rolled off his tongue like molasses, rich and smooth, tinged with an accent that evaded her understanding. It was a song from the Old West, laced with a hint of the exotic.

At his mention of her identity, Charlotte's eyes widened, and she glanced at Sir Thomas, who mirrored her surprise.

She had been careful, or so they thought, blending into the human world. Benny's laughter was deep and hearty, bouncing off the surrounding buildings. "Let's just say I have a knack for recognizing magical folk. I am an alchemist, banished from EverAfter for my...interesting experiments," he confessed, his eyes twinkling mischievously under the brim of his hat.

Charlotte shared a look with Sir Thomas, the busy street noises fading as they focused on this peculiar character. He was an enigma wrapped in the guise of a cowboy.

Sir Thomas quipped, "You know, Benny, you don't blend in with that get-up. Did you think Cincinnati was having a cowboy convention?"

Benny's grin was infectious, his white teeth a blazing

arc against his tanned skin. "I reckon the folks around here find it as charming as you do," he retorted.

Watching their exchange, Charlotte found herself smiling. It was rare to see Sir Thomas so entertained by someone else's eccentricities.

The afternoon sun cast long shadows as Sir Thomas pressed for more details. "Well, Benny, you've certainly piqued our interest. How did a brilliant alchemist from EverAfter find his way to Cincinnati, of all places?"

Leaning against a weathered post, Benny's eyes glazed over, the memories of his past surfacing like ripples in a pond. "Well, it all started with my fascination with transmutation. You know, turning one thing into another," he began, his voice a deep drawl that echoed the stories of old. He looked down at the cat. "I'd discovered a way to turn lead into gold—quite by accident, mind you." He smiled once more. "The lords of my land, they didn't take too kindly to that."

Benny's hands moved in the air, painting a vivid picture of a world where magic reigned supreme and his discovery threatened to topple the existing order. "They feared an economic collapse, an upheaval of the status quo. Gold is the backbone of our economy, you see. My discovery could devalue it overnight and plunge us into chaos."

With a sigh, he continued, "So, they banished me. Sent me to this realm with no magic, no familiar faces, nothing but the clothes on my back and the knowledge in my head." His shrug was nonchalant, but his eyes held the echoes of past pain and loss.

Listening to Benny's tale, Sir Thomas' gaze softened, a hint of understanding flickering in his eyes. "The struggle of adapting to a new world. I can relate." The cat's voice, usually brimming with sarcasm, held a rare note of sympathy.

Charlotte looked between the two, her heart aching at their stories. She, too, knew the disorientation and loneliness of being ripped from one's home and thrust into a new realm. The familiarity of EverAfter had been replaced by the concrete jungle of Cincinnati, a world devoid of magic and filled with strange customs and technologies.

As Charlotte watched them, a small smile tugged at her lips. Despite the hardships they faced, they had found camaraderie in the most unexpected of places. And maybe, just maybe, they could find a way to turn their misfortunes into a new beginning.

Benny's eyes, which had exuded warmth and kindness until now, suddenly darkened with a desperate intensity as they locked onto Charlotte's. With a slight tremor in his hand, he held up a page, torn and fragile, from what seemed to be her fairy godmother handbook. "I happened upon this rare find," he declared, his voice low and almost haunting.

Charlotte gasped, her gaze fixed on the delicate parchment. Her fingers involuntarily reached out, aching to reclaim it. "That's...that's impossible," she stammered, her voice betraying her shock. "The handbook is supposed to be indestructible. How did you..."

Benny shifted uneasily on the asphalt, the sound of his boots scraping against the ground echoing his discomfort. "Don't know the how, sweetheart," he admitted with a half-shrug. "But here it is. And I'm thinking, maybe it's a ticket back to EverAfter? With your help, of course."

As the implications of his words settled in, Charlotte's mind raced. The enchanting streets of EverAfter, the place she longed for every waking moment, felt so close yet so out of reach. Her magic had been erratic, and here was Benny, offering a glimmer of hope.

But at what cost?

The very essence of magic was thick in the air around them, and it was impossible to ignore its growing presence in the real world. Not too far from where they stood, a mermaid with iridescent scales tried to blend in, her fishtail barely concealed under a coat, while a shadowy figure, unmistakably a troll, observed from a concealed corner.

Benny, sensing her hesitation, leaned closer. "I'm not trying to strong-arm you, Charlotte," he said in a soft, urgent voice. His previous lighthearted demeanor was replaced with desperation, evident in the subtle twitches of his eyelids and the strain in his jaw. "But I need to get back. Can you understand that? EverAfter is my home."

Charlotte took a deep breath, trying to calm the torrent of emotions swirling within her. "I get it, Benny," she replied, her voice barely above a whisper. "But how can I help you when I can't even help myself? My magic is fractured and inconsistent. What you're asking? It's practically impossible."

A gust of wind blew through the market, sending newspapers and leaves swirling around them as if the elements themselves were reacting to the tension in the air. The once-familiar rhythm of the city was now overlaid with a hint of magic, creating an eerie symphony.

Benny took a step closer, his hands gripping the page tighter, crinkling the delicate hide. "Then teach me," he pleaded, looking at the stern buildings that seemed to be peering down at them, a parent's stern gaze oppressing him like a child who had been out of line. "Teach me how to use this," he gestured at the page, "to unlock the way back home. Maybe with both of us working together, we stand a better chance."

Charlotte looked at him, taking in the sincerity in his eyes. For a moment, she saw the Benny she had first met—kind, genuine, lost. She sighed, raking a hand through her hair. "It's not that simple," she began. "The handbook is more than just spells and incantations. It's tied to the fairy godmother's essence. Using it incorrectly could cause even more damage."

The shadows grew longer, casting the market in deep shadows. Somewhere, a dog barked, and the distant sounds of the city served as a reminder of the merging worlds.

Benny looked down, defeated, the weight of his desperation bearing down on him.

"I just... I need to find my way back," he whispered, looking up with tear-filled eyes. "EverAfter is all I've ever known."

Charlotte reached out, placing a reassuring hand on his shoulder. "We'll figure something out, Benny."

Cat bared his teeth, his imposing body tense and his very presence commanded attention as he came to stand at Charlotte's side, his low growl vibrating through the air. His eyes, sharp and alert, bored into Benny with a clear warning. Charlotte could feel the energy emanating from her companion, the protective aura that always surrounded her when danger was afoot.

With a distinct metallic sound, the soft slide of a sword

being sheathed echoed behind Benny. Sir Thomas, the feline embodiment of chivalry and flair, stepped into view, a smirk playing on his lips.

He shook the dust off his fine leather boots and tilted the feathered hat that seemed comically large for his small stature, then quipped, "Well, I'm quite pleased you two came to an understanding. The alternative would have been...messy."

Benny stiffened, realizing how outnumbered he was. He cleared his throat, offering the page to Charlotte with a deference he hadn't shown before. "I truly apologize for my earlier behavior," he began, his voice filled with genuine remorse. "Desperation makes us do strange things. But from now on, I shall be at your service, Charlotte. Until we find our way back."

Charlotte, taking the page, nodded, understanding the sentiment all too well. "Desperation is a powerful motivator, Benny. But remember, we're in this together. EverAfter is home to all of us."

She paused for a moment, then looked down at the large dog. "Except for Cat. He's from here."

Benny gave a rueful smile. "If you ever need assistance, or just some company from those who understand our...unique situation," he gestured vaguely around, indicating the hidden world of displaced magical beings, "just head to the fish market. You'd be surprised how many of us have taken refuge there. We look out for our own."

Charlotte smiled back, warmth flooding her. "Thank you, Benny. It's good to know we're not alone in this."

With a nod to Sir Thomas and a wary glance at Cat, Benny turned on his heel and walked away. Sir Thomas watched him go, his hand resting on the hilt of his sword. "You think he can be trusted?" he asked Charlotte.

Charlotte looked down at the page in her hand, then back at the retreating figure of Benny. "I think he's just as lost as we are," she replied. "And right now, that's reason enough to trust him." She looked around. "But I'm not stupid."

CHAPTER TWENTY-TWO

Charlotte tried to both walk and read the page that Benny had handed her. It recorded an elementary spell that allowed the caster to levitate objects without making contact.

A basic incantation, it was one of the first she had been taught during her initial days in EverAfter's fairy godmother training school. The ink was still fresh, but the edges of the parchment were tattered, making it evident that it had been ripped out of some book—and despite her shock, it was becoming evident that that book was her revered handbook.

"Why would someone remove this? And how?" Charlotte mused aloud, her brows furrowed.

Sir Thomas, trying to finish his snack of the day's catch he had swiped just before they left, cast her a sympathetic look. "Could be any number of reasons, dear lady," he began, always the gentleman, even in this bewildering new world.

Cat let out a low growl, communicating his unease at the page's unexpected presence.

Sir Thomas offered an educated guess, though he wasn't versed in magic. "Perhaps it's like a bookmark? A reminder or a warning of some sort?" He glanced at the paper, eyes reflecting curiosity.

Charlotte contemplated his words, her fingers tracing the intricate symbols on the parchment. "It could be. But who, and why?"

Lost in their thoughts and discussions, the trio's contemplative bubble was burst by a shrill scream from a nearby alley.

Reacting instinctively, Sir Thomas drew his sword, the blade glinting even in the dim light. Charlotte clutched the parchment, mentally preparing herself for a possible magical encounter.

Then they ran toward the trouble.

Rounding a corner, they were met with a scene straight out of a storybook—quite literally. Before them stood Little Bo Peep, her golden curls cascading like a waterfall. The white gown she wore was embroidered and edged with lace, the ruffles dancing with her every movement. She held a shepherd's crook with a lace bow at the curve.

A blue bonnet sat atop her head, providing contrast to her pale face, which was filled with fear. She was clearly outnumbered.

Surrounding her was a motley crew of thugs, each more menacing than the last. Tattoos snaked around their arms, peeking out from beneath tattered clothing. Some wielded sharp knives that menacingly caught the ambient light, while others sported brass knuckles, ready to strike.

Sir Thomas stepped forward, his posture threatening. "Unhand her, you brutes, or face the wrath of a skilled swordsman!"

Charlotte, rallying her powers, felt the energy from the parchment she held. Could it be of use?

Cat positioned himself defensively, ready to leap and protect.

The thugs, seeing the approach of the new defenders, shared uncertain glances but bolstered each other's courage with sneers and nods.

One of the brutes, a large man with a beard that reached his chest, sneered at Sir Thomas. "Think your fancy sword can take us all?" he spat before pulling and brandishing a wickedly curved knife.

Without waiting for an answer, he lunged at Sir Thomas, his blade slicing through the air. The cat parried the attack with grace and spun on his heel to deliver a retaliatory thrust.

The thug barely managed to sidestep, startled by Sir Thomas' agility.

Another thug, seeing an opportunity, tried to take Sir Thomas from behind, but Cat was already on the move.

Cat pounced and knocked the attacker off his feet. The thug struggled, trying to push the massive creature off, but the large dog's weight and strength kept the man pinned.

Charlotte's eyes narrowed. Her gaze was focused on the approaching attackers. "I might not be at full strength," she murmured to herself, "but I still have a few tricks up my sleeve." Her lips moved in a silent chant, drawing on the residual magic that lingered in the air around her.

Blue sparks erupted from her fingertips, shooting out

like mini fireworks. Some veered off-course, fizzling out in a shower of sparks, but a few landed true, striking their targets. "Feel the magic, jackass," she exclaimed as one of the attackers yelped in surprise and pain, stumbling back.

Bo Peep was proving to be more formidable than she'd appeared. "Don't underestimate a shepherdess," she warned, brandishing her crook like a weapon. With a swift movement, she swept it low, tripping one of the thugs.

He stumbled forward, colliding with another and causing both to falter.

Then, with a strength that belied her delicate stature, Bo Peep swung her crook like a batter at the plate. It connected solidly with another thug's gut, and he doubled over. "Home run," she stated, a fierce grin spreading across her face.

But the numbers were against them. Two more thugs, seeing Sir Thomas engaged with their comrade, tried to flank him. Swift as lightning, Sir Thomas pivoted, parrying a blow on his left while dodging another on his right.

His sword moved in a blur, each strike precise and calculated.

Sensing Sir Thomas' predicament, Charlotte tried focusing her energies. She whispered a chant, and the ground beneath the flanking thugs trembled. Vines, weak and thin but enough to entangle, shot up, wrapping around their legs, pulling them to the ground momentarily.

After ensuring his thug was incapacitated, Cat darted toward another who was aiming a kick at Bo Peep's head. With a fearsome growl, Cat intercepted, grabbing onto the thug's leg and dragging him down.

The battle was far from its conclusion. One thug, his

eyes trained on Charlotte's faltering form, believed her to be easy prey. He charged toward her with a guttural roar, his intentions clear.

Sir Thomas appeared out of nowhere, his blade meeting the thug's with a loud clang. "Not on my watch," he growled.

The fight escalated, and Charlotte realized they needed a strategy. They were holding their own, but for how long could they sustain this?

"The tide needs to turn in our favor," she muttered, her gaze darting around the chaotic scene.

Sir Thomas' grace belied his small size. His blade wove in a deadly dance, clashing with the blades of multiple opponents. He snaked through the battleground, leaving his adversaries disoriented and reeling. "Like a cat among pigeons," he mused aloud, a wry grin on his face despite the dire circumstances.

Cat was a formidable opponent. He lunged at any thug who dared approach, and his dagger-sharp teeth and powerful jaws were intimidating. One thug was audacious enough to wrestle with Cat but quickly realized his mistake.

Bo Peep was doing surprisingly well with her crook, finding inventive ways to use it. She managed to wedge it between one thug's legs, toppling him over before spinning to deflect a punch from another.

It was evident that while she might not be a trained fighter, sheer determination was a formidable force of its own.

Charlotte was starting to feel the weight of her weakened powers. Each spell drained her more than she anticipated.

Drawing from deep within, she began to chant a more complex spell. Her hands shimmered with a radiant blue glow, and the air around her seemed to thicken.

Noticing this, several thugs converged on her, sensing an opportunity.

Seeing the danger closing in, Cat and Sir Thomas sprang into action. "Back off," Sir Thomas hissed, fur bristling as he and Cat positioned themselves between Charlotte and the approaching assailants.

Charlotte's chant grew louder, her voice rising to match the tension in the alley. With a final, determined shout, she thrust her hands toward the sky. "*Ignis artificiosus!*"

Everyone braced themselves, expecting a wave of raw power. Instead, a series of small, erratic fireworks burst in the darkened sky.

They weren't threatening, but the sudden bright flashes and loud bangs startled the thugs. "What the—" one of them stuttered, dropping his weapon as he shielded his eyes.

For a fleeting moment, the alley was full of brilliant lights and echoing explosions. The thugs scattered, their bravado replaced with fear and confusion. "Didn't see that coming, did you?" Sir Thomas taunted, a smirk playing on his lips.

He seized the opportunity by jumping forward and slashing at several disoriented thugs, pushing them back farther. With a booming bark, Cat sent another group scuttling away in fright.

Bo Peep, catching onto the momentum, shouted, "Run if you value your lives!"

Their combined efforts, along with Charlotte's unplanned fireworks display, seemed to do the trick. The thugs, fearing they were up against a force beyond their understanding, began to retreat.

Their once-cocky demeanors were replaced with uncertainty and fear.

The alley, moments ago the scene of an intense battle, now held an eerie silence, broken only by the heavy breathing of the victors and the distant footfalls of retreating thugs.

Little Bo Peep, drawing breath in ragged gasps from the adrenaline-fueled encounter, studied the unlikely trio with a blend of bewilderment and appreciation. Her vibrant eyes flickered between the three figures before her. The shepherdess was visibly shaken as she tried to make sense of the surreal chain of events.

Her gaze lingered on Charlotte, whose magical sparks still danced around her fingertips, casting a glow on her face. It shifted to Sir Thomas, whose feline elegance was at odds with the lethal sword he held.

Finally, her eyes rested on Cat, his imposing form still bristling with barely contained energy.

Her bonnet, usually immaculate, was slashed and askew, a testament to the recent scuffle. Her usual rosy cheeks were pale, making the freckles across her nose stand out. The handle of her crook, clutched tightly in her hand, bore the imprint of her grip.

As she tried to reconcile the image of her rescuers with her understanding of the world, the twinkle in her eyes dimmed, replaced by confusion and disbelief as she spoke to all three. "Of all the tales and fables, never did I imagine being saved by such an eclectic mix of heroes. My heart holds an immeasurable depth of gratitude for each of you."

Charlotte approached the tired shepherdess gently, noting the signs of distress on her face. She brushed the dirt off Bo Peep's once-pristine gown and adjusted her bonnet.

"Every person deserves kindness and care, especially in unfamiliar lands," Charlotte murmured. Being in Cincinnati, far from the magical realm they knew, was disorienting.

Bo Peep hesitated for a moment before sharing, "In EverAfter, I cast a spell. A simple one I've done countless times to find my wandering sheep. Yet this time, something twisted, and instead of my beloved flock," she waved her crook around, "I found myself in this concrete jungle."

Charlotte, empathy filling her eyes, replied, "The lines between our worlds seem to be blurring. You're not the only one who's been thrown into this strange land. There's Peter, once Peter Pan of Neverland, who came here long before me, and here am I, both disoriented in this new realm."

Sir Thomas added his two cents to the mix. "It's as if the very threads that weave our stories and realities are fraying. Without intervention, the chaos that might ensue would not only endanger our tales but possibly this world as well."

With the danger of the alley behind them, the group began their journey through the streets, their unique appearances drawing curious glances as they exited the alley.

Aware of Bo Peep's anxiety, Charlotte spoke in a soothing tone. "Fear not, dear shepherdess. We're escorting you to a haven where others like us have found refuge."

As the group neared Peter's fish store, the familiar tinkle of the door's bell filled the air. Peter, his keen eyes immediately picking up on the newcomer's bewilderment, rushed out to greet them.

"Ah, welcome, welcome!" he exclaimed, his face breaking into a warm, welcoming grin. He extended his hand toward Bo Peep. "I see we have a new visitor. You're among friends, dear."

Bo Peep, taken aback by Peter's immediate warmth and acceptance, could only blink in surprise for a moment before recovering. She accepted his hand and gave a small, shy smile.

"Thank you, Peter," she said, her voice soft. "It's a bit overwhelming, all this, but it's comforting to know there are familiar faces...and places." She glanced around the store, her gaze lingering on the barrels of fish and the subtle hints of magic that threaded through the air.

After saying their goodbyes to Bo Peep, Charlotte, Cat, and Sir Thomas stepped into the embrace of the dusk, the city's lights twinkling like distant stars.

The fluorescent glow of the bus stop bathed them in an otherworldly light, making their already unusual appearance even more conspicuous. They hoped the evening crowd, too engrossed in their own worlds, might overlook their peculiarities. However, as they climbed onto the bus, the driver's stern countenance suggested that their journey home might be fraught with challenges.

The bus driver, a heavy man with a thick mustache that bristled under the harsh overhead lights, looked them over with a sneer. "What's the deal with the costumes?" he asked, his voice gruff. "You two supposed to be some kind of fairytale royalty or something?"

His gaze landed on Sir Thomas' sword, barely concealed disdain in his eyes. "What are you? And no pets allowed," he added, pointing a thick, accusatory finger at Cat.

"Actually," Sir Thomas began, an edge of irritation creeping into his voice, "we're cosplayers. I am a knight, and he," he gestured at Cat, "is a certified service animal."

"Certified service animal, my ass," the driver replied, "and I'm a king if you're a knight."

Sir Thomas, feeling both indignant and playful, couldn't resist a challenge. Drawing himself to his full, albeit short, height, he retorted, "Sir, that's no way to address a knight! I challenge thee to a duel for your disrespect!"

Charlotte, recognizing the growing tension, acted swiftly. With surprising strength, she grabbed Sir Thomas by the arm, hauling him away from the potentially disastrous confrontation. "Sir Thomas, this isn't EverAfter. Remember? No duels on Earth!"

To onlookers, it might've looked like a scene out of a Renaissance fair, with Charlotte playing the part of the peacemaker and Sir Thomas being the spirited duelist.

Unfortunately, they still had to get off the bus.

The bus left in a huff, and the small crowd that had formed during the commotion began to disperse, murmuring about "dedicated cosplayers" and "method actors."

Realizing they needed another mode of transport, they flagged down a nearby cab. The driver, unlike the bus driver, seemed to take their unique outfits in stride. "Been to a convention?" he inquired, his eyes twinkling with amusement.

"We're more than mere characters," Sir Thomas couldn't resist countering. "We hail from EverAfter, defending its magical realm and, apparently, now Cincinnati."

Charlotte, leaning into the playful narrative, introduced Cat. "And don't forget our brave mount, valiant in battle and loyal in service."

The driver chuckled heartily, navigating through the city streets. "Well, defenders of EverAfter or not, you've got a flair for the dramatic. You'll fit in well here."

The amber hue of the city lights painted the streets as the trio made their way to Alex's apartment. As they turned the corner, a peculiar sight greeted them. Sitting majestically atop a worn-out mailbox was a small blue squirrel. Its fur glinted in the soft glow from the streetlight, and its bushy tail flicked with purpose.

What caught their attention was its attire—a vibrant red cape that flowed behind it and an acorn medallion that hung around its neck, representing an unknown allegiance.

"We will get out here!" Charlotte told the man, providing him with bills Alex had given her so her gold coins wouldn't get her mugged or worse.

After they got out, the trio stopped to stare at the squirrel.

For a brief moment, the bustling city faded into the

background as the squirrel fixed its gaze on them. With an air of nobility, it raised a small paw in a salute and recognition.

Sir Thomas, ever the storyteller, leaned in, his voice hushed. "It's him again—the Squirrel of Destiny. Legends say he aids those on a noble quest."

Charlotte, ever pragmatic, chuckled. "Well, if squirrels are saluting us, we must be on the right track." A moment later, the squirrel jumped off and disappeared, and the trio continued the short distance to Alex's apartment.

CHAPTER TWENTY-THREE

Exhausted, Charlotte, Cat, and Sir Thomas shuffled into the apartment. They craved rest and recovery, and their minds wandered back to the familiar comfort of EverAfter.

Alex stepped into the living room, a mug of steaming coffee in hand. Immediately, his eyes landed on Sir Thomas, who was perched on the back of the couch, tail swishing.

The feline was looking at a shiny trinket precariously perched on a nearby stand. Alex was all too familiar with that concentrated gaze.

"Don't even think about it, Sir Thomas," Alex warned, setting his coffee on the counter and approaching the couch.

As Alex neared, Sir Thomas' eyes flicked toward him. He took on an air of innocence, brushing his feathered hat-covered head against Alex's leg and purring as if to say, "Who, me? Cause trouble?" Alex was not convinced and remained watchful, not taking his eyes off Sir Thomas.

Sensing that his plans had been foiled, Sir Thomas

diverted his gaze from the trinket and toward the window. Alex let out a relieved sigh.

"What is this, Alex?" Charlotte asked, examining the phone. "It looks like a mirror, but it's too thin."

Alex, still watching Sir Thomas since he knew what the feline could get up to, walked over and explained, "It's a smartphone, Charlotte. You can use it for communication, information, and entertainment."

"Ah, a magic mirror of sorts," she mused, her eyes wide with fascination. Sir Thomas stifled a laugh from the other end of the room.

Charlotte absentmindedly tapped on the smartphone, exploring its interface. The news app icon caught her eye, and curiosity compelled her to open it. As the headlines loaded, one in particular drew her immediate attention: **Prince Repel's Grand Public Appearance**.

She stood up, knocking the phone off her lap. "I have to go."

Alex, having caught the phone and read the headline, looked up at her. "Charlotte, you can't possibly intend to confront him out in the open amid all those people?"

Stopping and taking a deep breath, Charlotte met his gaze. "As much as every fiber of my being yearns to challenge him, I'm well aware of the limitations of my current magical capabilities. Even if I was at full strength, it would be reckless and dangerous to involve so many innocent bystanders."

A brief, relieved sigh escaped Alex's lips. "I'm glad you're thinking strategically. Going there to observe and glean some insight into his intentions—that could be hugely valuable. But after your unexpected encounter at

The Ascent, he's surely aware of your presence here. And he knows your appearance."

Charlotte's fingers fidgeted with the edge of her cape. "That does complicate things." A glint of consideration flashed in her eyes. "All right. Let's strategize."

Taking a moment, the group gathered around a table cluttered with maps, timelines, and odd trinkets. Sir Thomas spoke first. "What if we used a glamour spell? One that makes us invisible or at least inconspicuous?"

Charlotte hesitated, considering his suggestion. "Glamours are tricky here. The magic behaves...differently."

Alex nodded. "Even if Charlotte managed something magical, it might draw unwanted attention. What's natural in EverAfter is most likely not here."

As they debated, Sir Thomas looked hopefully at Charlotte. "But you *do* think there's a way to get in close without alerting someone as powerful as Repel?"

Charlotte paused for a moment before nodding, her thoughts racing. "Yes, but we need to be subtle. Blending in is our best option."

Sir Thomas' whiskers twitched. "What about normal disguises? In EverAfter, I once went to the Grand Masquerade as a griffon. Quite the spectacle."

Alex chuckled. "While that isn't exactly 'normal,' that does sound like an incredible sight. It might not help us here, though. We need to be inconspicuous. And, Sir Thomas, as much as I'd love to have you and Cat there with us, you two stand out a bit more than Charlotte does."

Sir Thomas looked at his feline body and over at Cat, who was batting at a beam of light on the wall. "Point taken."

Cat, sensing the serious mood, let out a soft, concerned whine, tail wagging slowly.

Charlotte knelt down, stroking Cat's head. "I know you want to help, but sometimes, staying behind is the best way you can."

Sir Thomas, attempting to lighten the mood, quipped, "Well, at least this way, Cat and I can work on our indoor games. Isn't that right?" He nudged the large dog with his paw, eliciting a playful bark.

As they continued their discussion, Charlotte glanced out the window, her eyes narrowing.

The world outside was dark, and not just because the sun had set. A layer of ice was slowly forming on the window panes, creeping like crystalline spiders.

Alex followed her gaze. His eyes narrowed, and his face paled. "That's not natural," he whispered.

Sir Thomas jumped onto the windowsill, his claws scratching at the icy surface. "Someone's watching us."

Charlotte's heart raced, her instincts on high alert. "We need to move *now*." Sir Thomas dove for the floor.

The room's temperature dropped precipitously, each breath forming a visible puff in the frigid air. The formerly cozy apartment was now bathed in a malevolent ice-blue hue.

Before they could fully register the change, there was a violent crash when the windows imploded, sending shards of glass and jagged pieces of ice flying in all directions.

Sir Thomas jumped back up and swiftly drew his blade, its gleaming edge reflecting the cold, unnatural light. Alex, ever protective, had already unholstered his Glock 26, its dark matte finish contrasting with the luminous fragments of ice littering the floor.

Cat, also protective, shielded Charlotte from the blast, his large frame taking the brunt of the flying debris. He then nudged her gently, helping her find her footing amid the chaos.

As the dust and frost settled, a chilling figure came into view. Framed by the remains of one of the shattered windows was the Snow Queen. Draped in a flowing robe that shimmered like fresh snow under moonlight, she wore her icy crown with an air of authority, but it was her smile, cold and devious, that truly captured the group's attention.

"Found you, little fairy godmother," she purred, her voice carrying a melodic yet sinister tone.

Charlotte, regaining her composure, responded with a mixture of defiance and caution. "What do you want, Snow Queen?"

The Snow Queen tilted her head slightly, the glint in her eyes revealing her amusement. "Why, to extend Prince Repel's greetings, of course. And perhaps have a bit of fun."

Alex, gripping his Glock firmly, intervened. "This is neither the time nor the place for your games."

Sir Thomas, blade still drawn and eyes narrowed, added, "Leave now before you regret this intrusion."

Cat gave a deep rumble that emphasized the threat. The room was thick with tension, each individual ready for the Snow Queen's next move.

She chuckled, a sound reminiscent of the tinkling of icicles. "So protective, but remember, fairy godmother, it's not just EverAfter that's in danger. This world is fragile, too." Her gaze swept over Alex and the room, taking in every detail.

Charlotte stepped forward, her determination evident. "We won't let you or Repel harm either world."

The Snow Queen's grin became predatory as she stepped into the apartment and pointed her katana at Charlotte. "You act as if you can do anything about it."

CHAPTER TWENTY-FOUR

The Snow Queen launched her assault with a flurry of ice and snow. Icy tendrils spread rapidly, covering walls and floor and turning the warm apartment into a frosty battlefield.

The four friends scattered. Alex ducked behind the remnants of his frozen couch, pulling Cat down with him. Sir Thomas darted beneath a table, his eyes fixed on the menacing Snow Queen. Charlotte stood her ground.

Drawing on her magic, Charlotte's fingers glowed purple as she fired a missile at the Snow Queen. It slammed into the Queen's chest, and the impact made her stumble, but when she looked up, it was clear that the attack had done little more than irritate her.

The Snow Queen jeered. "Is that all you have, Godmother?" Before she could launch a counterattack, Sir Thomas lunged from his hiding spot. With a fierce yowl, he went for her, claws bared. The Snow Queen, with reflexes befitting her legendary status, drew one of her icy katanas and deftly blocked Sir Thomas' assault.

The sharp blade clanged against his sword, and sparks flew.

"Bold kitty," she hissed, pushing him away with a wave of her hand. He slid across the floor.

Charlotte knew their chances were slim in these confined quarters. "We need a plan!" she shouted, trying to find an opening in the Snow Queen's defenses.

The apartment worked to the Queen's advantage. The close quarters gave the defenders little room to dodge her relentless onslaught, and she seemed to anticipate every move they made. The walls closed in on them, and the temperature dropped with every passing second.

They needed to regroup and strategize a way out.

Sir Thomas' claws glinted as they slashed at her robe, and he jeered. "Is that all the famous Snow Queen has to offer? Pathetic!"

Her eyes glinted with suppressed rage. "You're playing with forces you can't comprehend, feline!" she hissed. With a swift motion, she knocked him off balance and, taking advantage of the moment, unleashed a powerful icy blast at him.

Sir Thomas twisted in mid-air, narrowly avoiding a body hit. However, his tail wasn't as lucky. It was ensnared by the creeping frost, pinning him to the spot.

Seeing an opening, Alex fired at the Snow Queen, but she raised a shield of thick ice, and the bullets ricocheted harmlessly off its surface.

Her focus on Alex was the distraction Cat needed. He lunged, blindsiding the Snow Queen with his weight and momentum. His jaws snapped inches from her face, causing her to recoil.

Charlotte rushed to Sir Thomas' side. She murmured incantations under her breath, her fingers glowing as she tried to melt the ice trapping Sir Thomas' tail. Just as she managed to melt the ice that ensnared Sir Thomas' tail, the Snow Queen sent Cat hurtling across the room with a mighty heave. The dog crashed into a wall with a resounding thud.

Alex took the opportunity to fire another volley at the Snow Queen. The shots hit her, but to his shock, they bounced off, clattering on the floor. She had layered her skin with impenetrable sheets of ice as makeshift armor against the bullets below the shield.

Outside the apartment, a commotion grew. Their battle had not gone unnoticed. Neighbors from adjacent apartments pounded on the door while concerned shouts echoed from the street below.

Emergency vehicles' flashing lights pierced the darkness, painting the iced-over walls of the apartment red and blue.

Charlotte's eyes widened in alarm. "We need to get out of here. Our battle could endanger innocent people!"

Sir Thomas, his blood up from the battle and eager to finish the duel, took a moment to assess the situation. "Very well," he conceded, slightly out of breath. "I might not be one for magic as you are, madam, but I have my tricks. I'll provide the necessary diversion. You may wish to shield your eyes."

He plucked the long, ornate feather from his hat and stroked it, and the room filled with blinding light.

The Snow Queen shielded her eyes, disoriented.

"Now!" Charlotte shouted.

The group sprinted through the apartment door, their breathing fast and ragged. The hallway was overrun with concerned and terrified residents. Some were trying to exit their apartments, while others stared in shock at the frozen landscapes that had once been their neighbors' homes.

"Move! Everyone out!" Alex shouted, pulling open doors and urging people to flee. His cop instincts kicked in, and he took control of the situation even in its oddness.

When they reached the ground floor, the group emerged into the foyer, which had become a gathering point for bewildered residents. Among them was Mr. Lorenzo, the portly deli owner. He was a familiar face to Alex, always ready with a ham sandwich and friendly chat when Alex popped into his shop.

"Alex!" Mr. Lorenzo called, adjusting his glasses as he tried to make sense of the scene. "Are you okay? What in the world is going on? This is...well, even given your wild stories, this one takes the cake!"

Alex grimaced. He couldn't tell Mr. Lorenzo that they were fleeing from a magical ice queen. "Gas leak," he replied, thinking on his feet. "Some kind of chemical reaction. We think it caused these...frost formations. We're getting everyone out for safety."

Mr. Lorenzo looked askance but nodded. "All right, Detective. If you say so. Just be careful, okay? The world is weird these days."

As more police officers and emergency personnel arrived on the scene, their sirens added to the cacophony. Alex was pulled aside by a fellow officer, Detective Martinez, to explain the situation.

With every eye focused on the bizarre ice formations

and the new arrivals, it was the perfect time for Charlotte, Sir Thomas, and Cat to slip away. Charlotte pulled her cloak tightly around her, hiding her magical attire, while Sir Thomas, always one for theatrics, disguised himself as a house cat, purring and rubbing against people's legs. Cat relied on the shadows.

"We need to regroup," Charlotte whispered to the feline and the dog. "We need a new plan."

The three made their way to a nearby alley, away from prying eyes. Once they were safe within its shadowed confines, they paused to catch their breath and listen for any sign that the Snow Queen was giving chase.

Inside, Alex finished briefing Martinez, then scanned the crowd for his friends.

Charlotte's thoughts almost spiraled out of control as she contemplated the implications of their recent encounter, but before she could take a step, Sir Thomas' paw landed on her shoulder.

"Don't," he whispered, tilting his head toward the apartment windows. The icy glaze that had enveloped the building was gone, replaced by the warm yellow glow of the apartments' lights. "She's gone," he mused. "Was it an assassination attempt or a mere display of power to send us a message?"

Charlotte's gaze met Sir Thomas', and she took a deep breath as she thought about his question. "I wouldn't put it past the Snow Queen to kill us if she had the chance, but yes, it might have been a threat. A warning about what she's capable of."

Sir Thomas noted the frustration on her features. She looked down at her palms, the faint purple glow now dim.

"I should've been able to defend us better," she muttered. "It's maddening!"

As despair threatened to overwhelm her, a warm weight gently leaned against her leg. Sensing Charlotte's anguish, Cat pressed into her, doing his best to purr. The vibrations of his canine rumble seemed to weave a comforting spell and chase away some of her gloom.

She knelt, wrapping her arms around Cat's broad neck. "Thank you," she whispered into his fur. "You know, if my magic had been working as it should, I might never have met you. I'd still be lost in a new world. You, Alex, and Sir Thomas have brought light into my life."

Not one to let emotions get the better of him, Sir Thomas cleared his throat. "Ahem. Yes, well, we make quite the team," he agreed, a hint of warmth in his voice.

Charlotte got to her feet. "We do, and together, we'll find a way to stop Repel and the Snow Queen."

The trio settled down and watched the apartment building from a safe distance. The scene slowly returned to a semblance of normalcy. The fire trucks and ambulances dispersed, and the crowd of onlookers dwindled. Alex's familiar figure finally emerged from the entrance, looking weary but determined.

Seeing an opportunity, Sir Thomas took out his dimly glowing feather, and with a subtle wave, he captured Alex's attention. Recognizing the signal, the detective made his way discreetly toward the alley in which they were hidden.

"Are you all okay?" Alex asked when he reached them, his voice laced with concern.

Charlotte nodded. "We're fine, thanks to Sir Thomas' quick thinking."

"And your ability to stay under the radar," Sir Thomas added, nodding at Alex.

Alex rubbed the back of his neck. "It wasn't easy. Had to give the others a cover story about an attempted break-in and a scuffle. The water stains? Blamed it on a burst pipe." He looked around to check out the area. "The city's infrastructure isn't what it used to be, after all."

Charlotte's brow furrowed. "And your apartment?"

The detective sighed. "It's an active crime scene for now. The department is putting me up in a hotel until the investigation is over."

"Where does that leave us?" Sir Thomas inquired with a twinkle in his eye.

Alex smirked. "Two beds. Don't worry. It's pet-friendly."

Cat woofed, seemingly satisfied with the arrangement. Sir Thomas let out a mock groan. "I should have known you'd lump us in with the pets," he said with feigned indignation.

With a playful nudge, Charlotte teased, "Oh, come on, Sir Thomas. If they are anything like the hotels in Ever-After, a little pampering won't hurt. Maybe they'll even have tuna on the room service menu."

Sir Thomas huffed. "As long as they have a nice tea, I suppose I'll manage."

The group enjoyed the light moment, their spirits lifting. Then they made their way to the hotel, ready for a respite before preparing for the challenges the next day would undoubtedly bring.

CHAPTER TWENTY-FIVE

Alex's car groaned under the weight of its occupants. It was a sight to see. Sir Thomas awkwardly adjusted his position in the backseat. His long, ornate sword poked at odd angles, which was a challenge for Cat.

"For heaven's sake, Sir Thomas! Why didn't you leave your sword in the trunk?" Alex exclaimed, casting a wary eye on the rearview mirror as he tried to navigate through the dimly lit streets while simultaneously keeping an eye on his discomfited passengers.

Sir Thomas huffed. "A knight is never without his blade, especially after what happened with the Snow Queen. We must be ever vigilant!" He shifted, and the tip of his scabbard knocked Cat in the head.

Cat let out a low, disgruntled woof and shifted, trying to find a comfortable spot away from the offending blade. His big, expressive eyes fixed Sir Thomas with a reproachful look.

"My, um, sincerest apologies," Sir Thomas murmured, looking genuinely chagrined. He attempted to tuck the sword closer to his body, though it seemed an exercise in futility given the tight space and Cat's formidable dimensions.

Amid the shifting, a low grumble filled the car. All eyes turned to Cat's stomach, which was voicing its displeasure.

From the front passenger seat, Charlotte chuckled. "Sounds like we all could use some food." She shared a knowing glance with Alex. The events of the day had drained them emotionally and physically.

The car's atmosphere changed from mild irritation to jovial as everyone started discussing where and what to eat. The tantalizing thoughts of food distracted them from the dangers they had recently faced.

As they drove into the heart of Cincinnati, the group passed several restaurants, each evoking a different reaction from the occupants of the car. Charlotte mused about pasta, while the thought of tacos made Alex's stomach grumble along with Cat's.

Sir Thomas, who had been quiet for a moment, perked up. "What about Skyline Chili?" he proposed, recalling his past experience with the local delicacy. "It's a Cincinnati institution, and it would provide us with the sustenance we need."

"It was good enough to eat again," Charlotte agreed.

After a brief discussion, the group reached a consensus and pulled into a Skyline Chili drive-through. The colorful menu, coupled with the rich aroma of chili, brought smiles to their faces, momentarily pushing away their worries.

The ordering process was nothing short of chaotic, with Sir Thomas' request for "extra mustard" on his three-way coney causing an amused rise of the cashier's eyebrows. Soon, they were loaded up with bags of food, the car filled with the scent of dinner.

After they found a quiet parking spot, they dug into their meals. The conversation meandered from food to their recent adventures and back.

Sir Thomas let out a sudden belch, causing Cat to jump. "Ah," he said with a sly grin. "I believe I've discovered the source of my earlier discomfort."

Alex rolled his eyes. "And here I thought it was the sword."

"Sometimes, Detective, it's the simplest things that confound us the most."

Charlotte leaned back against the car seat, wiping her mouth with a napkin. "This chili!" she exclaimed, her eyes sparkling with fascination. "It's unlike anything we have in EverAfter. It's rich and comforting."

Sir Thomas, always one to voice his opinion, nodded in agreement. "True, but I have tasted something similar in my time, a type of stew. It's a tad more sour in flavor, which is why I have such a fondness for mustard."

Alex took a bite of his coney. "Well, Skyline Chili is a Cincinnati classic. I grew up with it, so it feels quite ordinary to me. But hearing you talk about it like this makes me realize I'm just fortunate to have it nearby." He took a sip from his drink and then turned to Charlotte. "EverAfter sounds incredible. From what you both have described, it's like something out of a fairytale. I guess, in essence, it is."

Charlotte nodded, her gaze distant. "Your world is just as fascinating, Alex. The enormous buildings, the technology, the hustle and bustle... In EverAfter, magic is our way of life, but here, it's technology. It's so...so *alien* to me."

Sir Thomas grunted and dabbed more mustard on his coney. "I agree. There's much that intrigues me here. Though," he paused, taking a deliberate bite, "I do wish the locals weren't so taken aback by my presence."

Charlotte giggled, recalling some of the reactions they'd encountered on their journey. "Oh, Sir Thomas. You've always been one to turn heads."

Sir Thomas straightened, feigning hurt pride. "I may not have been able to keep up my appearance in the time that I have been here, but I am still far more dashing than most I have come across."

Alex tried to stifle his laugh, but it burst out. "Sir Thomas," he began, trying to compose himself, "I don't think it's your lack of hygiene that shocks people. It's that you're a talking, sword-wielding cat. Most people assume you are a weirdo." He received a glare from Sir Thomas. "Or a very capable cosplayer who must be handsome as hell to pull off such a costume."

"Well, when you put it that way," Sir Thomas mused with a smirk, "I can see how it might be surprising."

Charlotte laughed. "That's an understatement."

As the trio's conversation flowed, a city bus rolled by, its sides adorned with advertisements. One ad caught Charlotte's eye—an image of a man, confident and regal, with the name Rafael Princeton emblazoned below it. To anyone else, it would have looked like a political ad, but to Charlotte, it held a deeper, more personal significance.

She huffed, her lips curving into a frown. The change in her demeanor didn't go unnoticed by Alex, who followed her gaze as the bus was about to disappear from view. "You really dislike that guy," he remarked, nodding at the vanishing bus. "Can't say I'm very fond of him either since he's tried to kill us more than once. Can you tell me more about him?"

Charlotte sighed, pushing away her half-eaten chili. "Well, it seems Prince Repel is known here as Rafael Princeton. In EverAfter, he's notorious, especially in the royal circles."

Alex raised an eyebrow, intrigued. "What did he do besides be generally a vile person? You have a history with him."

Charlotte hesitated for a moment, searching for the right words. "I was on guard duty the day he was banished. It was a spectacle, to say the least. Repel was Prince Charming's brother, and the two couldn't be more different. Prince Charming was loved and adored, and Repel was always envious of him. He desired more power, influence, and dominance, despite what he wielded as a prince."

She took a deep breath before continuing, "It's said he orchestrated an attempt on his brother's life. His treachery was discovered, and he should have faced the gallows, but his father and Prince Charming, in a final act of mercy, chose banishment over execution."

Sir Thomas nodded in agreement, adding, "Repel's banishment was a decision that split the court. Some thought it was too lenient, while others believed it was just."

Alex looked thoughtful. "But why send him here to our world? Is this where everyone from EverAfter gets banished?"

Charlotte leaned back and looked out the window. "The truth is, not many know where the banished go. The mages who create the portals keep it a well-guarded secret. Most of us in EverAfter assumed they were sent to some desolate, empty realm."

Alex smirked. "Well, if you have to banish people from EverAfter to Earth, maybe send them somewhere more fitting for their crimes like the middle of Antarctica or, I don't know, Wyoming."

Charlotte looked at him, curious. "Are those among the most desolate places here?"

Alex hid a small grin. "One is a tad less welcoming than the other." He pulled over, and it took only a minute to grab the group's trash, throw it in a garbage can, and get back in the car.

"You know, Charlotte," he began, adjusting the rearview mirror to get a glimpse of his passengers, "it might be best if we lie low for a while. Let things cool off."

Charlotte leaned her head against the window, her reflection superimposed on the passing lights. "I agree. The more I think about it, the less sense it makes to rush in without a solid plan. Repel will expect us, especially after what happened today."

A soft rumble of agreement came from the back, where Sir Thomas was nestled between bags of leftover food and Cat. "Wisdom often comes with time," Sir Thomas mused, rubbing his temples. "Rushing in heedlessly could spell our doom."

Alex smirked, glancing at Charlotte. "Our feline friend is quite the philosopher."

Charlotte chuckled. "You have no idea. In EverAfter, he is famous enough to have had songs written about him. He's so known for his proverbs, sometimes to an annoying extent, that there are some comedic lines about the 'philosophizing swashbuckler.'"

Sir Thomas feigned offense. "*Annoying?* I merely aim to enlighten my companions with the knowledge I've amassed over the years."

"As enlightening as it is," Alex interjected, "perhaps we can save the philosophy for another day. Right now, I think we all need some rest."

Sir Thomas yawned, stretching out as best he could in the tight confines of the car. "Indeed, Detective. Rest, and then we strategize. I have a few contacts in this realm who might provide us with useful information."

Alex raised an eyebrow. "Contacts? In this world?"

The cat smirked. "Did you think I've been idle during my time here? Even in a strange land, a knight finds allies."

Charlotte smiled, her eyes heavy with fatigue. "That's reassuring to hear, Thomas. I knew there was a reason I brought you along."

Sir Thomas wagged a finger. "Correction, my dear. You didn't bring me; I chose to come. One does not 'bring' Sir Thomas anywhere."

Alex laughed, keeping his eyes on the road. "Well, Sir Thomas, let's hope your contacts can help us unravel this mystery."

The drive was quiet after that, the soft hum of the car engine and the rhythmic beat of the city's pulse lulling them into a serene state. The brightly lit hotel sign finally came into view, signaling that the night's journey was at an end.

Pulling into a parking spot, Alex turned off the ignition and cast a glance at his companions. Cat was snoring softly, his large head resting on Sir Thomas' lap. The old knight seemed lost in thought as he absentmindedly stroked the dog's fur.

Charlotte stretched, exhaling deeply. "Thank you, Alex. For everything. We wouldn't have made it this far without you."

Alex smiled and patted her hand. "We're in this together. Tomorrow's another day and we'll face it head-on, but for now, sleep is our best ally."

The four exited the car, and Alex helped Sir Thomas bring in the bags of leftover food. The cool night air was refreshing, and the distant hum of the city was a reminder that despite the strangeness of their situation, life went on.

The hotel's lobby was quiet as they checked in, the night receptionist giving them a curious once-over but not questioning the motley group. Within minutes, they were settling into the adjoining rooms, the weight of the day sinking in.

As the night deepened, they all found solace in rest, dreams of EverAfter and Cincinnati intertwining in a dance of memories, hopes, and fears. Tomorrow would come with its own set of challenges, but tonight, they had each other.

Sometimes, that was enough.

CHAPTER TWENTY-SIX

In the mystical recesses of the Vent Haven Museum, a space that had celebrated the art of ventriloquism had been transformed into something out of legend.

The formerly ordinary room was saturated with an otherworldly glow, holding magic-imbued artifacts and symbols that weren't part of the museum's original collection. The walls, still lined with ventriloquists' dummies, bore magical enhancements courtesy of Prince Repel.

The dummies' lifeless eyes seemed to gleam, hinting at a semblance of awareness.

Within this chamber, Prince Repel stood at the heart of a summoning circle. The luminescence his hands emitted intensified, illuminating the dim room with an ethereal glow. As he murmured incantations from another realm, two imposing figures stood vigilantly at his side.

Lyra, a stunning nymph with iridescent wings that shimmered even in the muted light, watched Repel with a mixture of awe and caution. Her delicate features belied her fierce nature, and her sharp eyes darted around the room, ever alert.

Beside her stood Geb, a massive ogre whose size and brutish appearance made him a fearsome minion. His rough gray skin was like armor, and though his posture indicated deference to Repel, it was clear that he was on high alert.

Geb leaned down to whisper to Lyra, his voice rough but laced with concern. "I hope this goes better than the last time. That beast from EverAfter? It was a nightmare."

Lyra nodded, her eyes reflecting the memories of that fateful day. "Three guards gone just like that. At least Repel compensated us with their pay." She sighed softly, adding, "Though gold is cold comfort for lost comrades."

"He's taken precautions this time," Geb remarked to reassure both himself and Lyra. He gestured subtly at the magical wards that lined the periphery of the room, which glowed faintly but steadily. "Those should hold back whatever he summons."

Lyra exhaled, her wings fluttering slightly. "Let's hope so for all our sakes."

The room was momentarily swallowed by a thick purple haze. Every sound, even the flutter of Lyra's wings or the soft rumble of Geb's breathing, was amplified and distorted in the murk.

Their senses were on high alert, straining to detect any movement or noise that would give away the identity of the summoned creature.

As quickly as the mist had formed, it departed. At Prince Repel's command, the thick curtain of smoke was swept away, revealing the enigmatic centerpiece of their anxiety: a simple, slightly damaged doll.

The trio stared at the doll, then at each other, and then back at the doll. Its delicate porcelain features were marred by cracks and smudges, its painted lips slightly chipped, and its glassy blue eyes reflected nothing but the dim light. This lifeless figure, out of place amid the high stakes and heightened tension of the summoning ritual, was completely unexpected.

Geb, though usually reserved, found his voice first. "Master," he began hesitantly, "is that...is that what you intended to summon?"

Repel's gaze landed heavily on Geb, and the chilling intensity of those eyes made Lyra and the ogre flinch inwardly. They knew all too well the destructive power Repel wielded. A moment of his wrath could be deadly. After what felt like an eternity, Repel's gaze shifted back to the doll.

He cocked his head, and as curiosity replaced his fury, Repel approached the circle. The guards watched with bated breath as he extended a hand to touch the doll's head. The light touch caused it to topple over.

The tension remained in the room, but it was now born of confusion and curiosity rather than fear. Given Prince Repel's past reactions to failed endeavors, Lyra and Geb had anticipated an outburst of rage. Instead, Repel had an introspective demeanor, an unexpected side of their master.

The prince cradled the doll in his hands, examining it meticulously. Its porcelain skin, the slight scuffs on its cheeks, the tattered dress—all were scrutinized under his discerning gaze. "Could the wards have done this, or is it this place itself?" he mused, glancing around the room and taking note of the many dummies and dolls that watched the scene. The Vent Haven Museum, with its countless silent witnesses, might have interfered with the energies he had tried to channel.

He continued, "This museum is saturated with the remnants of old magic, residual energies left by the myriad of dolls and dummies. Could it be that the environment itself responded to my summoning?"

He twisted the doll around, searching for any trace of enchantment or possession. However, it seemed disappointingly mundane, no different from the other dolls around the museum. With a soft sigh of resignation, Repel carelessly tossed it to the floor, and it landed with a soft thud of the body and a crack of the head.

His attention shifted back to the summoning circle. The radiant and powerful lines now appeared dull, the intricate patterns fading. He traced a finger along its perimeter, feeling the residual magic dissipating.

"Should I attempt the spell again?" Repel mused more to himself than to his bodyguards. He was deep in thought, weighing the pros and cons, factoring in the unknown variables the museum might introduce. As he deliberated, Lyra and Geb exchanged a brief, uneasy glance, unsure of what their unpredictable master might decide.

As Repel's mutters faded, Lyra whispered to Geb, her voice imbued with a mixture of awe and incredulity. "I've never seen a summoning go awry for him. EverAfter has always responded to his call."

Geb was about to reply when someone, their voice

sharp and unmistakably regal, interjected, "Perhaps it's yet another sign that the magics here are out of balance."

Startled, both guards spun. Emerging from the ethereal haze was the Snow Queen. Her radiant beauty seemed out of place in the dimly lit chamber. Lyra and Geb instinctively stepped back, granting her passage. The temperature in the room dipped due to her presence.

The Snow Queen glided effortlessly toward Repel, every step exuding grace and dominance. He ceased his contemplation and turned to her, an unreadable expression on his face. "Ah, Snow Queen," he began with a sardonic smile. "How did *your* task fare?"

Her lips, pale but perfectly defined, pursed in irritation. "You could guess."

His chuckle filled the room, a warm juxtaposition to her frosty demeanor. "I do feel the lingering presence of the fairy godmother, our dear Charlotte. I assume your mission was less than successful?"

"You requested her capture," she responded coldly. "Not her demise."

His eyes sparkled. "An oversight. Perhaps I should have been clearer, but it's amusing to imagine the great Snow Queen *not* delivering a fatal blow."

The woman's stare could have frozen the sun. "Had I known you wanted her gone, she would be a memory now."

His gaze locked with hers, the tension palpable. "I find the chase exhilarating. Knowing she still breathes and plots adds a certain spice to our endeavors."

She smirked, the smile as cold as her title. "Careful, Repel. Games can backfire."

His attention shifted to the porcelain doll. "Speaking of unexpected outcomes." He motioned at the object of his current predicament. "Any insights, my queen?"

She eyed the doll, then glanced around the room, her gaze pausing on the many ventriloquist dummies. "This place thrums with ancient magics. Your summoning might have collided with residual energies. Then again," she smiled, "maybe you're simply losing your touch."

"Or perhaps," Repel's gaze hardened, "dear queen, there's another player in this game. One neither of us has considered."

A tense silence filled the chamber. It was a standoff between two titans of magic, observed by two beings caught in their intricate web.

The Snow Queen turned away, her gown flowing elegantly behind her. "I came to observe, not to aid. Consider this a courtesy visit." With that, she disappeared into the mist from which she had emerged.

Repel's face, usually a mask of confidence and arrogance, showed the briefest hint of concern, but as quickly as it appeared, it vanished. "The game has only begun," he murmured more to himself than to his guards.

Lyra and Geb exchanged glances. They realized they were on the cusp of events far greater than they had imagined, and in their master's grand scheme, they were but pawns on a mystical chessboard.

Standing amid the dissipating magical haze, Repel took a deep, steadying breath. He was a master of composure, but the unexpected twists of the evening had ruffled his feathers. Voice commanding, he snapped, "Guards."

Ever vigilant, Lyra and Geb immediately stepped to his

side. Their usually steeled expressions showed traces of the evening's stress.

"We're done here," Repel declared. "Clean this up."

The duo set to work, gathering the arcane paraphernalia they'd brought with them. As they did so, Repel turned his attention to the summoning circle. With a sweeping gesture, his fingers trailing faint wisps of energy, he erased the intricate patterns and wards protecting them.

The runes and symbols dissolved as if they were chalk being wiped off a slate.

However, as the room returned to its mundane state, a stubborn patch of the circle remained. Repel's brow furrowed in annoyance. He tried to wave it away, but it clung stubbornly. Temper flaring, he hissed, "Enough of this!" After a final and more forceful wave, the patch vanished.

"Pathetic world," he muttered with disdain. "If only the magics here were more potent. Then I wouldn't have to play these tiresome games."

In an instant, he transformed. His elaborate robe were replaced by a crisp, tailored suit, seamlessly blending modernity with sophistication. The polished shoes, the silk tie—every detail screamed authority. Repel ran his fingers through his hair, smoothing it to perfection.

Glancing at his reflection in a nearby glass case, he remarked, "Better." Turning to Lyra and Geb, he continued, "Come, there's much to do. We had an unexpected setback tonight, but the endgame is near. The rally and my speech are a lead-up to the final vote."

Geb gave a slight nod. "The city remains oblivious, just as you planned."

Repel smirked. "Yes. They see Mayor Repel, the city's hope. They have no idea of the storm that's brewing."

Always one for caution, Lyra remarked, "Let's ensure it stays that way."

With a shared sense of purpose, the trio made their exit from the Vent Haven Museum, leaving behind a room that seemed untouched by magic. However, for those who knew where to look, the residue of the evening's events lingered, a silent testament to the power struggles playing out in the shadows.

CHAPTER TWENTY-SEVEN

Charlotte slowly stirred from her sleep, blinking her eyes to adjust to the unfamiliar surroundings.

The soft early morning sun streamed through a gap in the heavy curtains, illuminating the room with a mellow amber hue. The plush bed beneath her felt alien yet invitingly cozy compared to her own in EverAfter.

Sitting up and rubbing the remnants of sleep from her eyes, she realized she was the last one to awaken. The first sight that greeted her was Cat lumbering about the room. His gentle eyes met hers briefly, his tail gently wagging in a muted morning greeting.

Her gaze shifted to Sir Thomas, who was engrossed in something on a sleek silver device. The sharp light from its screen made his gold eyes look even brighter. She could also hear Alex's voice, though muffled, from what she assumed was the adjoining room.

Stretching her limbs, she swung her feet to the side of the bed and made her way over to Cat, leaning down to give him a soft pat on his furry head. The dog let out a contented hum, nudging her hand for more affection.

"Good morning, Sir Thomas," she greeted, her curiosity piqued by his intense concentration. "What has you so engrossed?"

Sir Thomas looked up, a smirk playing on his feline lips. "Ah, Charlotte! Good morning to you, too. I've been acquainting myself with this fascinating device—Alex calls it a 'laptop.' It's similar to that smartphone you were fumbling with last evening and much smaller than the desktops I'm familiar with."

Charlotte tilted her head, trying to recall the gadget she'd been introduced to. "Oh! The one where I tapped the screen and saw pictures? This 'laptop' seems much bigger."

Sir Thomas chuckled. "Indeed. It is essentially a larger version, yet incredibly useful. One of those from our world whom I befriended upon my arrival here showed me its workings. They are remarkable tools, allowing one to access vast amounts of information with a few clicks."

Intrigued, Charlotte leaned closer, eager to learn and adapt. She could see the potential of the device to aid in their quest. "Then let's make the best use of it."

Sir Thomas gestured at the laptop, which displayed an image taken in Burnet Woods. The photo was grainy, capturing a fleeting moment in which a diminutive figure with pointed ears vanished behind a large oak. The headline accompanying the image posed the question, **Mysterious Elf-like Creature Spotted: Fact or Fiction?**

He scrolled down to reveal another intriguing headline. **Rapunzel Reenactment or Real-Life Fairytale?** Below it was a picture of an old tower in a historic district. A woman with lustrous golden hair cascading in a long braid was depicted letting down her hair from a window high above. The sight was oddly familiar, pulling at Charlotte's memories of tales told in EverAfter.

Before she could comment, Sir Thomas played a short video clip. In the muted light of a streetlamp danced the elusive shadows of otherwordly creatures. Their silhouettes suggested large, translucent wings reminiscent of fairies'. The caption below the clip read, *Strange Sightings: Fireflies or Fairies on Vine Street?*

"These tales," Sir Thomas began, drawing Charlotte's attention back to the task at hand, "though outlandish to the residents of this world, are commonplace for us. Most dismiss them as hoaxes or publicity stunts."

Charlotte nodded, absorbing the information. "How do you suppose they got here? The same way we did?"

Sir Thomas shrugged. "That's a mystery for another time unless we can ask Repel or the Snow Queen, neither of whom I expect to answer our questions. But look here." He zoomed in on a vibrant picture. The scene was from a bustling party, with people laughing, dancing, and enjoying themselves. The banner read, **Swingin' nights at the Swing House!**

One figure dominated the frame—a tall man with an unmistakably ovular figure, his bald head reflecting the party lights. He was raising a glass in a toast, his wide grin nearly splitting his face in two.

Charlotte leaned in, her intuition tingling. "He doesn't fit here. I've not seen anyone resembling him in this realm."

"You've got a keen eye," Sir Thomas said, then pointed at other figures in the background: a lady with butterfly wings shimmering in iridescent colors, a man with a tail peeking out from under his coat, and a couple with horns curling from their heads, which could easily be mistaken for elaborate headgear in the festive setting.

"These aren't mere costumes, Charlotte," Sir Thomas pointed out. "The Swing House seems to be more than just a trendy hotspot. It might be a sanctuary or gathering place for EverAfterans like us. And that man, given his prominence in the photo, could be someone of importance."

"EverAfterans? Hmm, I like that," Charlotte mused before nodding toward the photo. "A lead, perhaps?"

A knock on the door startled Charlotte, pulling her away from the captivating images on the laptop's screen. The door swung open to reveal Alex juggling plates and trays stacked with aromatic meals from room service.

"Good morning, sleepyhead!" he greeted with a cheery grin, his eyes twinkling with amusement. "I was starting to think you'd hibernate the day away. It's nearly 10:30."

Charlotte shot him a sheepish smile, her cheeks tinged with a blush. "This realm's comforts have a way of making one lose track of time," she remarked, her eyes drifting to the sumptuous spread he had brought.

Alex laid the trays on the desk with practiced ease, and a whiff of something deliciously savory filled the room. He took a bowl from one of the trays, filled it with kibble, and set it down for Cat.

The dog, distracted from his morning languor, ambled over, sniffing at the bowl before tucking in contentedly.

"I wasn't sure about your preferences, Charlotte," Alex admitted, pointing at the plates. "Given our conversations,

I thought you might enjoy these. Sorry, they didn't have chili on the menu."

Charlotte appreciated the gesture. "It's very kind of you, Alex. To be honest, my appetite is currently rivaled by my curiosity."

Following her gaze, Alex approached the laptop. "What did you find?"

Sir Thomas took a moment to summarize their findings, his fingers deftly maneuvering the touchpad to display the pictures and videos that had intrigued them. "It appears we're not the only EverAfterans making a home in Cincinnati. What's interesting is how brazen some of them are about their origins. No need for concealing charms or spells, it seems."

Alex frowned, leaning in to study the images more closely. "The Swing House," he mused, his brow furrowing in thought. "It's a popular spot known for its nightlife and eclectic, even odd, crowd. I've heard of it but never been there."

Charlotte looked at him, hope in her eyes. "Do you think it's worth visiting? It could provide a lead."

Alex pondered the idea, then nodded. "Could, but we'd need to be careful. If there are people from EverAfter there, there's no telling how they will react to newcomers. Especially if they're trying to keep a low profile."

Sir Thomas smirked. "From what we've seen, 'low profile' isn't their modus operandi."

As they continued discussing their next steps, Charlotte's stomach growled. That drew a chuckle from Alex, and he pointed at the food. "Perhaps we have time for breakfast before diving into detective work?"

Charlotte, though hungry, found herself drawn back to the enigmatic images on the laptop's screen. Each bite was punctuated with a glance at the pictures, a pattern Sir Thomas mirrored.

Alex broke the silence. "I've got some wiggle room in getting back to the precinct due to the mess over the last few days, but I want to go in and snoop around. See if I can dig up any dirt on this Prince Repel, or should I say 'Raphael Princeton.'"

"Be careful." Charlotte took a bite, then swallowed. "Repel and the Snow Queen aren't playing games. They've clearly found ways to manipulate the magic here better than I can."

Alex chewed his lip. "I'll be on my guard, but honestly, I have a feeling magic and this world's tech might not mix as seamlessly as they'd like. Otherwise, the prince would be using his spells to game the stock market instead of whatever he's up to."

The trio shared a laugh, but it was abruptly interrupted by an insistent tap from Sir Thomas. He pointed at a face in one of the pictures. Charlotte squinted, her eyes opening in recognition. "Peter Pan?"

He nodded.

The image showed the youthful, playful face of the fishmonger they'd encountered the day before. His trademark cap was missing, but the mischievous twinkle in his eyes was unmistakable.

The room was filled with a renewed sense of purpose. "It appears our adventure in Cincinnati just became a lot more interesting."

Sir Thomas nodded in agreement with Charlotte's words.

Alex looked at the two, raising an eyebrow in question. "Peter Pan? The fishmonger? What's he got to do with all this?"

Charlotte bit her lip, pondering how to best explain their connection. "In our world, Peter is... Well, he was a bit of a wildcard. Capable of great things but unpredictable. Finding him in these photos is not a coincidence."

Sir Thomas added, "He might know more about what's happening than he let on when we were there. We should seek him out before we venture to the Swing House."

Alex frowned. "You know, after everything that's transpired, I'm not comfortable with the two of you heading off alone."

Sir Thomas quirked an eyebrow, leaning back. "After the fight in the apartment, I'd hope you realize we're not helpless. Our worlds might be different, but our ability to protect ourselves remains."

Charlotte chimed in, "And remember, Alex, while this *is* Cincinnati, the places we're heading and the people we're likely to meet? It's as if we're stepping into our realm. We understand the rules and nuances."

Alex ran a hand through his hair, taking a deep breath. "I get it. I do, but danger has a way of finding people, especially in unfamiliar territory."

Charlotte placed a gentle hand on his arm. "We truly appreciate your concern, but we have a mission to accomplish. We can't always tread with caution."

Sir Thomas added with a smirk, "And should anything

go awry, wouldn't it be reassuring to know that the city's finest detective would be on the case?"

Alex couldn't help but chuckle, though the worry didn't leave his eyes. "All right, all right. I'll drop you off on my way to the precinct. But promise me something?"

Charlotte raised an eyebrow.

"If you do find yourselves in a tight spot, stay alive long enough for me to get there. Okay?"

The two shared a look, and Charlotte responded with a playful grin, "We promise to do our very best."

Sir Thomas nodded in agreement, his smile mirroring Charlotte's. "You have our word."

Alex eyed him twice to check for a mischievous glint in his eye. No glint. He was satisfied.

Cat barked happily, seemingly in approval of the arrangement. Alex rubbed his temples with a sigh. "Just try to take this carefully, will you?"

They had every intention of doing so for as much good as it would do them.

CHAPTER TWENTY-EIGHT

Alex pulled up at Peter's fish store. The hustle and bustle of the market enveloped them, filling the air with the sounds of commerce and the unmistakable scent of fresh fish and crustaceans.

Charlotte, Sir Thomas, and Cat unfolded from the vehicle and scanned the surroundings. As they stood on the sidewalk, Charlotte exchanged a final look with Alex.

"Take care, you three," Alex warned, worry evident in his voice although he tried to mask it with a casual demeanor.

"We promise, Alex," Charlotte replied, offering a smile. "Just remember to do the same. And if you stumble upon any other magical mysteries at the precinct, don't hesitate to give *us* a ring."

Sir Thomas added with a smirk, "Especially if it involves chili."

Alex let out a genuine laugh, shaking his head. "You two and your fascination with Cincinnati chili. Just be safe."

With a nod and a last wave, the trio ventured into the market.

Stalls upon stalls stretched out, with fishermen showcasing their catches. The shimmering scales of the fish reflected the sunlight.

Crabs scuttled about in their containers and lobsters lounged lazily, waiting for their next destination. Iridescent shells were displayed in neat rows, each possessing a unique pattern and sheen. The shouts of the vendors trying to lure customers to their stalls blended harmoniously with the general chatter, creating a lively symphony.

As they maneuvered through the crowd, certain people stood out. Among the human patrons and workers, some players were distinctly EverAfteran: a stall-keeper with mermaid scales on her legs as she waded through a water tank, a buyer haggling over the price of oysters, his gnome-like stature and pointed hat making him stand out, and a young girl, who, at a glance, appeared to be playing with a toy. Upon closer inspection, she was animatedly chatting with a pixie perched on her shoulder.

"What's interesting," Sir Thomas remarked, taking note of all three, "is that none of them seem concerned about hiding who they are. It's as if they're operating under an invisible shield."

Charlotte nodded. "There has to be some enchantment in play here. Perhaps an illusion spell or a ward that prevents regular folk from seeing their true forms. It would allow them to interact without fear of drawing undue attention."

They continued their search, and soon they spotted Peter Pan. He was in the midst of a lively conversation with a group of men who were unloading nets filled with the day's catch. His laughter was clear and contagious, and those around him responded with equal mirth.

Upon noticing the trio approach, Peter paused in his antics, his ever-playful eyes narrowing in curiosity. The twinkle in them suggested he was formulating a jest even before they exchanged words.

"Well, well, well," Peter began with a sly grin on his face. "What brings the fairy godmother, the charming cat, and the canine behemoth back to my market? Looking for another adventure, perhaps?"

Charlotte met his gaze. "Not just any adventure, Peter. We need answers, and you might be the one to provide them."

Peter's grin grew wider as he took in their serious expressions. The game was afoot, and he seemed more than ready to play his part.

The trio followed Peter as he led them through the busy market, maneuvering past stalls and workers until they reached the store. Peter led them through it and pushed open a different door than he had yesterday, revealing his office.

The office was a curious mix of business and Neverland nostalgia. The walls were painted a calming shade of aqua, reminiscent of the lagoons from his stories. One was adorned with maps and charts of fishing zones and trade routes. Another wall displayed a series of framed images—a younger Peter with the Lost Boys with Captain Hook's ship in the distance, and a serene-looking Tinker Bell, glowing ethereally.

The furniture was a blend of modern and antique. A

mahogany desk stood in the center, covered with papers and artifacts. It had comfortable plush chairs arranged around it.

The room smelled like the ocean, a combination of salt, seaweed, and fish, which wasn't surprising given what was outside. On his desk was an ornate lamp shaped like a conch shell that emitted a warm golden light.

"Please, make yourselves comfortable," Peter said with a sweep of his hand, his jocular tone returning. "Would you like something to drink? Water, tea, or perhaps something stronger?"

Sir Thomas raised an eyebrow. "It's a tad early for 'something stronger,' isn't it?"

Peter smirked. "In my new Neverland, it's always the right time."

Ever the pragmatist, Charlotte cleared her throat. "Focus, Peter," she said, pulling the printouts out of her bag and spreading them on the desk. The images showed a sprawling house with a large swing at its center. The most prominent object was the large man, whose odd figure dominated the photos.

"We want to know about this," she said, tapping the image of the Swing House. "And more importantly, about him." Her finger hovered over the large man.

Peter's playful demeanor faded. He picked up the photograph, studying it for a long moment. "Why are you involving yourselves with him?" he finally asked as he looked up, his voice noticeably graver. "Whatever you've heard about this man? Believe me, it's not true."

Sir Thomas leaned forward, his voice firm. "We don't know anything about him, but we've come across several

EverAfterans who either revere or fear the man. We need to understand what's going on, especially if it's related to Prince Repel."

Peter sank into his chair, rubbing his temples, then pointed at the photograph. "He isn't as malevolent as Repel, but don't be mistaken. He's not one of the good guys, either."

The room went silent as the trio processed Peter's words, realizing the complexity of the situation they had found themselves in.

Peter leaned back, looking contemplative. "He is not just any EverAfteran. That," he pointed at the picture again, "is Humpty Dumpty."

Charlotte's eyebrows knitted in confusion. "The egg man?"

Peter nodded. "Exactly, but as you can see, he's not egg-shaped anymore. He was banished after insulting the king of his district. Humpty always had a penchant for humor, often at others' expense. Unfortunately for him, he cracked a joke, pun intended, right in front of the king during a grand feast. That didn't sit well."

Sir Thomas huffed. "Given his appearance, I can only imagine the kinds of jests he made."

Peter chuckled. "You have no idea. The king, instead of shattering his fragile ego—again, pun absolutely intended—opted for a more merciful punishment. Humpty was transformed into a human or something that resembles one by the king's skilled mages. It was believed that his fragile egg form wouldn't last a day in a realm other than EverAfter, but he's made a fortune in eggs."

Charlotte mused, "How did he come to make a fortune selling eggs? It seems a bit ironic."

Peter grinned. "Ah, Fate. After he arrived here, Humpty used his knowledge of eggs, having been one himself, to venture into the business. He found a niche in the market and became the top egg supplier in the Midwest."

"He sells his own kind?" Sir Thomas looked horrified. "That's macabre."

Peter raised a hand. "Not exactly. Remember, he's not an egg anymore, just a former ovoid. I think he saw it as a way to adapt and reclaim his narrative. Regardless, he's made a fortune."

Charlotte interjected, "And the Swing House?"

"Ah." Peter sighed. "That's his sanctuary. After he amassed his wealth, he bought that property. The giant swing is his way of connecting to his past. From what I've heard, the gentle back-and-forth motion reminds him of the safety and comfort of EverAfter, a place he can't return to but desperately misses."

Charlotte tilted her head, studying Peter. "Why the disdain for Humpty? From what you've told us, he sounds more like a jester than a genuine threat. Did he crack a joke about you, too?"

Peter huffed, crossing his arms. "I can handle a joke. After all, I've traded more than my fair share of jests with the likes of Hook. What I can't stomach is a charlatan. Someone who preys on the vulnerable, especially those from our realm."

Charlotte frowned. "What are you getting at?"

Peter leaned forward, his face serious. "Humpty has been luring banished EverAfterans to him with promises to mend their broken stories and give them a way back home. Many of those, driven by desperation and homesickness, have flocked to him."

Sir Thomas adjusted his hat thoughtfully. "If he truly possesses such abilities, why hasn't he returned to Ever-After himself? Wouldn't he want to undo his own banishment?"

"Exactly," Peter said, pointing a finger at Sir Thomas. "That's the crux of it. He doesn't really have the means to mend anyone's tales, but he's crafted a facsimile of Ever-After here in Cincinnati. He keeps those poor souls in his Swing House, constantly throwing grandiose parties. The attendees lose themselves in the music, the dancing, and the merriment. Anything to numb the pain of their lost world."

Charlotte's eyes widened in realization. "So, the constant state of euphoria you mentioned. It's just a ruse?"

Peter nodded. "It's all a show. An opiate for the disillusioned. I approached him, thinking we could collaborate to genuinely help displaced EverAfterans, but it didn't take me long to see through his façade. Beneath the boisterous laughter and grand gestures, he's a bitter, banished being seeking company in his misery."

Sir Thomas, who had been quietly observing the conversation, spoke up, his eyes sharp. "Let me guess, he didn't take kindly to you seeing through his act."

Peter smirked. "You could say that. He's got a thin shell, after all. Our last meeting ended in quite a heated exchange."

Charlotte, agitated by the tangled web they were now enmeshed in, ran a hand through her hair. "This affair is becoming more complex by the minute. I thought we might have a lead with Humpty."

Peter leaned against his desk thoughtfully. "While Humpty might not have the answers you seek, that doesn't mean he's devoid of utility. He's one of the most connected EverAfterans in the city. I haven't seen him directly liaise with Repel, but that doesn't discount shared acquaintances or mutual deals."

Sir Thomas leaned in. "So, you're thinking we should pay him a visit?"

Peter injected a cautionary note into his voice. "If you do, be circumspect. Don't reveal your true intentions, especially your urgency. Humpty relishes playing with those he perceives as desperate."

Charlotte nodded. "Thanks for the guidance, Peter. As always, your insights are invaluable."

As the group began to exit, Charlotte paused at the door. "By the way, Peter. How's Bo Peep? Has she been adjusting well?"

Peter's stern demeanor melted into a soft smile. "She's recuperating but still resting. She wants to express her gratitude for all you've done. Says she's in your debt. If you ever need her aid, she's more than willing."

"That's good to hear," Charlotte replied, touched.

The trio made their way back out of the store, and the shouts of the vendors and the scent of fresh seafood enveloped them. When they reached the exit, Charlotte hailed a taxi, determination in her stance. They were heading to the Swing House, and come what may, they would confront the enigmatic Humpty Dumpty.

CHAPTER TWENTY-NINE

Charlotte, Sir Thomas, and Cat stepped out of the taxi.

The urban surroundings juxtaposed oddly with the whimsical feeling the trio got as they approached the Swing House. The modern skyline served as a reminder that they were in a bustling city, not a fairytale, yet something about the location felt like it had come straight out of a storybook.

Tall and out of place amid the typical brick buildings, the Swing House seemed to beckon them. The architecture was a delightful fusion of old and new, as if a medieval castle had been plucked from its original site and planted in the heart of Cincinnati.

Though there were no turrets, the irregular balconies and ornate ironwork hinted at a place where the mundane met the magical.

As they approached, a centaur trotted by, drawing stares from the locals. They quickly dismissed it as performance art or festival gimmick. A gnome perched on a windowsill waved at Cat, who barked hesitantly.

Sir Thomas whispered to Charlotte, " Cincinnati is known for its arts and culture, but this is something else!"

Before Charlotte could respond, the heavy front door swung open to reveal a poised butler. He eyed Charlotte with recognition. "Ah, Miss Charlotte, Sir Thomas, and Cat. We've been expecting you."

Cat cocked her head to the side. "How do you know about us? We only found out about Swing House this morning."

The butler, maintaining his composed demeanor, replied, "The Swing House has its ways, and in Cincinnati, as vibrant and bustling as it is, magic still finds its corners." He gestured for them to enter. "Please, Master Dumpty awaits."

Sir Thomas exchanged a puzzled glance with Charlotte.

Upon entering the Swing House, Charlotte, Sir Thomas, and Cat were drawn to the opulent interiors. The mansion's expansive foyer was adorned with rich crimson and gold draperies, providing a warm, regal ambiance.

Gilded frames holding exquisite works of art lined the walls while the polished marble floors gleamed softly under the crystal chandeliers that dangled overhead. Painted in a celestial theme, the ceiling seemed to move like the night sky, its twinkling stars and nebulous clouds creating a sense of timeless wonder.

As they ventured farther into the building, Charlotte's eyes widened in recognition. Many of the paintings depicted scenes familiar to her—whimsical landscapes, towering castles, and mythical creatures.

These weren't random fairytale settings. They mirrored the very essence of EverAfter, her beloved home.

"Where is this?" she whispered to herself, tracing the frame of a painting that showcased a forest she was certain she had once roamed.

The main hall was a lavish expanse in which several EverAfterans lounged on plush velvet settees, chaise longues, and plump floor cushions.

Sir Thomas took in the scene with concern. "Something's not right," he murmured, noting the vacant expressions and the telltale haze of intoxication that enveloped some of the inhabitants.

"Look!" Charlotte whispered, drawing their attention to the centerpiece of the room.

At the back, a huge swing with ropes as thick as vines and a seat upholstered in a rich brocade held the unmistakable figure of Humpty Dumpty. This transformed version of Humpty was an exaggerated human, a grotesque blend of man and egg.

His immense body seemed at odds with the delicate swing, and his bald pate contrasted sharply with the tufts of twisted blond hair sprouting from the sides of his head. His fingers, chubby and adorned with multiple rings, clutched the swing's ropes as he gently swayed.

As the trio approached, Humpty's eyes snapped to them, and his lips stretched into an unsettlingly wide grin, revealing a set of impossibly large teeth.

"Ah, the guests of honor!" he exclaimed, voice dripping feigned sweetness. "Charlotte, Sir Thomas, and Cat! How *delightful* to finally meet you."

Charlotte took a deep breath, recalling Peter's cautionary words. It was essential to navigate this encounter with finesse, avoiding any traps laid by the enigmatic Humpty Dumpty. She stepped forward, exuding an air of quiet confidence. "Mr. Dumpty!" she began, allowing a genuine smile to grace her lips. "I must admit, your abode is unlike any I've ever seen. The Swing House is truly a marvel, an artful blend of this world and EverAfter."

Humpty's grin widened, and his amusement was clear in his eyes. He slowed the swing as if he were savoring her words. "Ah, Fairy Godmother," he purred. "It's indeed a rarity to have one such as you grace my halls. Especially under such pressing circumstances."

Charlotte's gaze didn't waver, betraying none of the apprehension she felt. "I'm here in pursuit of understanding," she replied evenly. "To engage with those who have been cast out from EverAfter, like you. From the looks of it," she continued, glancing around the opulent hall and at its dazed occupants before returning her attention to him, "you've created quite a niche for yourself in Cincinnati."

Humpty's smile shrank. "Being banished from EverAfter was no simple ordeal," he admitted, a hint of vulnerability creeping into his voice. "But one learns to adapt, even in a place as eclectic as this one. The city offers a temporary respite, yes, but it's my family," he said, gesturing with a flourish at the entranced individuals behind Charlotte, "who truly brings me solace."

Charlotte nodded thoughtfully, picking up on the subtle undercurrents of his words. He had a depth that she hadn't anticipated, a complex tapestry of pain, ambition, and a longing for something lost. She hoped to use this insight while navigating the treacherous waters of their impending negotiations.

"Tell me, Humpty," Charlotte began, her voice soft but

probing. "How do the banished EverAfterans fare in this vibrant city? It must be challenging to adjust to such a contrasting world."

As she spoke, she wove in her own curiosities and concerns. "I've heard whispers that Prince Repel might be plotting something unusual. Are you aware of any such thing?" She glanced at him, trying to discern any signs of recognition without giving away the full scope of her knowledge.

Humpty's grin was back, and he observed Charlotte with a depth that was hard to read. He pumped his feet on the grand swing, its ropes creaking in rhythm with his movements, each oscillation seeming to be a moment of contemplation.

After what felt like an eternity, Humpty finally spoke, his voice holding an undertone of mischief. "Ah, the banished ones. They find solace here in various ways. For all its quirks and peculiarities, Cincinnati offers them a semblance of belonging. As for Prince Repel? Well, whispers travel fast, don't they?"

Charlotte tilted her head. "Surely you understand my concern. As a fairy godmother, it is my responsibility to care for all from EverAfter, even those who no longer call it home."

Humpty let out a chuckle. "That's a noble endeavor. However," he said, leaning forward and momentarily halting the swing, "I had thought your primary reason for coming here was slightly different."

He reached into his jacket, producing a wrinkled parchment. Charlotte's heart leaped at the sight of another page.

He teased, holding it just out of her reach, "This is

something you might find very interesting, don't you think?" He started swinging again.

Charlotte blinked, then fixed her gaze on the parchment Humpty dangled between his pudgy fingers. That page had unmistakably come from her treasured handbook, the ultimate guide to her magical responsibilities. Every page was essential since each contained a spell, a potion, or a tale from EverAfter's rich history. The loss of even one page would be catastrophic.

Humpty noticed her reaction and his smile widened, if that was possible. "Recognize this, do you?" He swung a bit higher, letting the page dangle tantalizingly out of reach.

She tried to maintain her composure, masking the urgency in her voice. "I'd appreciate it if you'd return that to me, Mr. Dumpty. It's personal."

Humpty chuckled, and some of the dazed EverAfterans glanced at him. "Dear Charlotte, everything comes at a price in this city, especially something as invaluable as a page from a fairy godmother's handbook."

Charlotte sighed inwardly. This wasn't going to be as straightforward as she'd hoped. "What is it that you desire, Humpty?"

He leaned forward, the swing's ropes groaning under his weight. "Information, for starters. Tell me, why are you really here? Is it for these lost souls," he waved dismissively at the entranced individuals behind her, "or is it for something...or someone…else?"

Charlotte hesitated, considering her words carefully. "EverAfter is vast, with countless tales, characters, and histories. I am here for many reasons. One is the well-being of the banished since it's my duty to care for all. But," she added, voice firm, "I am also in search of answers. Answers I believe you possess."

Humpty regarded her for a moment, then laughed softly. "Oh, Fairy Godmother, you play your cards close to your chest. But I do admire your spirit." He twirled the page in his fingers. "Very well. Let's strike a deal. This page for some truth."

Charlotte nodded, taking a deep breath. "Ask your questions, then."

Humpty's smile didn't waver as he prepared to unravel the depths of Charlotte's intentions.

Charlotte's keen eyes studied him, sensing a shift in the dynamics between them. Here in the majestic Swing House, under the mesmerizing chandeliers and surrounded by opulence, she felt like she was facing Humpty in a chess game.

Humpty swayed on the swing, his face betraying a hint of mischief. "Now, now, Fairy Godmother. It's not often I get to ask the questions. Indulge me, will you?" He leaned forward, eyes glinting with anticipation.

"Of course," Charlotte replied, bracing herself for whatever query Humpty would throw her way.

"Do you have a way back to EverAfter?" Humpty asked, twirling the page from her handbook as he spoke.

Charlotte hesitated before replying, "No. As of now, I do not. And to be honest," she added, looking vulnerable, "I'm not even sure how I got here. A portal just materialized out of nowhere and swallowed me."

Humpty raised an eyebrow, intrigued. "Ah, the unpredictability of magic. And your handbook?" he pressed. "I was told that fairy godmother handbooks are indestructible, yet I found a page from yours in my garden."

She nodded, her face reflecting her concern. "I believed the same. The handbook is a cherished artifact of my position and is supposed to be resilient to all harm, but it seems this realm doesn't play by the rules of EverAfter."

Humpty contemplated her words, the atmosphere in the room becoming increasingly charged. "One last question." His tone was very solemn. "If you were to find a way back to EverAfter, would you take it?"

Charlotte's gaze became distant as memories of her beloved homeland flooded her mind. After a thoughtful pause, she said, "My primary duty as a fairy godmother is to protect and guide those in EverAfter. However, having been thrust into this realm and witnessing its unique challenges, I realize there are issues here that also require my attention. Until I find a way back, I'll continue to fulfill my duties here."

For a brief moment, Humpty's perpetual grin faltered, revealing a glimpse of some hidden emotion—respect, or even empathy. Then, as if catching himself, the twinkle returned to his eyes.

"Well played, Fairy Godmother," he responded, his tone dripping amusement and admiration. "Well played."

The page, delicate and ornate, floated gently downward like a feather.

Charlotte extended a graceful hand and caught it in mid-air, then caressed the script. The scrying spell wasn't particularly powerful or a secret, but in this unfamiliar realm, every piece of her handbook was valuable.

As she examined the page, Humpty gracefully brought his swing to a standstill. The playful glint in his eyes didn't fade. "So, Fairy Godmother, any more pressing questions? Or perhaps," he gestured around the room, "you and your companions would like to stay and revel in the festivities tonight?"

Sir Thomas, looking out of place amid the opulence, glanced at Humpty's followers. Their faces were uniformly cheerful, their attire impeccable, but their eyes... Those lacked any semblance of life or consciousness.

They smiled, yes, but it was the smile of marionettes, the joy not reaching the depth of their souls.

Sir Thomas grimaced subtly, a cold shiver coursing down his spine. The scene was too eerie for his liking.

Charlotte sensed Sir Thomas' unease, and while she was genuinely grateful for Humpty's hospitality, she also felt an underlying tension that she couldn't quite place. With a polite nod, she responded, "Thank you for the generous offer, Humpty, but pressing matters and quests await us. We must decline."

Humpty tilted his head, his smile undiminished. "A shame, but I understand. Duties call." He gave a dramatic sigh. "The life of a fairy godmother and her brave knight is indeed a busy one."

Charlotte tucked the page into a hidden pocket in her gown. "Indeed it is. Thank you for your time, Humpty. And for the page."

With a wave, Humpty replied, "Always a pleasure to entertain royalty and legends. Safe travels, Fairy Godmother. And remember, my Swing House is always available for a dance or two."

Charlotte paused at the doorway, curiosity in her eyes. "Before we part, Humpty, I do wonder. What are your thoughts on Prince Repel's aspiration to claim the mayorship?"

Humpty chuckled, the sound rich and genuine. "Ah, the ambitious fallen prince. To be honest, I've always found it best to steer clear of Repel. He plays a dangerous game, one far removed from my taste. He's not...fun, you could say. But now that you mention it," he wagged a finger playfully, "the prospect of you two locking horns piques my interest. It promises to be quite the spectacle!"

Sir Thomas tightened his grip on his sword hilt in a subtle warning. Charlotte gracefully inclined her head. "Well, I hope not to disappoint."

With Cat in tow, the trio made their exit, their footfalls drowned out by the laughter that followed them from inside.

No sooner had the door clicked shut than Humpty beckoned for his butler with a swift hand motion. "Be a dear and send word to the prince. Inform him about our visitors today."

The butler, as impeccable as always, raised an eyebrow. "Are you planning to ally with Prince Repel, sir?"

Humpty smirked, lazily twirling a finger in the air. "Oh, not at all. I'm just...accelerating the drama. It's been dreadfully dull of late, but now, with a foot in both camps, I'm in a delightful position to dance between the two." He paused, gazing out a window at the moonlit night. "After all, in this uncertain world, I must look out for myself. Gone are the days of relying on king's horses or king's men."

The butler nodded, acknowledging the sentiment, and with a swift bow, he left to execute his master's bidding. Humpty, alone but for his dazed followers, swung back into the air, reveling in the intricate game he'd set in motion.

CHAPTER THIRTY

The gold chandeliers in the hotel's lobby cast a soft glow, under which the marble floors gleamed. Weary from their journey, Charlotte, Sir Thomas, and Cat trudged through the revolving doors of the hotel in which they were staying.

The weight of their mission seemed heavier as they realized that their meetings with Humpty Dumpty and Peter Pan, while enlightening, hadn't provided a solid strategy to deal with Prince Repel.

As they rode the elevator to their floor, Charlotte looked reflective. "I'm beginning to wonder if a head-on attack against Prince Repel is wise," she confessed, her fingers absentmindedly petting Cat as the large black dog stood faithfully by her side. "Maybe a more covert tactical approach would serve us better."

Adjusting his fur as if to emphasize his readiness for any challenge, Sir Thomas responded, "A stealthy approach does seem prudent, given how little we truly know. That

Ascent building we tracked him to? It might be a red herring. He could be anywhere."

The elevator's doors opened on their richly carpeted hallway, but before they could step out, a familiar face rounded the corner. Alex's eyes widened in relief when he spotted them. His hurried breaths indicated that he had been searching for a while.

"There you are!" he exclaimed, his voice filled with relief. "I was half-tempted to get in the car and scour Cincinnati for you. This vast city is full of nooks and crannies, after all."

Charlotte smiled weakly, appreciating Alex's concern as they entered their hotel room. "We're here now, and we'll figure out our next move together."

Sir Thomas' stomach groaned, and he let out an embarrassed cough. "Certainly, but, uh, perhaps our minds would work better with a bit of food to fuel them."

Alex chuckled as he settled onto the plush couch, stretching his legs in relief. Reaching beside him, he grabbed the room service menu and handed it to the cat.

Sir Thomas carefully studied the offerings, humming occasionally at dishes that caught his fancy. Charlotte, always attentive to Cat's needs, fetched a gleaming silver bowl from a cupboard and poured a generous serving of kibble into it.

The large dog wagged his tail in approval, then padded over to gobble up his meal.

While Cat enjoyed his dinner, the mood in the room shifted from casual to serious. Alex cleared his throat, drawing everyone's attention. "So, about our dear Prince Repel," he began, his fingers tracing the embossed gold logo on the menu. "Or should I say, Raphael Princeton, the aspiring mayor?"

Charlotte's eyes sharpened with interest. "What did you find out?"

Taking a deep breath, Alex recounted his findings. "According to his official biography, Raphael Princeton hails from Elyria, Ohio."

Charlotte interrupted with a raised eyebrow, "Funny. There's an Elyria in EverAfter, too."

Alex nodded. "Probably why he chose that. He's crafted a detailed backstory for himself. He claims to have gone to Yale, not Princeton, ironically, and says he's had a string of political odd jobs leading up to this mayoral run."

Sir Thomas chimed in, "That's impossible. He was banished from EverAfter to Cincinnati not long ago. How could he have such a detailed history in this world?"

"That's what's baffling me," Alex admitted, a hint of frustration in his voice. "Every record and reference I dug into checks out. It's as if he's been living this life for decades. My best guess? He used magic to create an impeccable façade."

Charlotte leaned back, her mind racing. "If this prince had been this much of a master of deception back in EverAfter, his coup might have been successful. I shudder to think of the implications of that."

Sir Thomas took a final glance at the menu and made his choice. "I'll have the grilled salmon and roasted vegetables," he declared, finger tracing the description.

Charlotte scanned the options. "I'll take the chicken Caesar salad."

"I'll have the club sandwich," Alex added, handing the

menu back to Sir Thomas. "Mind making the call?"

Sir Thomas raised an eyebrow. "Why don't you do it?"

"I'd like to hear about your recent meetings," Alex replied, eyes fixed on Charlotte, his curiosity evident.

Sighing, Sir Thomas muttered under his breath, "Fine, but I'm ordering dessert for myself." His fingers danced on the hotel phone, and moments later, he was placing their order on the speaker. Before hanging up, he added, "And a slice of the triple chocolate mousse cake."

Charlotte waited for Sir Thomas to finish, then turned to Alex. "All right, where to begin?"

"Peter Pan," Alex prompted.

Charlotte nodded. "We met him in the fish market, and he was much more helpful than I feared, given what we were thinking. He gave us insight into Humpty Dumpty. He apparently runs an egg business that is popular around here and afar."

Alex thought it over and his eyes widened. "Wait, the man behind Kingsmen's eggs? I've seen those in markets! I've only seen him in pictures. He always looked...odd."

Charlotte chuckled. "Yes, he's an EverAfteran. Apparently, he's made quite a name for himself here. Anyway, we went to his mansion, the Swing House. Stunning place, by the way. And after our chat, he returned one of my lost pages."

"Repel's plans?" Alex asked.

Charlotte exhaled. "That's the concerning part. From what I gathered, he is running a legitimate campaign. Humpty also seemed to be in the dark about any ulterior motives."

Alex smirked. "If you believe you've found a politician

running a legit campaign, magical or not, I'd say you've discovered a real fairytale."

Charlotte shrugged, a playful smile dancing on her lips. "True, but what choice do we have? Right now, confronting Repel might be our only option."

Alex's determination was evident in his eyes. "I've witnessed the chaos at The Ascent firsthand. There's no doubt in my mind that Repel's up to no good, but without hard evidence, I can't loop in the other officers. They'd think I've lost it."

Charlotte sighed, rubbing her temples. "It seems we'll be navigating this minefield on our own."

Before anyone could comment further, a knock on the window diverted their attention. They scanned the room, puzzled, and finally, Sir Thomas' sharp eyes locked onto the source of the disturbance—a blue squirrel perched on the windowsill.

Sir Thomas' face registered a flash of recognition. "You!" He lunged forward, throwing open the window to snatch the squirrel.

Alex jumped up, his cop instincts kicking in. "Is it a threat? Should I—"

"No, he's not dangerous. Just...elusive," Sir Thomas grumbled, tightly gripping the wriggling rodent. "Every time he shows up, he slips away before we can get any answers."

The squirrel, far from being intimidated, turned his fierce gaze to Sir Thomas. "Unhand me, you overgrown feline!" He gave the cat a feisty bite, making Sir Thomas yelp and drop him.

The squirrel nimbly jumped atop a nearby chair, raising

his arms as if he were preparing for a grand declaration. "I am the Squirrel of Destiny foretold in the prophecies!"

Charlotte and Sir Thomas exchanged knowing glances, but Alex stared blankly, clearly flummoxed.

"The Squirrel of Destiny?" Alex questioned, his brow furrowing. "I've read my share of fairytales, but that is a new one."

Sir Thomas sighed. "He's a part of our world's lore. The Squirrel of Destiny is said to appear at critical moments, bearing pivotal messages. He's also known to be quite capricious."

Alex eyed him. "A capricious talking squirrel?"

The squirrel preened, evidently pleased by the attention. "Capricious? I prefer to think of it as maintaining an air of mystery. Now, are you ready to hear what I have to say, or shall I vanish into the winds of destiny again?"

Throughout the exchange, Cat was silent, ears perked and tail wagging slightly. He seemed to be intrigued by the unfolding drama since his head went from person to person as they spoke.

The squirrel tilted his head, his tiny eyes impatiently darting between the astonished faces of the room's occupants. "I haven't the luxury of time, mortals," he declared with a grandeur that contrasted sharply with his petite stature.

Charlotte blinked. "Then tell us, O Squirrel of Destiny," she urged, her voice a mix of curiosity and mild amusement. "What must I do?"

Drawing himself up to his full height, the squirrel replied, "For you to uncover more pages of your precious tome, you must journey to Skyline Chili. Be there precisely at 3:10 p.m., and once there, place an order for the Four-Way chili. But—and this is crucial—insist upon onions."

Sir Thomas' brows furrowed in confusion. "Chili? Onions? Is that a coded message?"

"What is it with Skyline and you guys from EverAfter?" Alex asked at the same time.

The squirrel huffed. "Pay heed! When you request onions, they will inform you that, regrettably, they are momentarily out. However, in a stroke of serendipity, the delivery truck bearing said onions will arrive just then. Discreetly follow the person who ventures out back to receive the shipment."

Charlotte's fingers tapped the table as she considered the squirrel's words. "And then?"

"Board the truck," the squirrel instructed, his voice grave.

Charlotte raised an eyebrow. "Should I wait for my chili order?"

The squirrel twitched his fluffy tail in frustration. "This isn't a gastronomic adventure, madam! It's not about the chili! Do not tarry, or you'll miss the truck." He took a moment to steady his breath, clearly trying to maintain his composure. "Remember to alight from the truck at its penultimate stop. From there, destiny will chart its course."

Sir Thomas opened his mouth, a multitude of questions on his tongue, but before he could articulate one, the Squirrel of Destiny vanished, true to his nature, leaving the faintest rustle of curtains in his wake.

Alex was struggling to process the surreal encounter. "Did we just get our next lead from a..." he turned to Charlotte, "a *squirrel?*"

Charlotte took a moment to gather her thoughts. "Squirrel or sorcerer, if he points the way to recovering my book, I'll heed his advice. Tomorrow at Skyline Chili it is."

Alex leaned back, his fingers massaging his temples as he tried to process the bizarre turn of events. "Do a lot of the beings from EverAfter speak in that cryptic manner?" he inquired, his voice tinged with exasperation.

Charlotte chuckled, her eyes twinkling. "Oh, yes. Riddles, cryptic clues, and vague prophecies are a popular pastime in our realm. It gives us all something to ponder during the long winter nights."

Sir Thomas, who had been silently contemplating the ornate pattern of the room's wallpaper, chimed in. "It's a cultural thing, you could say. Keeps our minds sharp and agile, not entirely unlike the game shows you humans are so fond of."

Alex shot Sir Thomas a surprised glance. "You've been watching our shows?"

Sir Thomas grinned, his whiskers twitching with amusement. "I've picked up on a few of your peculiar pastimes, like game shows, reality TV, and infomercials. Quite the fascinating world you've got here."

Charlotte laughed, shaking her head at the unlikely image of Sir Thomas engrossed in late-night TV marathons. "Well, I suppose every world has its quirks."

The trio settled into a reflective silence, the weight of the upcoming mission pressing down on them. With guidance from the mysterious Squirrel of Destiny, they hoped they were one step closer to unraveling the enigma of Prince Repel and reclaiming Charlotte's book.

CHAPTER THIRTY-ONE

Skyline Chili was bustling when they arrived, the unmistakable aroma of simmering meat and spices filling the air. Locals chatted at tables while newcomers studied the menu on the wall intently.

Alex parked the car while Charlotte, Sir Thomas, and Cat headed toward the entrance. They paused, devising a quick plan.

"You and Cat keep an eye on the back," Charlotte whispered to Sir Thomas. "The moment you see the delivery truck, let us know."

Sir Thomas nodded, glancing down at Cat, who was trying to look nonchalant despite the obvious excitement in his eyes. The pair stealthily made their way to the rear of the building.

Alex caught up with Charlotte, an amused look on his face. "You know, for a moment there, I felt like you guys were planning a bank heist."

Charlotte chuckled. "I never thought my life would come to strategizing over chili orders."

As they stepped into Skyline Chili, Alex glanced around. "Remember the specifics?"

Charlotte recited, "A Four-Way. Insist on onions."

Alex arched an eyebrow. "Do you think there's wiggle room with these prophecies? Like, what if I casually mentioned onions?"

She considered his question. "This is the first time I've followed a predestined squirrel's plan, so who knows? I wouldn't risk it, though."

They queued, and as they approached the counter, a friendly server greeted them. "What can I get you today?"

"Hi! We'll have two Four-Ways," Charlotte began, exchanging a knowing look with Alex. "And, uh, it's really important that it comes with onions. We love onions."

Alex chimed in, laying it on thick. "Yeah, can't have the Four-Way without onions. It's just not the same."

The server raised an eyebrow but nodded, typing in their order. "Sure thing! We might be out of onions, though. Let me check."

Charlotte feigned disappointment, exchanging a victorious glance with Alex. Their plan was in motion.

As the squirrel foretold, a commotion arose from the back as another employee shouted, "The onion delivery's here!"

The server smiled apologetically at Charlotte and Alex. "If you don't mind waiting a few minutes, we'll have those onions for your chili soon."

"We'll wait," Charlotte replied with a knowing smile.

As the sous chef headed to the back to receive the shipment, Charlotte and Alex followed discreetly. From a distance, they could see Sir Thomas and Cat keeping an eye out.

With every step, their anticipation built. The Squirrel of Destiny's cryptic instructions were falling into place, and they were one step closer to uncovering the next piece of the puzzle.

Charlotte and Alex quietly watched the delivery men unload crates of onions and other goods. Sir Thomas and Cat lurked in the shadows nearby, eyes focused on the open back of the truck.

"I overheard them talking," Sir Thomas whispered. "They have two more stops on their route."

Alex furrowed his brows, struggling to remember the instructions the squirrel had given them. "If I'm not mistaken, we were told to disembark at the 'penultimate' stop, correct?"

Sir Thomas nodded in agreement. Cat, gifted with the best hearing among them, continued to keep his ears on the ongoing conversation.

Alex, still mulling their peculiar situation, voiced his thoughts. "It's astonishing that a squirrel can foresee what's to come, isn't it? It's like something from a dream."

Her eyes darting around, Charlotte responded, "At this moment, our focus should be on the now." She motioned at the truck, where the delivery men were chatting with the chef before he returned to the restaurant.

Amused by the conversation, Sir Thomas added, "*I* can't believe a squirrel used the word 'penultimate.' Quite a vocabulary for a small creature."

Charlotte chuckled. "Well, maybe being the 'Squirrel of Destiny' requires a large vocabulary. It's not just about seeing the future, but also having the words to describe it."

"Quick! This is our chance!" Alex urged.

The quartet snuck toward the truck. The metal floor was cold as they clambered inside, and they ducked behind the few remaining boxes and were silent.

The storage compartment's temperature was significantly lower than the outside air, designed to keep perishables fresh. The chill bit through Charlotte and Alex's clothing, making them shiver involuntarily.

"Why didn't I wear a thicker jacket?" Charlotte muttered, hugging herself.

Sensitive to her discomfort, Cat huddled against her, his fur providing a modicum of warmth. She chuckled and patted his back. "Always be prepared."

Sir Thomas couldn't resist a jab at Alex. "Bet you wish you had a fur coat right about now, eh?"

Alex shot him a smirk. "Well, since you mention it..." Without warning, he scooped up Sir Thomas, wrapping the fluffy creature around him like a fur blanket.

"Unhand me, you brute!" Sir Thomas exclaimed, trying to squirm free. But Alex's grip was firm, and the combined warmth of their bodies was undeniably comforting.

"See? This is why I always say you should make friends with furred creatures," Alex teased.

"As if you have ever said that!" Sir Thomas sighed in mock exasperation. "I am a knight, not a blanket or a pet!"

The delivery men approached, forcing the group to quiet down. The doors were closed, darkness enveloped them, and the truck roared to life.

The metallic interior rang with every bump in the road.

The tight quarters were filled with shallow breathing, the overpowering scent of onions, and a looming sense of anticipation. The air was not only cold but damp, making their clothes cling uncomfortably to their skin.

"I wonder what awaits us at the end of this ride. Perhaps another clue or a key to the prophecy?"

Trying to keep her teeth from chattering, Charlotte replied, "As long as it's warmer than in here, I'll be happy."

Alex huffed, his warm breath forming a small cloud in the cold. "Honestly? With our current trajectory, I'm expecting another eatery. Maybe a gourmet onion shop or a farmers' market."

Sir Thomas shot Alex a sidelong glance. "'Gourmet onion shop?' Really?"

Alex shrugged. "Hey, after a prophecy from a squirrel, anything is possible."

There was a jarring lurch, causing everyone to grip the crates around them. Cat growled softly, his ears perking up in alert.

"I think we hit something," Charlotte said, steadying herself.

"Or something hit us," Alex added, peering through a crack between the crates.

The truck's engine idled for a few moments, its vibrations seeping through the metal beneath them. Then there was an eerie silence. They waited, expecting to hear the voices of the delivery men or the sound of the doors being opened, but nothing happened.

Cat's growl deepened and he bared his teeth, sensing something amiss. Sir Thomas placed a gentle hand on the dog's head to calm him.

"Maybe they're just taking a break," Alex whispered, though uncertainty laced his voice.

The group barely had time to exchange worried glances before the doors of the truck were flung open, allowing a blinding stream of daylight to pierce the darkness. An unfamiliar gruff voice ordered, "All right! The four of you, out. Now!"

Charlotte's heart raced. They had been discovered, but by whom?

The truck doors swung wide, revealing a scene out of a fantasy realm. Towering above them was an ogre, its muscular green frame covered with dirt and sweat and its eyes gleaming with cruel amusement.

Around it scampered an assortment of henchmen—goblins, trolls, and several unknown creatures—all grinning maliciously.

Using brute force, the ogre plucked them out one by one, dropping them unceremoniously on the dusty ground. The change from the chill and darkness of the truck to the glaring sunlight was disorienting. Charlotte squinted against the light, struggling to take in their surroundings.

The dilapidated buildings and overgrown vegetation suggested an abandoned city, and the air was heavy with a sense of decay. This realm had been abandoned by time and was now home to these bizarre creatures.

As they were forced to their knees, Charlotte's mind raced. The emblem on the ogre's torn vest was unmistakable—Prince Repel's insignia. Her blood ran cold. These were the prince's henchmen.

With all the authority she could muster, Charlotte

shouted, "By the power vested in me as a fairy godmother, I demand you release us at once!"

Her proclamation was met with laughter from the goblins and trolls. Then a nymph emerged from the crowd, her delicate wings shimmering in the sunlight. Her eyes held no kindness, only a cold determination that sent shivers down Charlotte's spine.

The nymph leaned close, her breath smelling of moss and damp earth. "Your title carries no sway here, Fairy Godmother, especially without the magic to back it up."

Charlotte opened her mouth to retort, but no words came out. The nymph was right. With her magical powers still in chaos, she was close to helpless.

The ogre barked an order, and the henchmen scampered off. They returned moments later with an assortment of vehicles—sleek cars and large, dark vans.

The ogre and his minions descended upon the quartet like a whirlwind of brute strength and malice.

Before Charlotte could react, someone clamped a foul-smelling cloth over her nose and mouth. A thick, nauseating stench invaded her senses, making her head spin.

She struggled, her fists pounding the solid mass of the ogre and her legs kicking out in a futile attempt to break free. Her resistance was short-lived since her strength waned and her consciousness slipped away.

As the world around her dimmed, she had a vague sensation of being lifted, the ogre's grip unyielding. Then came the harsh confinement of a small space, her body crumpled in an uncomfortable position. The last thing she heard before surrendering to the darkness was the ominous sound of a trunk slamming shut, the noise resonating ominously.

Their surroundings had changed from the abandoned city to the suffocating darkness of the vehicles' trunks. They were being taken away, but Charlotte had no idea where they were going.

Her consciousness returned in fragments, her mind foggy and disoriented. Gradually, she pieced together the situation. She was lying on a cold, hard surface, and the air was damp and stale, tinged with the scent of rotting wood. Slowly, she pushed up into a sitting position and took stock of her surroundings.

The room was small and barren, illuminated by a single flickering bulb hanging from the ceiling. The walls were rough-hewn stone with moss in the crevices. There were no windows, and the only exit appeared to be a sturdy wooden door on the opposite wall.

Charlotte turned her attention to the unmoving form lying next to her. Alex. She crawled over to him, her muscles protesting. After placing two fingers on his neck, she sighed in relief when she felt his steady heartbeat and shook him. "Alex. *Alex*! Wake up."

His eyes fluttered open, and he groaned as he tried to sit up. "What... Where are we?"

Before Charlotte could respond, he took in their surroundings, and his face twisted in anger. "I'm going to turn that squirrel into a hat. I knew we couldn't trust it! Is this what it wanted? To have us captured by Repel's goons?"

Charlotte shook her head, her voice steady. "The squirrel doesn't take sides, Alex. It listens only to Destiny."

She stood up, her legs shaky, and went over to the door. She tried the handle, but it was locked. She concentrated, trying to summon a spell to unlock it, but nothing happened. That was when she noticed a rune etched into the doorframe, a counter-spell to neutralize her magic. She sighed and leaned against the door. "We've been taken prisoner."

Alex joined her at the door and banged on it with his fist, but there was no response. "Great. Just great."

Charlotte turned to face him, offering a comforting smile. "Listen, Alex. I promise we will get out of this. I might not have my full powers, but I still have tricks up my sleeve."

His eyes met hers, and despite the situation, a small smile tugged at the corners of his mouth. "You've gotten me to believe in crazier things."

There was a loud bang on the door, causing both of them to jump. They exchanged a glance, both bracing themselves for whatever was coming next.

From the sound of it, whatever was next was here.

CHAPTER THIRTY-TWO

As Charlotte and Alex braced for what was coming, the door swung open to reveal the ogre they had encountered earlier.

They tensed, preparing to be attacked or dragged away, but the ogre just stood in the doorway for a moment, then let out a guttural groan and collapsed onto the floor with a heavy thud that shook the room.

Sir Thomas emerged from behind him with a triumphant glint in his eyes as he slid his blade back into its scabbard. Charlotte and Alex are overjoyed to see their friend safe and sound.

Breathless with relief, Charlotte asked, "Sir Thomas! How did you manage to escape?"

Sir Thomas chuckled and gave a dismissive wave. "By this point in my life, I've escaped from no less than fifty dungeons, jails, and prisons. I must say," he touched the doorframe, "this one hardly cracks the bottom ten in terms of difficulty. A simple lockpick and a well-placed strike were all it took."

His tone was serious as he explained the situation. "However, we must make haste. I overheard from my captors that we are at The Ascent, and Prince Repel has taken Cat to a different chamber. Since Charlotte's magic transformed him, Repel wishes to conduct experiments."

Charlotte felt a surge of anger and fear. "We have to save him!"

Sir Thomas nodded and presented her with a familiar object: her wand. "Indeed, and this should aid our cause."

He handed Alex a Glock 26 and a Desert Eagle pilfered from a guard during his daring escape.

Alex raised an eyebrow at the impressive weaponry now in his possession. "Feels like overkill," he remarked with a hint of sarcasm, "but I'll take it."

Sir Thomas allowed a smirk to play on his lips. "Better to be overprepared than caught off-guard, don't you think?"

With a renewed sense of determination, the trio ventured out of the cell, their senses alert and primed for the unexpected. The gloomy corridor stretched before them, seemingly endless and fraught with hidden dangers.

Sir Thomas took the lead, his sword drawn. "I must confess…" he looked left, then right, "I'm unsure of where Cat was taken."

Alex glanced around warily. "Then we'll have to find someone who knows."

On cue, five henchmen appeared from around a corner.

All were from EverAfter, but their malicious grins and twisted features showed a delight that was far from wondrous. Their eyes had a menacing gleam when they spotted the trio.

Sir Thomas advanced, his sword slicing the air, and with a powerful stroke, he took down one henchman. He then engaged in a fierce duel with another.

Alex, wary of using his guns and alerting others to their location, squared off against a third. He landed a solid punch that sent the henchman staggering back, dazed.

Charlotte focused her magic and cast a spell, trapping the remaining two henchmen inside the walls. They thrashed and screamed, and the walls crackled with magical energy that shocked them.

With one of the henchmen incapacitated and at their mercy, Alex grabbed him by the collar, pulling him up to face him. "Where's Cat? Where did you take him?"

The goon spat in response, his eyes filled with defiance. "You can't make me talk."

Alex's gaze shifted to Charlotte, who was maintaining the spell on the two henchmen. A sinister smile played on his lips as he turned back to the goon. "You sure about that? You could talk to her instead."

The goon's eyes widened in terror as he took in Charlotte's fearsome display of power. He gulped and shook his head. "All right, all right! I'll help you. Just keep her away from me!"

Sir Thomas finished off his opponent with a well-placed strike, wiping his blade clean as the goon crumpled to the floor. They then turned their attention to the minion who was eagerly sharing the location of the lab in which Cat was being held.

After he finished speaking, Sir Thomas sauntered over and used the hilt of his sword to knock the goon unconscious. "We won't be needing him anymore," he said as he turned to lead the way toward the lab.

The trio navigated through the intricate maze in the tower, on alert for danger. They managed to avoid running into any more of Prince Repel's henchmen before they reached the lab.

Cat was locked in a glass chamber in the middle of the lab. He barked with joy upon seeing his rescuers. As Charlotte was about to break the glass, two of Prince Repel's goons happened to walk by and notice them. Alex and Sir Thomas knocked them both unconscious in a matter of seconds.

The way now clear, Charlotte shattered the glass chamber and freed Cat. The reunion was brief but filled with relief and happiness as the friends embraced the dog.

Their celebration was short-lived, however. As they were preparing to depart, several guards appeared at the door, blocking their way. The group was preparing to fight their way out when a sinister voice spoke behind them.

"Well, well, well. What do we have here?"

The group turned to see Prince Repel standing there with a wicked grin on his face. He was dressed in a suit, but as he approached, a dark mist surrounded his form and morphed it into a hooded black robe.

His eyes glinted with malevolence as he stepped forward, his intentions clear.

The air in the room filled with tension as Alex drew both the Desert Eagle and the Glock 26 and held them at the ready. He glanced at Sir Thomas and Charlotte. "They won't lock us up again," Alex said, his voice steady. "Not after we've seen all this."

Three of the quartet stood in a unified front, their determination evident in their stances. Instead of joining the fray, Charlotte took a step forward and confronted Prince Repel.

"What are you doing to this realm? Why?" she demanded, her voice echoing off the walls of the laboratory.

Repel's eyes glinted as he gave a fake sigh of hurt. "My dear Charlotte, I'm merely trying to make this place more suitable for our kind."

He swept his arm around the room. "Those who are banished from EverAfter are invariably drawn here. Even the few who land elsewhere on this planet are inexplicably pulled to this city. There is a type of magic here I can't describe. I plan to make Cincinnati the first true safe haven for EverAfterans. I'll start as mayor, and in time, I will be king."

Alex snorted. "You should've chosen a different place for your little utopia. Americans hate their politicians, and they'll never stand for a king."

Repel's eyes twinkled with malevolence. "Oh, don't worry. I'll *make* them accept me as their new ruler. Every good fairytale has a happy ending, doesn't it? I will have mine."

Charlotte's eyes flashed with anger as she demanded, "Have you been pulling people from EverAfter to Cincinnati?"

Repel gave a slight nod, a smug smile playing on his lips. "Why, yes. I'll need subjects for my kingdom to flourish, won't I?"

His voice was darker as he continued, "How long will it be until more are banished, given all the idiots in power?"

Sir Thomas couldn't help but chuckle. "*There's* the lunacy I was expecting. You're still a spoiled child, always in the shadow of your brother."

Repel's eyes narrowed dangerously, and there was pure rage in his voice when he spat, "Shut it, Thomas."

Just as quickly, he cooled down. He turned his gaze to Charlotte, his eyes narrowing in thought. "It seems there have been some unintended side effects from my plans. I had no intention of summoning you or Thomas. I don't know how you arrived here to be such a thorn in my side."

Charlotte and Sir Thomas exchanged a look of utter bewilderment. Repel wasn't responsible for bringing them here? Charlotte's voice quivered with fury as she snapped, "If it wasn't you, *who* brought us here?"

Repel shrugged his shoulders, a dismissive smile on his lips. "I just told you that I don't know. If I did, rest assured, I would have personally dealt with the annoyance by now."

He leaned in, his eyes boring into Charlotte's. "I had no reason to go after you. I already have what I wanted from your kind."

With a flourish, he produced a book from his robe, and Charlotte's breath caught in her throat. For a moment, she thought it was her handbook, but then she saw the name "Belinda" etched on the cover, and her heart sank.

"What do you want with that book? What have you done to my fellow fairy godmother?" she demanded, her voice shaking with anger and fear.

Repel chuckled as he caressed the cover. "Belinda is also

an annoyance I still have to deal with, but that can come later." He paused before continuing. "After I find her again."

His eyes glinted with malevolence as he opened the book and flipped through it.

"As for why I wanted the book," he added, his voice satisfied, "it's simple, really. In this realm, magic is faint and chaotic, but with this book as a focus, I and several others have been able to tap into the magic of the realm more easily and use it effectively. On top of that, we've been able to learn some of the spells contained within."

He gave a sinister smile as he snapped the book closed and tucked it back into his robe. "I must say, now I understand why you godmothers value these handbooks so highly. There are a lot of supposed rules and guidelines inside, but I had no time for those. I take what I need and discard the rest."

Prince Repel raised a hand. "I have a few questions for our lovely fairy godmother. Have you considered why you are so dead set on stopping me? We don't have any history together other than the wedding fiasco, so, it can't be a vendetta. It's not loyalty to my brother either, given that fairy godmothers are loyal only to their cause. Do you not think that those who are banished here deserve a better fate than to be left in a world where they are not wanted and is almost incompatible with their way of life?"

Charlotte took a deep breath before responding, her voice steady and clear.

"Stop with the theatrics, Repel. You're not the benevolent savior you're painting yourself to be. All you want is power and control, the same things you desired in Ever-After. You are ripping people from their realm against their will and deceiving the people in this one. You are no hero or savior. You're just a villain who wishes to play at being a god."

Silence followed Charlotte's fierce retort. Repel glared at the fairy godmother, but his fury was quickly replaced by a gentle smile.

"Perhaps you are right," he conceded, his tone laced with a chilling calmness. "I *am* playing god. And as God," he flicked his eyes to the other three and back to Charlotte, "I get to decide whether you and your friends live or die."

Repel unleashed a spell at Charlotte, the air crackling with energy as a bolt of light shot toward her. Simultaneously, he ordered his henchmen, "Kill them!"

As the light hurtled toward Charlotte, she raised her wand, summoning the most powerful shield she was capable of. A brilliant flash illuminated the room as the two spells collided, sending out shockwaves that knocked the henchmen off balance and her back a step.

Charlotte and her group sprang into action.

CHAPTER THIRTY-THREE

As Repel's henchmen charged them, Charlotte summoned a spell she hoped would incapacitate them. Her wand glowed brightly, and a stream of light shot toward the oncoming attackers, but instead of the expected stunning spell, her magic produced a series of dazzling fireworks that exploded in the air, momentarily blinding the henchmen and causing confusion in their ranks.

Alex took advantage of the distraction and launched into the fray, guns blazing. He took down two goblins with precise double-taps before his ammo ran out. Discarding the guns, he switched to hand-to-hand combat, using his martial arts training to take down a troll that had joined the fight.

Sir Thomas was a whirlwind of fur and steel as he fought a group of orcs. His agility and skill with the blade allowed him to dance around his larger and clumsier opponents and cut them down one by one.

Cat was fighting a giant lizard that had charged him.

Despite its size and ferocity, Cat dodged its attacks while landing powerful blows of his own. The lizard roared in frustration as it tried to catch the nimble canine.

While her friends fought the henchmen, Charlotte faced off against Repel, who was casting more spells. His dark robe billowed as he summoned fireballs, which he hurled at Charlotte. She raised her wand to summon a shield, but a burst of water extinguished the fireballs before they reached her.

Charlotte cursed under her breath. Her powers were still not cooperating.

She focused on her wand as she summoned another spell. This time, a bolt of lightning struck Repel, causing him to stumble back in surprise. Charlotte enjoyed a brief moment of triumph before he recovered and retaliated.

"Oh, *crap*." She dove out of the way too late.

A wave of energy hit Charlotte, and she hit the wall behind her and slid down. She groaned as she struggled to get back on her feet. Her energy was waning, her powers drained by the continuous use of magic.

Once upright, Charlotte gathered her strength for the next spell. As Repel launched another ball of dark energy toward her, she cast a spell to create a mirror-like shield. To her relief, the shield materialized as she intended, reflecting Repel's attack back at him.

The dark energy hit him square in the chest, and he sprawled on the floor.

She cast another spell, this time successfully creating a rope of light that wrapped around Repel, trapping him in place.

Alex had managed to disarm an orc and was using its

club to fend off a group of goblins. Its weight was a challenge, but he wielded it with precision, knocking the goblins down one by one.

Sir Thomas was in his element. His sword stepped through an intricate dance as he took on a group of orcs. With a final flourish, he took down the last orc, its body collapsing to the floor with a thud.

Cat had bested the giant lizard and pinned it to the floor. He let out a victorious bark, his tail wagging triumphantly.

With the henchmen down, Charlotte, Alex, Sir Thomas, and Cat turned their attention to Repel, who was still struggling against the bonds of light. Charlotte approached him cautiously, her wand raised.

"Your reign will end before it starts, Repel," she declared.

As she was about to cast the final spell, dark energy burst from Repel, shattering the bonds and sending Charlotte flying back. She crashed into a table, the impact knocking the breath out of her.

"I think not." Repel stood up, his eyes glowing with fury. With a wave of his hand, he summoned a group of more powerful creatures—ogres, trolls, and other dark beings—who materialized beside him, ready to fight. "Rather, it's your time to die, Charlotte."

The tide of the battle had shifted. Charlotte and her friends were now facing a much more formidable force.

As the new henchmen charged them, dread settled in her stomach. She had used up most of her energy, and her powers were waning. "Oh, for all the goddesses' sake." She pushed up from the floor, wand at the ready, as she prepared to face the new wave of attackers.

The room erupted into chaos.

Alex swung the club at an approaching ogre, but it was like hitting a brick wall.

The ogre barely flinched and immediately retaliated with a punch. Alex almost dodged, but the edge of the blow sent him to the floor. He was out of ammo and out of options. Glancing around, he saw a sword lying a few feet away. It was his only chance, so he crawled toward it, reaching for it as an orc raised its axe.

Sir Thomas was surrounded by trolls, their lumbering forms closing in on him from all sides. He fought fiercely, his sword a blur as he parried and struck, but he was tiring. A blow from a troll's club sent him to his knees and he struggled to rise, his blade wavering.

Cat was fending off a group of goblins, but they were quick and agile and darted in and out, slashing at him with their knives. He managed to catch one with his paw and it flew across the room, but the others were relentless, and their attacks got bolder.

Armed with the sword he had appropriated, Alex was struggling to keep a group of ogres at bay. He swung the sword with all his might, managing to cut one of them down, but he was no match for their brute strength. A blow from another ogre sent him sprawling to the ground, his sword skittering out of reach.

Charlotte's and Repel's magical powers collided in an explosion of light and dark. Charlotte's energy was almost gone, and she stumbled back, wand slipping from her hand.

Charlotte and her friends were losing. Repel laughed as he savored his impending victory.

A voice in her head whispered, "*You are not alone.*"

Warmth swelled within Charlotte and spread outward, coursing through her veins like a river of liquid sunlight. The sensation was akin to standing in the sun at noon on Midsummer's Day.

After she bent down to retrieve it, her fingers curled around the familiar hilt of her wand. The wand, a delicate extension of her will, pulsed with a light that echoed her newfound hope.

She pivoted on her heel, the marble beneath her feet grounding her. Her gaze met Repel's, her dark eyes reflecting the faint glow of her wand.

Her voice didn't waver, and each word was delivered in time with the steady beat of her heart. "You. Will. Not. Win." Her words sliced through the tension like a finely honed blade. Her defiance demonstrated a courage that would not be forgotten.

Repel scoffed, raising his hand to cast the final spell.

The air in the room shifted, and a shadow fell across the doorway. Charlotte and her friends and Repel and his creatures turned to see a dark figure whose presence commanded the attention of everyone in the room.

It looked like the Grim Reaper, clad from head to toe in a pitch-black robe. A hood obscured its face, creating an impenetrable shadow where its visage should be.

The sheer malevolence that emanated from the figure was enough to make everyone in the room feel terror, though they could not comprehend what stood before them.

Charlotte's eyes darted between the figure and Repel, searching for a sign that he had summoned this evil being.

However, Repel's face mirrored her confusion and shock. It was evident that he was as taken aback by the figure's appearance as she was.

The newcomer turned to face Repel, raised one arm, and pointed at the prince. "*You*," it accused, its soft voice filling the cavernous room. "*You* broke the sanctity of the veil."

Repel's confusion deepened, his mind racing to comprehend the accusation the being had leveled at him.

What was this veil the figure spoke of, and how had he broken its sanctity? Before he could formulate a response, the figure glided toward him, its movements smooth and inexorable.

His panic rising, Repel pivoted and cast the spell he had intended for Charlotte at the figure.

The spell hit its target, and the figure dropped to the floor in a heap. A triumphant smirk spread across Repel's face since he mistakenly believed he had vanquished the foe.

His confidence restored, he laughed, the sound filling the room with its malevolence.

His merriment was short-lived. To everyone's amazement, the being rose from the floor with an ease that contradicted the force of the spell that had struck it. Its robe rippled and undulated as if they were made of smoke as it got to its feet and stood tall and unharmed.

It resumed its slow, deliberate advance toward the prince.

Terror crossed Repel's face as he realized the gravity of

the situation. His previous confidence evaporated, replaced by frantic desperation as he cast spell after spell at the advancing figure.

The spells hit the target, but the being absorbed them all, its form flickering but not dissipating. The air crackled with the magical energy, but the figure was unfazed, and its progress toward Repel didn't slow.

The figure seemed unstoppable, impervious to Repel's most powerful magic. The balance of power had shifted again, and this new entity now held the upper hand.

When the newcomer reached Repel, the prince made a futile attempt to flee, but the figure snatched him by the back of his head with a hand that looked like an elongated skeletal claw.

The people in the room held their breath as a guttural scream ripped from Repel's throat, sending shivers down everyone's spine.

The others in the room watched in horror as Repel's body underwent a gruesome transformation. His skin darkened and took on a translucent quality, as if his very essence were being drained. His body faded until there was nothing left of him but his robe, which fluttered to the floor in a heap.

The figure stood over the empty robe, head tilted as it regarded the garment. Then it swiveled its faceless hood to the rest of the people in the room.

Concern washed over everyone present. The prince's henchmen, once so formidable and imposing, were reduced to cowering in fear. With Repel dead, they fled, their shouts getting louder and angrier as they stumbled over one another in their haste to escape.

Alex reached down and helped Charlotte to her feet. Both kept their eyes on the newcomer. "We have to go. *Now*!" His voice was tense.

Charlotte was rooted to the spot, staring at the figure and beyond it. Recognition tickled the edge of her consciousness. She had never seen this person before, yet deep inside her, she knew who it was.

That left her torn between the urge to flee and the desire...no, the *need* to understand the enigma before her.

After it retrieved the handbook, the person's attention turned to Charlotte. With a defiant yell, she lunged for the handbook, but Alex and Sir Thomas caught her arms, pulling her back just in time.

Time hung suspended as they regarded each other, the air thick with tension. Charlotte thought she saw a glimpse of something familiar in the darkness of the hood.

Then it was gone.

Charlotte and her friends braced for the figure's next move, but instead of attacking, the newcomer turned on its heel and glided away. It melted into shadows and vanished, leaving them staring at the empty spot it had occupied.

The silence in the room was broken by sounds of chaos from the rest of the tower.

The loss of the fairy godmother handbook weighed heavily on Charlotte's heart. The potential it held was again a distant dream.

"We need to go while the tower is still in chaos," Alex urged, his voice steady and calm.

With a heavy heart, Charlotte acquiesced, allowing her friends to lead her out of the room. As they departed, Cat darted toward a table with a playful bark and snatched a book, wagging his tail as he caught up with the group.

They disappeared into the tower, leaving behind an empty room with shadows that seemed to linger in the corners as if the figure might reappear at any moment.

They were right to fear the possibility.

CHAPTER THIRTY-FOUR

Known for a glass façade that seemingly defied the laws of physics, the tower felt like a treacherous maze concealing dangers at every turn. As they maneuvered through the maze-like corridors, the group was prepared to face guards or any other threat that might arise.

However, as they moved through the building, it became clear that the tale of Prince Repel's gruesome demise at the hands of the mysterious figure had spread like wildfire. Guards and residents were fleeing in all directions, faces contorted with fear and horror as they screamed about the monster that had claimed the prince's life.

When they reached the bottom floor, Charlotte surveyed the lobby, her gaze sharp as she processed their next move. "We're not getting through that crowd," she hissed in frustration. "It's too big a risk."

Sir Thomas nodded, his eyes reflecting the same concern. "Agreed. We'd be sitting ducks in there."

Charlotte's eyes darted to one of the large windows

lining the lobby. "We're going to have to make our own exit," she announced, determination coloring her voice as she pointed at the glass. Without waiting for a response, she sprinted toward the window, and her companions followed. "Hope you trust me!"

Alex jumped, then looked. "Oh, shit!" He reconsidered his life's choices. This wasn't the short drop he had expected. If they hit the ground from three stories up, he wasn't sure he would survive.

The cool night air hit their faces, a sharp contrast to the stifling heat created by the throng inside. The ground rushed up to meet them.

"Brace yourselves!" Charlotte warned, her voice whisked away by the wind. She muttered an incantation, her voice barely audible over the rush of air. The enchantment enveloped her and her companions in a protective shield.

Their landing was surprisingly soft, the enchantment absorbing the impact. They hit the ground running, their footsteps echoing on the pavement as they sprinted away from the menacing glass tower.

The edifice, a haunting silhouette against the night sky, soon faded in the distance. This part of Cincinnati, normally bustling with activity, was eerily deserted since the chaos from The Ascent had spilled out into the surrounding area. The group sprinted past the Roebling Suspension Bridge and the winding pathways of Smale Riverfront Park, their lungs burning with exertion.

Finally, when they felt they were a safe distance from the building, they slowed to a walk, gasping as they tried to catch their breath. The twinkling lights of the city cast a surreal glow on the empty streets.

Exhausted, Charlotte and her friends found a small patch of grass on the side of the road and dropped down on it to rest, weary from the events of the day.

Charlotte couldn't help going over their situation as she caught her breath. The loss of the handbook weighed heavily on her heart, as did the quandary of who Belinda was. Charlotte was both angry and frustrated by the evening's events. The mystery of the figure that had taken the handbook was particularly vexing. There was something familiar about it, as if she should know who or what it was, yet the answer eluded her.

Charlotte looked down at the handbook she still had in her possession. Its pages were tattered, and some were missing, but she knew that if she could find a way to repair it and retrieve the missing pages, she could regain some of the powerful magic that had once been at her fingertips.

Sir Thomas, who was seated beside her, asked the question that had been lingering in everyone's minds. "Do you have any idea who that figure was?" he asked gently.

Charlotte hesitated for a moment before answering. "I...I don't know," she admitted. "But it feels familiar, like I should know what it is, but I can't quite place it. The answer is just out of reach." She sighed. "It's driving me crazy."

She looked down at her hands, feeling as lost and confused as she had when she had first arrived in Cincinnati from EverAfter.

Sensing her distress, Cat trotted over and gently nudged her with his nose. Charlotte looked at the canine, who had a book in his mouth. To her surprise, it was a tome she hadn't seen before.

Cat dropped the book at her feet, and Charlotte's heart skipped a beat when she realized that it was one of the books from the laboratory. She looked at Cat with gratitude and astonishment. "Where did you get this?" she asked, her voice filled with wonder.

Cat wagged his tail. His face seemed to say, "I thought you might need this."

Alex, Sir Thomas, and Charlotte huddled around the book, their heads close together as they scrutinized its contents—pages upon pages of notes, drawings, and seemingly incoherent ramblings.

Some notes were meticulous, while others looked like they had been scribbled down in a hurry. As they flipped through, they saw drawings of spell symbols and intricate diagrams that only someone with a deep understanding of magic could comprehend.

Amongst the spellwork and notes on the campaign, they also found sketches and pictures of a peculiar building.

"It's like he's from a different time," Alex noted, holding the book up to get a better look at the sketches. "All this could easily fit into a smartphone, but I guess Prince Repel hasn't quite caught up with modern technology."

Charlotte was drawn to a series of pictures of a unique building she recognized as the Spaceship House, which was famous in Cincinnati for its futuristic design. Next to one of the pictures, she saw several phrases written in a language she didn't recognize. The words glowed on the page as if they were alive.

"This place must have held some significance for him," Charlotte mused, tracing the picture. "I think we should go there."

Alex and Sir Thomas looked at each other, clearly yearning for rest. However, they couldn't let Charlotte go alone after everything that had just happened.

Sir Thomas stood up. "I was fully prepared to spend the rest of my evening vanquishing the evil prince, but that task was taken care of for us, so my dance card is blank. Let's go see this Spaceship House."

They took a ten-minute taxi ride around the confusion and got dropped off two blocks from the building.

The group approached the Spaceship House, delighted by the futuristic design. The circular shape and silver color gave the impression that it had just landed.

"I haven't been in this part of town since I was a teenager," Alex remarked, scanning the structure. "That always seemed like something out of a sci-fi movie."

Sir Thomas took in the building. "It's a remarkable piece of architecture," he mused. "Although it's smaller than I had imagined."

Charlotte approached the door, her heart racing in anticipation of what they might find inside. As she touched the knob, a surge of energy rippled through her, and she stumbled back.

A barrier of light had formed around the door, shimmering with an intensity that spoke of very powerful magic.

"It's enchanted," Charlotte declared, awe and frustration in her voice. "A lock spell. It won't open without the correct phrase."

Alex flipped the book open, turning to a page filled with drawings of the Spaceship House. Next to the sketches were a series of phrases written in a flowing script. He handed the book to Charlotte. "Maybe one of those?"

Charlotte studied the phrases. Each seemed more ominous than the last, like something a villain in a fairytale might devise to keep prying eyes away. Charlotte's eyes settled on the phrase at the bottom of the page.

"By moon's pale light and star's sharp gleam, thy passage barred, save by this theme. Speak now the words of darkened dream and enter the realm of the unseen."

After she took a deep breath, Charlotte spoke the phrase, her voice resonating in the still air. The barrier flickered, then disappeared, leaving the door unguarded. Charlotte turned the handle, and the door swung open with a creak.

The group exchanged glances before stepping into the dark interior, unsure of what they would find. As they entered the foyer, they were shocked to see a turkey, an owl, and a mouse perched on small chairs in the main room, intently focused on the playing cards in their hands.

The room contained older furniture, and a faded rug covered the wooden floor. The walls were lined with shelves filled with books and artifacts, and the antique chandelier cast a warm glow over the room.

Alex turned to Charlotte, eyebrows raised in surprise. "Are they a threat?"

Charlotte squinted at the animals, reaching out with her senses to detect any danger. "There's magic on them, but it's not very strong. I don't think they're a threat."

The mouse sniffed the air and turned its small head in their direction. "Oi, Geb! Is that you? Got another delivery?"

The turkey clucked her tongue and shook her head. "If that was Geb, this entire building would be rumbling."

The owl let out a hoot of laughter. "Then it seems we have guests."

The group exchanged glances. There was no point in trying to hide. They stepped into the main room, watching the three magical creatures.

The mouse looked at them, his small eyes gleaming with curiosity. "All right. Who are you, then?"

Charlotte cleared her throat, unsure of how to answer.

Were they pets or more of Prince Repel's henchmen? They didn't seem menacing, but looks could be deceiving.

"We're...we're looking for something," she began cautiously. "Something that belongs to us."

The turkey raised an eyebrow, and the mouse chuckled. "Is that so? Well, you'll have to speak to the master about that."

The owl nodded solemnly. "Yes, the master will know what to do with you." He studied the group, tilting his head to the side in a thoughtful manner. "You lot don't seem like the master's usual type."

The turkey chimed in, ruffling her feathers. "Except for the knight. He seems like a feisty one."

Sir Thomas wasn't sure how to take that, and his hand moved to the hilt of his sword.

To gain control of the situation, Alex decided to bluff. "The prince sent us here to collect something of importance."

The mouse was quick to counter that. "That can't be true. We didn't receive any message, and that's protocol. Why are you really here?"

Taken aback by the creatures' nonchalance, Charlotte decided to lay all her cards on the table. She pulled out her wand and held it up for them to see. "I am a fairy godmother, and Prince Repel is dead. We were led here by one of his notebooks, and we want to know what he was hiding."

Sir Thomas shook his head, a small smile playing on his lips. "You are too honest for your own good, my lady."

The three creatures burst into hysterics. Their howling laughter filled the room.

The turkey managed to catch her breath long enough to ask, "The prince really is dead?"

The group nodded, and the animals' laughter got louder and more jubilant.

The owl wiped a tear from his eye, still chuckling. "Well, that is quite the turn of events."

Sir Thomas stood with his arms crossed and a bewildered look on his face. "Are you *happy* that your master is dead?"

The mouse, who had managed to contain his laughter, shook his head. "'Master' is just the term we use because he'd fry us if we didn't. We have no love for that jackass."

The owl chimed in, a stern expression on his face. "We were among the first beings the prince brought to this realm from EverAfter when he began his experiments. Since then, we have been slaves."

The turkey nodded in agreement. "After he gathered some real muscle and made friends with others of ill intent, he locked us up in this house and made us look after his knickknacks."

Charlotte's eyes widened in surprise.

"Have you come to free us?" asked the mouse.

Charlotte hesitated. "We didn't know you were here, but you are free from the prince now. I would suggest heading to the fish market and searching for Peter. It's a good place to start anew."

The animals seemed more than happy to take her advice, but before they stood to leave, Charlotte made a request. "Would you mind showing us what you were looking after for the prince?"

The turkey considered her question before nodding. "We shall. In fact, there is something you will probably find useful. The prince was particularly keen on them."

She walked over to a cupboard under the sink and pulled out a small box. After she handed it to Charlotte, she watched as the fairy godmother opened it and gasped. Inside was a stack of pages that looked like they came from Charlotte's handbook.

"My pages!" she exclaimed in surprise. "How did he get these?"

The owl, still perched on its chair, ruffled his feathers. "The prince was intrigued by the magic in these pages," the owl explained. "After he realized how much power they had, he sent his minions far and wide in search of them, desperate to get his hands on every single page."

Charlotte eagerly sifted through the stack. Each page had been meticulously preserved, a testament to their importance. With a joyous gasp, she began placing the pages in their rightful order.

As the sheets came together, a magical force brought them to life. The pages fluttered and danced in the air, aligning themselves perfectly. Charlotte watched in awe as her handbook reassembled itself and the simple white cover that bore her name appeared from nowhere. Her smiling friends stood by her side, sharing in her triumph.

Their happiness was short-lived.

The room darkened, as if an unseen cloud hovered over them. The quartet looked around in confusion, their smiles changing to concern.

Charlotte was still admiring her handbook when she felt a shift in the air. A loud voice in her head said, *Congratulations, Charlotte. You successfully pieced together what was once lost, but I'm afraid your journey ends here. I will take that handbook.*

An unknown force dragged them into an abyss.

CHAPTER THIRTY-FIVE

With a *whoosh* that seemed to emanate from all directions, the darkness lifted. Charlotte blinked as her eyes adjusted to her new surroundings. She was in a realm that was the antithesis of the Spaceship House.

The sky was inky-black, filled with blots of lights that looked like distant stars. Odd shapes and shadows on the horizon gave the illusion of buildings and trees, but nothing was clear or defined.

Charlotte turned her attention to the others. Alex stood nearby, his jaw slack as he took in the surreal landscape. "Where are we?" he asked, his voice barely above a whisper.

Charlotte shook her head, unable to provide an answer. She looked for Cat and found him standing with his hackles raised, senses on high alert. The sight of her loyal companion in that state fueled her worry.

Sir Thomas was the most composed, but he had unsheathed his sword, and the blade glinted in what light there was. "This place has as much trickery as EverAfter," he muttered, scanning their surroundings for danger.

The turkey, the owl, and the mouse were there as well, and they were in the midst of a heated argument. "I told you not to touch that!" the turkey squawked at the mouse.

"I didn't touch anything!" the mouse retorted, his whiskers quivering with indignation.

The owl was attempting to mediate to no avail. "Now, now. Let's not jump to conclusions."

Their bickering cut off when someone emerged from the shadows—the dark figure from the lab. Its presence chilled the air, and everyone, even Cat, froze, transfixed by its appearance.

The only sound was the soft rustling of the figure's robe as it glided closer to them.

The mouse squinted at the new arrival and muttered, "Er, any of you have a clue 'oo that is?"

Sir Thomas gravely replied, "The person who killed Prince Repel."

"Really?" The mouse's whiskers twitched. "I'd shake his hand if he wasn't so bloody terrifying."

Charlotte clutched her handbook to her chest and took a step forward. "Who are you, and why do you want fairy godmother handbooks?"

The figure, which was staring at Charlotte with an intensity that made her shiver, gave a low, irritated rumble. "I was once known as Miraval, and I was a lowly wizard in minor tales. However, Fate had other plans for me. I was sent here to guard the gate between your world and this one and ensure that no one who lands here goes back."

Sir Thomas quirked an eyebrow. "You looked like that in EverAfter? You'd think you'd get more play."

Miraval pointed a finger and burned a line on the

ground between them. Flames danced over the earth as he bellowed, "I was transformed and given power beyond what any other being in your world has in exchange for my services."

Sir Thomas glanced at the flames. "Looks like a punishment to me."

Miraval scoffed. "I was given a sacred duty. I will live forever, and I am invincible. There is no way back to Ever-After, so you must learn to adapt and survive here. Do not challenge me or disrupt the balance I am duty-bound to maintain. I am the Gatekeeper, the guardian of all realms, and *you will heed my command*."

Everything that had bothered Charlotte since she first saw Miraval coalesced, and she pointed at him. "Wait a minute. I know you, and I know this story. The Gatekeeper was turned to sand and then back to bone, but only bone. A skeleton of their former self." She jabbed a finger in the air for emphasis. "That's straight from the handbook—the pages buried deep in the back that never get used. No one knew you were real."

For a moment, the Gatekeeper remained silent. Then he lifted a hand to his hood. With a slow, deliberate motion, he pulled it down to reveal his true form. His skeletal face was etched with the sorrows of ages. His hollow eyes seemed to bore into Charlotte's soul as he asked in a grim tone, "Do you now believe me to be real?"

The turkey, ruffling her feathers, leaned close to the owl and mouse, whispering, "I, for one, believe him to be real." Her voice was shaking.

The owl and the mouse exchanged worried glances, then nodded solemnly, tensing in unison.

Charlotte frowned. "Why can't we return?" she demanded, the fervor in her voice resonating through the space. "None of us chose to be here in this realm. We were either tricked by Repel's twisted games or sent here against our will for reasons unknown. If you truly care about preserving the balance between the realms, it's your duty to let us return to our rightful home!" Each word landed with the force of a hammer's strike.

The Gatekeeper responded by drawing his hood back up, his features swallowed by the shadows once more. His frosty and uncompromising voice rang out. "No. I will not allow any of you to return. The damage is already done." He pointed a skeletal finger at the handbook Charlotte clutched protectively to her chest.

"Hand over the book," he commanded.

Charlotte's mind whirred into overdrive, and she held the book closer. The book thrummed with a life of its own against her chest. She remembered the hidden knowledge stashed in the book's latter pages, the secrets she had stumbled upon during her initial reading of the handbook.

Her hands trembled as she flipped to the back of the book, uncovering the truth about the Gatekeeper's existence. "You're not invincible, Miraval! There's a loophole, a way to overthrow the Gatekeeper!" she proclaimed, a triumphant edge to her voice.

The Gatekeeper bellowed in rage, and as if provoked, the wind surged around them, forcing the group to steady themselves by clutching each other lest they be lifted off their feet.

Cloak swirling, Sir Thomas unsheathed his sword and shouted over the wind's roar. "Does he have an Achilles heel? Could this explain his insatiable pursuit of the fairy godmother handbooks?"

The Gatekeeper's pupils flared with wrath as Charlotte thumbed through to the last page to read about ways to make him fall.

The turkey gasped and huddled closer to the owl, whispering, "She has pushed him over the edge."

The owl nodded, its eyes wide with dread.

The mouse grinned. "I appreciate her boldness."

Alex drew his Glock and shouted to make himself heard over the tumult. "He was trying to destroy your book?"

Charlotte lifted an arm to block the wind. "It couldn't be destroyed. The pages wouldn't burn, and he knew the torn-out pages would eventually find each other and knit themselves back together. It couldn't be done. He just wanted them hidden!"

Miraval pointed a finger at Charlotte as his roar shook the ground beneath their feet. "*Give me the book, or face the consequences!*"

Charlotte stood her ground, the wind whipping her hair around her face. "I will *not* give you the book. We will find a way back to EverAfter, and we *will* stop you!" she declared defiantly.

The wind abruptly ceased, leaving an eerie calmness in its wake. Miraval towered over the group, imposing and terrifying. His eyes gleamed with an unholy light as he stated in a voice that rumbled like thunder, "You, Charlotte, are defying your sacred calling as a fairy godmother. Your duty, like mine, is to protect the realms and maintain balance."

Charlotte lifted her chin, eyes burning with a fierce resolve as she shot back, "I protect those from EverAfter, and I see no difference between you and Repel. Both of you are nothing but villains, driven by a lust for power and control." Her voice was steady in the face of the looming threat.

With a guttural growl and a wave of his hand, Miraval conjured a blade formed of magic, its edges shimmering with supernatural energy. Raising it high, he passed his sentence. "You are a disgrace to your kind and an enemy of the order and balance of the realms. As the Gatekeeper, it is my duty to eliminate threats to that balance. Prepare to face the consequences of your defiance."

With a determined glint in her eyes, Charlotte pointed her wand at Miraval. Her handbook glowed, and its pages fluttered. A luminescent shield materialized in front of and blocked the gatekeeper's fierce attack.

The impact of the blade striking the shield sent shockwaves through the realm, yet the shield held strong, to Miraval's surprise. For the first time since their confrontation began, he felt a flicker of doubt.

Using the momentum from the clash, Charlotte pushed the shield forward with all her might, which sent the gatekeeper staggering back a few steps.

"And it is *my* duty to eliminate threats to my people!" she declared.

A triumphant yell pierced the air as Sir Thomas bounded onto the scene, riding Cat like a noble steed from days of old. Cat had grown, and his raised hackles made him look even larger. His eyes gleamed with a fierce determination to protect his owner.

Sir Thomas parried another vicious blow from the Gatekeeper and landed on the ground next to Cat, sword at the ready. The blade gleamed even in this dark expanse.

"And it is *our* duty to help her with *her* duty," Sir Thomas declared with a proud grin as Cat growled at the evil figure. "*En garde*, Gatekeeper."

CHAPTER THIRTY-SIX

When Sir Thomas and Cat engaged Miraval in battle, Charlotte moved to join the fray but was stopped by a firm hand on her shoulder. She turned to see Alex looking at her with concern and determination.

"Wait, Charlotte! Do you know how to beat him?"

Charlotte bit her lip and shook her head. "The answer is in the back section of my handbook, but I'll need to find the right page."

Alex nodded. "Well, I hope you're a fast reader since we need that information and fast. The rest of us will keep Marvin, or Minerval, or Miravain…whatever the hell his name is…distracted."

Charlotte's eyes expressed her worry. "Alex! This being is more of a threat than Repel ever was. I don't want any of you to get hurt!"

Alex gave her a small smile. "As a police officer, it's my duty to protect people, and just like you, I do everything I can to keep them safe. I'd also like to live to keep doing that, and the best way for that to happen is for you to figure out how to beat that guy."

Charlotte hesitated, but Alex was right. With a nod, she turned to her handbook and frantically began flipping through the pages, searching for the information that would let her defeat Miraval.

Alex drew his gun and joined Sir Thomas and Cat.

Charlotte's heart pounded as she read through the section on the Gatekeeper. The pages seemed to blur as she tried to take in all the information at once.

"Is there anything we can do to help?" asked the owl, fluffing his feathers in concern.

The mouse and the turkey nodded in agreement, though the turkey added with a self-deprecating laugh, "We're not much in the way of fighting, I'm afraid. We're crap at that, actually."

Charlotte glanced at the trio and gave them a small smile. "Just give me a moment. I need to find the right passage, and there's a lot to go through here." She turned her attention back to the book.

The turkey leaned over her shoulder and read the pages with Charlotte. "Hey, look at this! He's got a housekey." She pointed to a picture of the Gatekeeper. In the illustration, a key hung from his waist.

The owl leaned in for a closer look. "That's not just any key," he said, his eyes widening in realization. "That's a celestial key. It has the power to open any door. Even those between worlds, supposedly."

Charlotte's head snapped up. "A celestial key?" she echoed, her eyes narrowing in thought. She glanced at

Miraval, who was locked in a fierce duel with Sir Thomas, and saw a glint of metal below his waist.

The key! It was there, just like in the picture.

The mouse snorted in amusement. "So, all one needs to be a Gatekeeper is a special key? Any knobhead can do that."

Charlotte shook her head. "It's not that simple. To wield the celestial key, you must possess powerful magic or have a powerful source of magic with you. Otherwise, the key is nothing more than a fancy trinket."

The owl tilted his head thoughtfully. "Are you powerful enough to use it? If so, you could open a portal and toss the gatekeeper through it."

Charlotte bit her lip, wishing it was that simple. Then she got an idea and flipped to the front of her handbook, searching for a particular passage.

"Aha!" she exclaimed, showing them a picture of a crystal. "My *handbook* is a powerful source of magic, made from a luminous crystal. If I can return it to that state, I can use the celestial key."

The turkey frowned in confusion. "Okay, so then you'll have a fancy rock. What's that good for?"

Charlotte grinned. "With the crystal, I can power the key and do exactly what the owl suggested. I can cast Miraval into another dimension." She returned her focus to her book. "But first, I need to get my hands on that key."

Charlotte turned to a specific page and began to chant the words of a spell she hoped would allow her to magically wrest the celestial key from Miraval. As she spoke the final word, a blue light emanated from her hand and extended toward the gatekeeper. As the light was about to wrap around the key, it rebounded as if it had hit an invisible wall.

"Oof!" She hit the ground, and her handbook flew out of her hand. The owl and the turkey rushed to her side and helped her up while the mouse looked on with a thoughtful expression.

"Are you all right?" the owl asked, fluffing his feathers in concern.

Charlotte nodded, still dazed. "I'm fine, but it seems the key is protected against magic."

The mouse tapped his chin. "You've got the right idea, luv. Just need to focus on something different." He looked at his companions with a grin. "Are you blokes still in the mood for a gamble?"

The two birds looked worried, but that shifted into amusement when the owl asked, "What have you got in mind?"

Sir Thomas, Cat, and Alex continued their attack on Miraval. Alex emptied his guns, his bullets hitting and shattering the gatekeeper's bones, only for the pieces to reform almost instantly.

Sir Thomas and Cat weren't faring much better. Every sword slash repaired itself, and any time Cat charged or bit Miraval, he was either blocked or tossed aside like a rag doll.

Their attacks slowed the Gatekeeper, but they didn't seem to hurt him. Mostly, they angered him.

Sweat poured down Alex's face when he realized he was out of bullets. "Damn it!"

Sir Thomas grunted as he swung his sword at Miraval again. "We must hold on. Charlotte will find a way."

Cat growled in agreement and lunged at Miraval.

Miraval seemed to have reached the end of his patience. With a roar, he knocked Cat away, then slammed his blade into the ground, releasing a magical explosion. The trio was thrown back, and pain coursed through their bodies as the magic latched onto them.

Miraval moved toward Alex, who was struggling to get up, intending to finish him off. Before he could reach him, the owl swooped in and struck Miraval in the head with his talons.

"Take that, you brute!" the owl hooted, barely dodging a retaliatory swipe.

The Gatekeeper growled, "Flying rodent!"

The owl huffed in offense. "I am insulted. I am not a pigeon!" With a flick of his wings, the owl cast a spell to speed up its movements to avoid another attack from Miraval.

Below and slightly behind the owl, the turkey did her best to distract Miraval. "Hey, look at me! I'm a turkey!" she yelled, flapping her wings and running in circles around the Gatekeeper's feet.

Miraval grimaced as he tried to step over the turkey. "Did the fairy godmother send you simple animals to fight on her behalf?"

The turkey laughed as she continued to run around, then called over her shoulder as she fled, "Well, we're not fighters. We know we're crap at it. But we're good distractions!"

Miraval felt a tug at his waist. He looked down in horror and saw that the celestial key was gone. Panicked, he looked for it and saw the mouse holding it, grinning cheekily.

Charlotte, who had watched the scene unfold, took advantage of the distraction and cast the spell she had attempted earlier. With the key in the mouse's possession, the spell worked.

The blue light grabbed the mouse instead of the key, and as he flew toward Charlotte, key in hand, he shouted, "Hey, Gatekeeper! Maybe you should've kept a closer watch on your keys! You're not just a lousy wizard. You're a lousy Gatekeeper, too!"

Charlotte caught the mouse in one hand, giving him a warm smile as she thanked him for his valiant efforts. He disappeared, leaving Charlotte to focus on the task at hand.

The pages of the handbook pages dissolved in a cocoon of light. Moments later, a radiant crystal emerged, pulsing in sync with Charlotte's heartbeat.

Holding the celestial key in her other hand, she brought the two objects together. When they touched, the resulting surge of power created a symphony of light and magic.

Miraval roared in frustration and raised his hands to conjure a powerful spell he hoped would turn the tide in his favor, but before he could complete the incantation, a giant portal ripped open the fabric of reality behind him. Tendrils emerged from the swirling vortex, wrapped around Miraval, and pulled him in.

Miraval struggled and dug his feet into the ground as he fought to resist. "No!" he bellowed as he battled the invisible forces that sought to claim him.

The portal was relentless. As it sucked Miraval toward its gaping maw, the realm he had crafted crumbled and dissolved, and the pieces were drawn into the portal with him. The ground split open as trees, rocks, and everything else was pulled into the vortex.

Charlotte stood her ground, the luminous crystal and celestial key held aloft as she concentrated on the spell. The power coursed through her veins as well, both exhilarating and terrifying. She asked the portal to expand beyond Miraval and his domain, using the celestial key as a conduit, and directed the spell to seek out and capture all of Prince Repel's minions who remained in Cincinnati.

One, then two, then many flew past and were sucked into the portal, their cries of surprise and fear echoing as they were pulled in.

The portal eventually encompassed the entire area. Then the sky darkened, casting the realm into gloom. The air was charged with energy, the hairs on the back of Charlotte's neck standing on end as the portal worked its magic.

Miraval fumbled in his robe and pulled out the other fairy handbook in a last-ditch effort to find a counterspell that could save him from his impending doom, but the powerful winds generated by the portal whipped the book out of his grasp and sent it soaring into the sky, its pages fluttering like the wings of a bird.

Anger consumed Miraval, and he planted his feet firmly on the ground and drew on his remaining power to cast a final spell at Charlotte.

The resulting bolt of light caused her to stagger back as pain coursed through her body, but gritting her teeth, she fought through it. However, the onslaught disrupted her concentration, causing the portal to waver and lose some of its strength.

Seizing the opportunity, Miraval headed toward Charlotte, his robe billowing behind him as he charged through the flying minions who were being sucked into the portal. They screamed as they were pulled past him, but he paid them no mind, focused as he was on reaching Charlotte and reclaiming the key and crystal.

Miraval leaped at Charlotte and held onto the key and the crystal as they grappled. Charlotte was almost overwhelmed by the Gatekeeper's immense strength as they struggled for control. She funneled all her energy into the portal, amplifying its power until the air hummed.

Miraval's grip faltered as he was pulled toward the portal, but with a final burst of magic, he transformed the crystal back into the handbook. A brilliant explosion of light caused its pages to scatter in all directions.

The celestial key clattered to the ground, now dull and lifeless. Charlotte stumbled back, gasping for breath as she surveyed the aftermath of the explosion. She expected to find Miraval ready to continue their battle, but when she looked up, he was nowhere in sight.

Confused, she looked around. Gone were the distorted landscape and looming portal. In their place was the field outside the Spaceship House, the grass swaying gently in the breeze as if nothing had happened.

The weight of the world lifted off Charlotte's shoulders when she realized it was over. Her knees gave out, and she sank to the ground in relief.

Her moment of respite was short-lived.

She heard groans and muffled curses nearby. Her head snapped up and she looked around, panicking when she saw her friends lying on the ground.

She rushed over to Alex, who was lying on his chest. She carefully turned him over and begged him to speak. He took several deep breaths before muttering, "That felt like the worst full-body charley horse I've ever experienced." He gingerly sat up and added, "I've only experienced that one, but I don't need another to compare."

Cat barked as he got to his feet, stretching his legs and letting his tongue loll out of his mouth. Sir Thomas muttered that he felt like he was experiencing the worst hangover of his life, and he didn't even have the memories of the party to account for it.

Relief flooded Charlotte when she realized her friends were fine, albeit battered and bruised. The owl, the mouse, and the turkey joined the group, and the birds complimented Charlotte on her victory.

Alex asked, "Did you get him?"

The mouse piped up, "It looked to me like the Gatekeeper got himself. While attempting to stop Charlotte, he blew himself up."

Alex looked at Charlotte, brows furrowing in concern. "Is he truly gone?"

Charlotte glanced at the dull celestial key, then picked it up and turned it over in her hands. "I can't say for sure, but if he *is* still alive, he's trapped somewhere without this key."

The owl let out a hoot of laughter. "Not much of a Gatekeeper without his key!"

The mouse added, "Yeah, he's probably right pissed, considering how high and mighty he sounded about his job."

Charlotte sat down on the grass and sighed, then glanced at the scattered pages of her handbook. "I should be happy about how things turned out, but my book was torn apart in the process. I'll have to collect all the pages again."

Alex put a comforting arm around her shoulders. "We did it once, and we can do it again."

Charlotte raised an eyebrow. "'We?'"

He grinned at her. "Well, yeah. I *am* a detective. Finding things, especially if they are hard to find, is part of the job. You're not alone in this."

Sir Thomas, still trying to catch his breath, chimed in. "Of course you have my sword and my loyalty, Lady."

The bird and the mouse nodded in agreement, and the owl puffed out his chest. "We shall keep a vigilant watch from above and below. No page shall go unfound!"

The turkey gave a hearty gobble. "More excitement in one day than I've had in years. I'm in!"

"Count me in, too!" the mouse chimed in with a squeak. "But after I take a little nap."

The owl turned to Charlotte and tilted his head. "About that fish market you mentioned when we first met. What's waiting for us there?"

Charlotte smiled and got to her feet, brushing the grass off her dress. "Let's find out, shall we? We've got good news to spread."

CHAPTER THIRTY-SEVEN

The air inside Peter Pan's fish store was rich with the scent of the ocean, augmented by the delicious aroma of freshly grilled fish and other delightful treats. Strings of fairy lights hung from the ceiling, casting a warm glow over the festivities. The place had been closed for a private party, and it was filled with laughter and the clinks of glasses as fairytale creatures and characters from EverAfter celebrated the end of Prince Repel's takeover attempt.

At the center of the party, Charlotte, Cat, Sir Thomas, Alex, and the trio of owl, mouse, and turkey were surrounded by a crowd of curious onlookers eager to hear the details of their adventure. The crowd was an eclectic mix, from werewolves and witches to former knights and dragons in human form—even mermaids in large tanks filled with water. They had come together to support one another in this unfamiliar realm and celebrate the victory over their common enemy.

Peter Pan, dressed in a green tunic and hat, leaned against a counter, nursing a drink as he listened to the group's tale. His eyes widened in amazement as Charlotte recounted their battles with Repel and the Gatekeeper.

"So, you not only took care of Repel but a Gatekeeper as well?" he asked after taking a long drink.

Sir Thomas chuckled and clarified, "Technically, the Gatekeeper took care of Repel, and we took care of the Gatekeeper, but I think we can take credit." The crowd cheered and raised their glasses in salute.

Peter Pan let out an impressed whistle, leaning back as he processed what he had just heard. "I know we're just legends and stories to the people of this world, but we have our own legends. A real Gatekeeper, huh? Wish I could have seen him."

Alex grimaced as he finished his drink. "You really don't. Creepy bastard. Full of himself, too. I hope he's really gone for good. Good riddance."

Peter raised an eyebrow mischievously. "Not just saying that because he kicked your ass before Charlotte came in?"

Alex shot him a side-eye. "Did our new mouse friend really have to tell you everything?"

The drunken mouse declared with a hiccup, "The best stories are full of details, and it was funny!" Before anyone could reply, he passed out. The turkey gently scooped him up off the floor to ensure that no one accidentally stepped on him.

Peter turned his attention to Charlotte, asking about the key and the portal. "So, does this mean you have a way back to EverAfter?"

Charlotte sighed, her eyes drifting to the dull celestial key lying on a nearby table. "I might, but not until I reassemble my book. It's scattered across the city. Well, I hope it is just the city."

Peter patted her on the back in genuine support. "That's more hope than most of us had before now. You've only been here a few days, and you've already changed our entire outlook. That's pretty impressive since the banished are usually a gloomy lot."

Sir Thomas furrowed his brow, an important question weighing on his mind. "Charlotte, where did you send all the evil EverAfterans who sided with Prince Repel? Surely you didn't send them back to EverAfter, where they are just going to cause havoc."

Charlotte shook her head, a knowing smile on her lips. "I did send them back to EverAfter, but not just anywhere. I sent them to the fairy godmothers' headquarters. Considering that Repel only had eyes for the worst among our people, my fellow godmothers will have no issue dealing with them if they try to cause more trouble."

Having somehow acquired another drink, Alex took a sip, his mind working through the implications. "What if they are just banished again? They could come right back here to Cincinnati."

Charlotte's eyes twinkled. "That's the beauty of it. The mandatory sentence for banished EverAfterans who somehow make it back is eternal imprisonment in one of our most secure facilities. It's not a common practice since it's nearly impossible to return once banished, but the law is there."

She paused, her gaze becoming distant as she looked out over the crowd. "I hope the incidents with Repel and the Gatekeeper will cause such a commotion that fairy godmother headquarters will look into the banishments and what happened. Hopefully, we will get some help from them."

Peter leaned back with a sly grin on his lips. "The fairy godmothers' resistance to taking swift action is legendary."

Charlotte shot him a playful pout. "Hey, look at what *I* accomplished!"

Peter raised his hands in mock surrender, but there was a twinkle in his eye as he responded, "Oh, I give you credit, Charlotte, but you're alone in this world now. You'll have to make your own rules. As for the fairy godmothers back home, I'm sure they'll do something...eventually. After all the bureaucracy is sorted out." He winked. "I'm just saying you probably shouldn't hold your breath. Start collecting those pages."

Charlotte sighed, mind already working on the task. "I suppose you're right. It's going to take a while, especially since I don't have Prince Repel and his goons to search for them this time."

Peter finished his drink and turned his attention to Alex. "Speaking of Repel, are you going to report him missing? He was on the campaign trail, and people are going to notice that he's gone."

Alex rubbed his chin thoughtfully. "I suppose I'll have to. Can't tell them he's dead."

Peter's eyes gleamed. "Mind holding off on that for a bit?"

Alex raised an eyebrow. "Why?"

Peter leaned in, voice dropping to a conspiratorial whisper. "I, and I'm assuming the rest of us, would like to take a gander at The Ascent. See what we can find. If anyone has something interesting or useful from either here or EverAfter, it would certainly be Repel."

Alex's brow furrowed. "That's not lawful."

Peter smirked. "He wasn't from here. Are you sure it's even in your jurisdiction?"

Alex sighed, running a hand through his hair. "Funny, man-child."

Their conversation terminated as the room filled with the melodic strumming of guitars, the soulful notes of a violin, and the rhythmic beat of drums.

Then more musically inclined party-goers brought out instruments, from a beautifully carved wooden harp to gleaming silver flutes, elevating the fish store with sound and celebration.

Peter's laughter was infectious as he declared, "Questions will keep for another time. Tonight, we celebrate! Let's party hard enough to make Humpty Dumpty turn green with envy!" With a mischievous wink, he disappeared into the crowd, the twinkling of lights glimmering off his tunic and hat.

Alex watched him go with a smile on his face and said to no one in particular, "He was asking most of the questions, you know."

Tapping his foot in time with the music, Sir Thomas chuckled. "I agree, but I also agree with Pan's statement that it looks like the party is just getting started. I, for one, am not about to pass up a chance to dance and work off the aches from our last battle." With a wink, he told Alex and Charlotte, "You two should join us!"

Without waiting for an answer, Sir Thomas joined the

dancers, with Cat close behind, and the pair was lost to sight.

The room was a kaleidoscope of colors as werewolves in bright costumes twirled witches in flowing robes and dragons in human form swayed with former knights in shining armor. The air was thick with laughter as well as the scent of the ocean, and the fairy lights cast a warm glow over it all, creating a scene that was both magical and otherworldly.

Charlotte looked at Alex with a twinkle in her eye. "Do you dance, Detective?"

Alex laughed. "I almost learned how to once. I was about to go undercover, and dancing was part of the case, but when my chief saw my moves, he assigned someone else."

Charlotte's giggle was light and melodic as she extended her hand to him. "I'm not much of a dancer either, but we could learn together. It will be fun."

Alex hesitated, glancing at the swirling crowd. His eyes landed on a couple of shots sitting on a nearby table, and he downed them in quick succession before turning back to Charlotte with a resigned smile. "Even if it doesn't turn out to be fun, it could be good for a laugh."

With that, the pair joined the melee as the music became more spirited. The soaring violins and other instruments intertwined with the drumbeats to create a lively melody that had even the most reluctant participants tapping their feet.

For the first time in a long while, the banished had a reason to celebrate. They were in a realm that had little magic of its own, but tonight, they were creating plenty of their own.

This celebration would be remembered for a long time.

The Snow Queen gracefully glided among the silent ruins of the once-majestic Ascent. The imposing structure, now an example of the transience of power, was empty, forsaken by all who had dwelled within its walls. She felt an icy chill in her bones that had nothing to do with the frosty air around her and everything to do with the rapid and unforeseen downfall of Prince Repel.

She had known that Repel's arrogance and grandiosity would be his undoing. However, she hadn't anticipated the swiftness and severity of his collapse. It was as if the universe had conspired against him, orchestrating his demise with a precision that was both awe-inspiring and terrifying.

As she perused the empty halls and desolate rooms, she kept a lookout for artifacts and other objects that might catch her fancy. She had no intention of lingering in this forsaken place. The risk was far too great, especially now that Repel's protection was no longer at her disposal.

Fortuitously, her plans had never been dependent on the deceased prince, but though his demise didn't upend them, it presented complications.

Chief among them was the loss of the myriad minions who had served Repel. On occasion, she had co-opted them for her own ends. Their absence would slow her progress, a delay she could ill afford.

As she walked through the crumbling halls and devasted rooms, ice spread across the floor and crept up the walls as if the building itself was reacting to her fury. Her mind was awhirl with thoughts of vengeance, and at the center of her rage was Charlotte, that infernal fairy godmother.

Who would have imagined that a member of the fairy godmothers' guild, along with a motley crew of misfits—including a human, of all creatures!—would have the audacity and capability to stand in her way? The thought was inconceivable, yet here she was, dealing with the fallout from their actions.

A cold fire burned within her, fueling her determination to not only overcome this setback but to emerge from it stronger.

She would not allow Charlotte and her ragtag band of insurgents to have the last laugh. The Snow Queen was a force to be reckoned with, and she would see to it that the world knew and feared her name.

However, she understood the importance of patience and strategic calculation. Her adversary had proven herself to be a formidable foe, far more powerful and resourceful than she had given her credit for. Rushing headlong into a confrontation without adequate preparation and knowledge of Charlotte's whereabouts would be a fool's gambit.

She would bide her time, gather her strength, and devise a meticulous plan to vanquish the godmother.

The Snow Queen was not one to admit defeat, and she would use this time to her advantage. When she did strike, it would be with the precision and ferocity of a winter storm, leaving nothing but devastation in its wake.

As she delved into the recesses of her voluminous dress, her fingers brushed the leathery cover of a book. Pulling it out, she gazed at the name etched into its cover—Belinda. A small but triumphant smile played on her lips. This book was the key to unlocking the power she needed to defeat Charlotte and reassert her dominance.

She would use fairy godmother magic to bring her foes and this realm to their knees.

THE STORY CONTINUES

The story continues with book two, Spells, Wishes & Quests, coming soon to Amazon and Kindle Unlimited.

Get sneak peeks, exclusive giveaways, behind the scenes content, and more. PLUS you'll be notified of special **one day only fan pricing** on new releases.

Sign up today to get free stories.

Visit: https://marthacarr.com/read-free-stories/

AUTHOR NOTES - MARTHA CARR
OCTOBER 23, 2023

A note from my garden. If you're new to these author notes, a little background. I have a pretty typical suburban lot. Not all that big, but there's some space back there with an eight foot fence and room down the sides.

Just enough space to make all of it one large garden. There are fig trees down one side that really put out this summer, despite the heat and lack of rainfall, silver ponyfoot and frog fruit for ground cover on that side and a nice row of Moses in the Cradle. Plus an enormous water tank to catch whatever rainfall comes my way and a screen in front of the AC unit that is covered in vines.

On the other side are peach trees and native grasses. It's Texas so that sort of combo is pretty typical. The porch goes out into the yard a little ways with a trellis and café lights.

In the back corner is everyone's favorite spot. A metal arch I designed that's covered in trumpet vines, over a wooden bench. Lots of pictures get taken on that bench.

The majority of the backyard is a garden of flowers and

grasses that Lois loves to meander through, plus a few large trees.

It's my secret garden that's full of lizards and spiders and birds and a vole family and probably a few snakes. Again, this is Texas. Snakes are the reason boots were invented. I tend to roll with what is and save my fist shaking at the sky for better things.

Lately, I've been very busy elsewhere and couldn't get back to the garden. And, I was wondering why I was feeling more stress than usual. Little things were bothering me that I normally didn't notice. What was up?

Well, the boyfriend went out of town this weekend to see family and I dove into working in the garden. In Texas, we have two distinct growing seasons – spring and fall - and two seasons that are more about patience and tending to nutrients and water and cutting back – winter and summer. We have just entered the second growing season and that frog fruit took notice and was starting to cover everything. The rains have finally returned and a lot of other things were growing thick trunks and leaning over other plants. The banana peppers and green peppers were overflowing. It took a solid day to get most of it cut back and stand back to see where I might need to add something.

That's gardening for you. Things flourish and wither, side by side sometimes. I do my best to figure out why either one took the path they did, do what I can and then move on to something else. Gardens are very good at humbling humans in the best possible way because they can be forgiving if you just try but will ask you to pay attention as well.

However, even in my absence this summer, the garden was flourishing, and I felt a connection to the earth and the good dirt full of worms once more.

We all have outward regulators we use to keep us sane, or maybe drive us crazier. One of my bigger ones is putting my hands in dirt, moving things around, and helping plants grow. Then taking a lot of early morning breaks or just at dusk, to sit on the porch and admire what Mother Nature and I figured out together.

Fortunately, another one of my regulators is writing about magic. Time to get back to that. Leira and the troll are waiting for me. We'll talk again soon. More adventures to follow.

AUTHOR NOTES - MICHAEL ANDERLE

OCTOBER 25, 2023

First and foremost, thank you for not just delving into this story but also these authors' notes hidden away at the end. I appreciate you hanging around to let me chat with you a little!

The Giddy Excitement of New Concepts and Story Ideas

Creativity, as you well know, can be a fickle beast. Sometimes, it flows with abundance, and other times, it's like trying to squeeze water from a stone. Lately, I've been experiencing the latter, feeling like my well of ideas had run dry. However, last weekend, I stumbled upon a new methodology for brainstorming concepts, allowing me to play with ideas and see where they might lead. The result? A newfound excitement for a world I'm eager to create and share with you.

Sort of share.

My initial concept revolved around the son of a Genghis Khan-type character. But after delving into some books I've enjoyed for quite some time (particularly The

Riss Project), I decided to put a twist on the idea and show the world and its inhabitants in a different light. I'm super excited about this new direction and look forward to seeing this concept take flight.

I realize I'm being vague here, but that's because I don't want to jinx myself. There's always the chance that this idea might not pan out the way I hope, and if that's the case, I don't want to disappoint anyone. But for now, I'm riding this wave of enthusiasm, eager to explore the possibilities this new creative approach has unlocked for me.

So, here's to the exhilarating journey of discovery that lies ahead, both for me as a creator and for you, my readers. I'm eager to share this new world with you, and I can't wait to see where it takes us!

Talk to you in the next story!

Ad Aeternitatem,

Michael Anderle

MORE STORIES with Michael HERE:
https://michael.beehiiv.com/

BOOKS BY MARTHA CARR

Other Series in the Oriceran Universe:

THE LEIRA CHRONICLES
CASE FILES OF AN URBAN WITCH
SOUL STONE MAGE
THE KACY CHRONICLES
MIDWEST MAGIC CHRONICLES
THE FAIRHAVEN CHRONICLES
I FEAR NO EVIL
THE DANIEL CODEX SERIES
SCHOOL OF NECESSARY MAGIC
SCHOOL OF NECESSARY MAGIC: RAINE CAMPBELL
ALISON BROWNSTONE
FEDERAL AGENTS OF MAGIC
SCIONS OF MAGIC
THE UNBELIEVABLE MR. BROWNSTONE
DWARF BOUNTY HUNTER
ACADEMY OF NECESSARY MAGIC
MAGIC CITY CHRONICLES
ROGUE AGENTS OF MAGIC

OTHER BOOKS BY JUDITH BERENS

OTHER BOOKS BY MARTHA CARR

JOIN THE ORICERAN UNIVERSE FAN GROUP ON FACEBOOK!

BOOKS BY MICHAEL ANDERLE

Sign up for the LMBPN email list to be notified of new releases and special deals!

https://lmbpn.com/email/

For a complete list of books by Michael Anderle, please visit:

www.lmbpn.com/ma-books/

CONNECT WITH THE AUTHORS

Martha Carr Social

Website: http://www.marthacarr.com

Facebook: https://www.facebook.com/groups/MarthaCarrFans/

Michael Anderle Social

Website: http://lmbpn.com

Email List: https://michael.beehiiv.com/

https://www.facebook.com/LMBPNPublishing

https://twitter.com/MichaelAnderle

https://www.instagram.com/lmbpn_publishing/

https://www.bookbub.com/authors/michael-anderle

www.ingramcontent.com/pod-product-compliance
Lightning Source LLC
LaVergne TN
LVHW041746060526
838201LV00046B/919